Welcome to Opine

MATTHEW MARULLO

This is a work of fiction. Names, characters, places, and incidents are either the product of the author's imagination or are used fictitiously. Any resemblance to actual persons, living or dead, is purely coincidental.

Marullo Publications

Cover design and book production by Adam Hess

ISBN-979-8-218-05523-3
Library of Congress Control Number 2022915213

Printed in the United States

"It is difficult to free fools from the chains they revere."

—VOLTAIRE

Prologue

Old Opine Rhyme:

O pale blue sun in thy blue sky,
How doth thee light upon mine eye!
Haloed with thy white corona,
Art thou bloomed from fair Pomona?

Old Opine Parable:

A Negro at a slave auction crawls over to a white man, begging for water. When a slave trader sees this, he walks up to the white man.
"Kick that nigger!" the slave trader says to him.
The white man turns and kicks the slave trader.
"Why'd you do that for?" the slave trader says. "I said kick the nigger!"
"It makes no difference to me," the white man replies, "I'm blind!"

Excerpt from *People's Guide to Foolery*, by Clover Watsonia:

"Mr. Chazos, would you like the newest model smart phone, or the model from last year, which is almost exactly the same?"

"Which is the more expensive?"

"The newer model."

"Then it's the best. I'll take it!"

"Mr. Chazos, would you like the newest model car that comes with all the newest technology, or last year's model, which has last year's technology but has a better safety record?"

"Which is the more expensive?"

"The newer model."

"Then it's the best. I'll take it!"

"Mr. Chazos, would you like your son to attend our new trade school, which will train him how to speculate on the stock market and profit off the financial economy; or our liberal arts school, which will prepare your son for graduate study while offering exposure to a more broad-based curriculum studying the greatest achievements in art, literature, music, history, philosophy, ethics, and all the social and natural sciences?"

"I'll take the trade school!"

"Really? But the liberal arts school is the more expensive!"

"Hey buddy, I'm not buying a lousy phone or car here! This is my son's future we're talking about!"

One

'Twas the blood squibs that mattered the most.

The device was simple enough for use by an elementary school morality play about the Fools: like a tiny stick of dynamite, a small tube encloses a detonator wired to an electronic trigger, linked remotely. Press the button and it launches a jet of fake blood. A convincing blood spurt was crucial to ensure the comic element was not diminished in the slightest. After all, what good is any morality play about the Fools without the comic element? Laughter was the undisputed panacea for all social stresses in Opine. Laughter was the catharsis through which the Fool's Bane was lampooned. The social, mental, and physical benefits of laughter were true way back then, billions of years ago, for the Ancients, as they were now.

As always, the topic for the play was chosen at random. There were way too many viable topics to warrant a hierarchy of value, or relevance. And way too many to exhaust over a lifetime of morality plays. Any one would do just fine. The Find, which we shall address shortly, provided more than enough material for ages to come.

This particular play was dealing with the inception of the Americas. You cannot fully appreciate one of these morality plays unless you are there. The exhilaration of the spurting blood, the laughter, the release, it all had to be experienced firsthand. Morality plays were a catharsis for the ancient Greeks, as were the Olympic games. The gladiatorial spectacles were a catharsis for the ancient Romans, as was the insatiable bloodlust back then. And, in the absence of violence and war, dramatic portrayals of violence and war, for thousands upon thousands of generations. This, however, was a different kind of catharsis. This was psychological purification of the highest order. This was fostering a State of Contentment, in real time.

The parents beam with delight as second grader Aster Bottlebrush, dressed as a Spaniard, approaches another child dressed as a Native American. "We Spaniards are here to take over your land of Hispaniola," Aster says, in that wonderfully placid monotone, like it was the first reading. "You will dig in the mines for gold." The other child answers, "But this is our land. You can't do this to a peaceful people. Can we please live together in peace?" "No," Aster answers, "you will do as we say. We are your masters now." "That is cruel and unjust," the Native American answers, "and we will resist you." Aster raises a plastic match-lock musket. "Then you shall all die," he says. "By 1508 we will massacre three million of your people." Aster pulls the trigger, snap. Blood squirts from the wound in a thin jet. The child wheels around and the blood sprays the parents. They roar in laughter. The grinning teacher claps.

The next two boys step up, pockets of laughter still lingering, one boy dressed as a Native American, the other as an English settler. "Powhatan," the settler says, "some of our friends ran away to you. Please return them." "They were starving, and came to us for food," Powhatan answers. The English settler raises his musket. "If you do not comply, you will die." Powhatan replies, "It was you who settled on our land, yet we did not attack you." The English settler says, "None of that matters. We will burn your houses down, burn your crops, take your queen from you, and then take your children in our boats and blow their brains out." Snap, the blood squirts, the range especially impressive. As the child falls, some of it spurts into a woman's mouth as she laughs. Her laugh becomes gargled: "Ha-guhguh-guhguh, ha-guhguhguhguh," though she doesn't mind because fake blood at public events like these was always washable, and flavored, this one as strawberry vegan cheesecake, and it was considered a privilege to be showered with fake blood ridiculing the Fools. The entire room is resplendent with pride and delight. Their children were learning, educating, entertaining, and purifying, all at once.

Now it was time for a pair of girls. It didn't matter that they were girls. The point would come across, regardless. And the comic element. "One of your Pequot Native Americans killed one of our white men," the girl dressed as an English settler begins, with the same monotone as the boys, the same wooden expression. "We shall punish him," the other girl responds. "But you should know the white man he killed kidnapped one of our own." The English settler raises her musket. "None of that matters," she says. "We shall make war on the Pequots. We will massacre your people. Not only the warriors, but also your innocent men, women, and children. We will set fire to your villages. We will cut to pieces anybody who does not burn in the fire." Pop, squirt. And then half the class dressed as settlers closes in on the other half dressed as Native Americans, firing their toy plastic muskets and the spurting is a sprightly celebration of thin red streamers, bathing kids, bathing the parents, all in uproarious guffawing as the classroom quickly becomes showered in the joyous revelry of meditative therapeutic purifying Opine bliss and how the parents were so proud and how the teacher was so proud and there was more ha-guhguhguhguh and this was only the first act, there was so much more to come, so much more teaching and so much more learning, and don't forget laughter, the panacea for all social stresses, the beloved unlimited reservoir of laughter supplied by the unlimited reservoir of the Fools.

'Twas the blood squibs that mattered the most.

Two

Chunky happy Nerine Bayberry, dressed in the customary Opine colorful flower pastels, entered the Boxwood Borough Revelation Chamber, the room full of exactly one hundred children, dancing what amounted to a cross between an Irish jig and a Scottish highland dance, although those places, Scotland and Ireland, were meaningful only insofar as they represented long-lost territories inhabited by the Ancients, some of whom, of course, were the Fools. "Some" was the best quantitative approximation one could ever say about the population density of the Fools, as everybody knew the relevance of their legacy rested solely on their influence upon Opine's present State of Contentment, to be presently revealed by the all-important rite of passage ceremony at hand, the Revelation.

The term Revelation was of course taken from the Bible, one of the many, many digital documents recovered from The Find, though it must be understood that the people of Opine, the Opinions (the first "i" pronounced with a long vowel), completely disregarded its Biblical significance when selecting an apt designation for this all-important event enlightening eight-year-old children to the wonderful history of their existence. The story of the Biblical Revelation was well-known, but of course not taken seriously. Indeed, it was lampooned regularly among the other myths, not because they were myths—indeed, the historical and moral teachings of myths were of paramount literary and sociological importance—but because there were actually people back then who read similar passages from the Bible and took them at face value, as if they actually happened, or as if the dark, foreboding portents within *would* actually happen. As a professor quipped, "Let me know if the world ends, so I can say I told you so!" The Opinions were trained at very early ages to separate the sublime from the ridiculous, and the ridiculous offered exhaustive opportunities for education, entertainment, and therapy, all critical to maintaining a balanced State of Contentment.

There were one hundred children dressed in adorable cute flowery outfits in the chamber because one hundred was a nice round number and every bubbly Revelation teacher was responsible for one hundred children. Every child is told by their parents this was a very important event in their lives and their Revelation was the first step to their understanding of how they came to be Opinions. The beautiful part is that all the children would completely accept what they heard because in Opine, the word "opinion" was not in circulation as a common noun, except in Ancient parlance, but as a proper noun to describe their common heritage as the people of Opine. Opinions had tastes but they didn't have opinions about what was true, because to have an opinion about what was true would imply there are facts independent of universal truths, and anything other than a universal truth to an Opinion would be very much like anything other than a fact to us, like saying the daytime sky is yellow when it is in fact blue. The Opinions cannot distinguish between a fact, like "the sky is blue," and a universal truth, like "no one individual possesses more natural human worth than another," because each of these statements occupy the same plane of truthfulness.

So when chubby chirpy Nerine Bayberry stopped dancing and the children stopped laughing, the children never questioned what Ms. Bayberry had to tell them in her characteristically Opine-bubbly style. Because questioning her would be like questioning the existence of the blue sun in the blue sky. She told them the truth and they all knew it was the truth before she even told them the truth. She told them that the planet they were living on, Opine, used to be called Earth. That billions of years ago it had been revolving around another star the ancient inhabitants (christened the Ancients) had called the Sun, in a completely different solar system in a completely separate galaxy. Then, around five billions years later, just about when the Sun was beginning its red giant phase, the galaxy known as the Milky Way had merged with the galaxy known as the Andromeda, and somewhere along the line Earth had been gravitationally ejected out of its orbit, spending a million years as a rogue planet before being gravitationally captured by a blue star, a very unique type of blue star called a blue dwarf, evolved from a red dwarf.

Ms. Bayberry was very lively as she danced around the screen pointing to happy bubbly graphics of ancient Earth and its white star (it was not yellow but white, that is the truth), and then to its new star, a star that used to be a red dwarf but was now a blue dwarf because it had increased its surface temperature over many millions of years and would eventually cool to a white dwarf and finally a black dwarf. And how wonderfully lucky they were that what used to be called

Earth had been gravitationally captured, along with a single moon about three-quarters the size of the Ancient moon, by this puny little blue dwarf star, and how lucky they were that billions of years later the evolutionary process that had led to complex life on Earth, beginning with a primordial soup and ending with all the richly variegated plant and animal species so meticulously preserved on the digital documents within The Find, had all risen again, and that this most likely happens quite often in the universe, for as long as there was a planet the right distance from a star, life would indeed be resilient, it would arise, given the right conditions to trigger the processes and feedback loops and chemical reactions necessary to eventually spawn self-replicating complex life, given the happy coincidences of time and circumstance, because that is what the Opinions knew and understood it to be, happy coincidences, not preordained fate, not divine fortune, not some supreme being's will, but just another universal truth, another lucky roll of the cosmic dice, another validation of the way things have been, and are, and always will be. Time and circumstance rule all.

All told, modern Opinion astrophysicists calculated that it took approximately nine billion Earth 1.0 years from the demise of Homo Sapiens 1.0 on Earth 1.0 to the emergence of Homo Sapiens on Earth 2.0 (this translates to about fourteen billion four hundred million years on Opine, where the year is 228 days). It sounds like an eternity, but nine billion years is a blink of the eye in the lifetime of the Cosmos.

The children, among them Aster Bottlebrush, were wide-eyed and amazed, entranced and fascinated with the narrative, as Opinions always were about the extraordinary story of their existence, and how can one not be thoroughly enraptured when one is completely enveloped in an all-encompassing State of Contentment. Ms. Nerine Bayberry took a moment to make the children laugh with a jaunty little Russian-like folk dance before continuing with how the Fools, who the children had already heard so much about since they could walk and talk, had ruined their own species and the entire planet, long before the Milky Way galaxy was anywhere near the Andromeda galaxy, long before the inception of the new primordial soup that would eventually replicate millions of years of human evolution, except this time around one of the Ancients had left the newly evolving Homo Sapiens the most precious, consequential, miraculous gift one could imagine, a gift that the Opinions indeed regarded as a "miracle," not in the Ancient supernatural sense of the word but miraculous in the sense of an amazing stroke of time and circumstance.

It was The Find. A digital record of ancient Earth's achievements in all the arts and sciences—the social and natural sciences, art, music, literature—encoded on a small quantum computer, the size of an ancient twenty-first-century tablet computer, vacuum-sealed in a pure AM-III glass box, buried deep in the earth by an unnamed individual who had the presence of mind to collect and preserve millions of petabytes of interactive texts and documents, a grand compendium of human history and achievement. Thousands of years of history, innovation, acquired knowledge—not exhaustive, but ample. The Find had been recovered an unspecified number of millennia ago by the Proto-Humans 2.0, most likely as a result of a geological event. The AM-III glass encasement protecting its contents, sustaining a single two-inch crack, was made of spheroidal carbon molecules called fullerenes. This kind of synthesized glass is harder than diamond. The Proto-Humans 2.0 had no idea what to make of this box and the strange metallic object within, finally owing its existence to divine forces well beyond their comprehension. Fear of the object's unknown power encouraged its preservation for thousands of years. They treated it as a talisman, a sacrosanct idol, not to be meddled with, but admired, worshipped.

Any archaeologist or anthropologist on Earth or Opine would be utterly amazed at the close parallels between ancient cultures on both worlds. It seems the trajectory of cognitive evolution in the areas of technological innovation, cultural norms, and artistic sensibility are codified within a preordained genetic template, independent of time or physical circumstance. The Opinions had their version of, for example, Earth's San People, dating to as old as 200,000 BCE. Cultural artifacts bearing a generic similarity to ancient civilizations like Çatalhöyük, the Sumerians, the Harappans, and even the Egyptians were unearthed on Opine. While there were obvious glaring differences in early scripts, and the absence of large monuments in Opine, such as the pyramids, the similarities between cultural artifacts on both ancient worlds, particularly in the areas of architecture, tools, and ornaments, were striking. For millennia, civilizations rose and fell, following historical paradigms reminiscent of their Ancient counterparts. The predilection for one group of people to dominate another was still robust within the human genome, and those traits defining "the stronger" were just as arbitrary and just as unnecessary.

It was The Find that would completely alter, and accelerate, the timescale of Opinion advancement, as compared to their lost ancient cousins. For thousands of years, The Find would remain a hallowed, mystical enigma, revered, feared, coveted, passed on from generation to generation, culture to culture, remaining secure in the hands of those strong enough to lay a claim as its custodian. On Ancient Opine, the stuff of legend was often the Keeper of The Find.

Thus legends were written, stories were told, until Homo Sapiens 2.0, comparatively early in their evolutionary development, had finally figured out how to manipulate the quantum computer, analyze its components, and extract what they could of the quantum data. However imperfect and incomplete the recovery effort was, as an estimated 60% of the data was irretrievable, it was still a monumental achievement, one that would transform the character of their race forever, helping to eventually purge their self-destructive behaviors, thereby paving the path to the present State of Contentment they now enjoyed, a State of Contentment inconceivable without the wealth of scientific knowledge and history handed to them by utter serendipity, a happenstance recalling so many of those amusing Ancient stories about visits from advanced alien civilizations.

It is true this was nothing less than a gift from an alien civilization, one that had managed to extinguish itself billions of years ago, but one which had left a digital imprint of its greatest successes and its greatest failures. It was a gift of language as well as a gift of knowledge. The Homo Sapiens 2.0 analog of the Homo Sapiens 1.0 Bronze Age had been given a monumental head start on the development of language, as it was all laid out in millions of gigabytes worth of digital encyclopedias, complete with primer texts and accompanying pictures. The hardy quantum computer activated automatically from its energy source, solar power. Thus it would always stay on as long as there was a blue sun in the sky, the late twenty-first-century quantum chip lasting in its pressurized earthbound encasement. Once a single, brave individual had endeavored to risk cutting through the sacred glass casing, it didn't take long to figure out how to swipe a finger across the screen and navigate the menus with the tap of the finger.

When a civilization is given a Rosetta Stone with the key to its encryption, it also doesn't take long to decipher a foreign language. The Ur-Speech was, in a relatively short time, supplanted with the much more efficient modern English. Twenty-six symbols arranged in different permutations, permutations called words, words arranged in different configurations, configurations called sentences, sentences juxtaposed to illustrative digital pictures. A Rosetta Stone with a free key.

And what need does an emerging civilization have for a trial and error exploration of modern agricultural methods when all the secrets of modern agriculture are there for the taking? None whatsoever. No trial and error, just follow the guide. And what need does an emerging civilization have for a trial and error exploration of industrialization, with all its hundreds of years of failures and abuses and health hazards and social upheaval and oppression, when all the secrets of the most efficient and environmentally safe industrial methods are there for the taking? None whatsoever. No trial and error, just follow the guide. And what about a trial and error exploration of what constitutes the best educational system for an emerging civilization? The fairest income distribution? The fairest way to levy taxes? The fairest economic system? The fairest healthcare system? No trial and error necessary.

And when an emerging civilization is also handed a blueprint outlining in meticulous detail the most efficient technology for publishing and disseminating the greatest intellectual achievements that Homo Sapiens 1.0 has to offer, such a sweeping mass dissemination of knowledge serves to render unnecessary the historical imperative of trial and error. There is no room for error when you are told the errors in advance.

Although Ms. Bayberry touched on these particulars in only the most general terms, questions abounded, of course, for all Opinions were wired to be intellectual sponges. Ms. Nerine Bayberry assured them that it was through the Opinions' peerless educational system that all of their questions would be answered, for the purpose of the Revelation was to provide an exhilarating introduction to what would blossom as a lifetime of intellectual and emotional fulfillment, and why spoil the veritable treasure trove of surprises to come? She added, in the spirit of the Opinions' idolatry of nature, that if you "nurture your roots, the tree will follow."

Noticing the beckoning gleam in their eyes, Ms. Nerene Bayberry alleviated their lingering curiosity with a hint that the demise of the Ancients billions of years ago was due to a very compelling coincidence of many factors, a kind of "systems failure," brought upon the Ancients by the Fools themselves during the course of many hundreds of years.

"And do you know what?" Ms. Bayberry winked. "They knew how to avoid it, but did *nothing!*"

"*Nothing?*" a child gasped.

"Nothing!"

"What Fools!" another child marveled.

"Fools, in*cah-BLLeeeehCH...*"

There were plenty of recyclable canisters spread throughout the room, providing Ms. Nerene Bayberry with ample time to grab one before releasing a pint or two of pale yellow vomit. The children barely noticed, you see. They were as accustomed to vomiting as we are to coughing or sneezing. The Opinions vomited often, sometimes every few days, for a very important physiological reason, though for now, we shall not spoil the veritable treasure trove of surprises to come.

Three

Aster Bottlebrush of Boxwood Borough in Cockspur Coral County, a boy of eight with an admirable Opine cider complexion, has just arrived home from the aforementioned Revelation with his proud, glowing parents of admirable Opine cider complexions, Kaffir and Gaura Bottlebrush. Aster does not have any siblings, but his parents were free to have one more child. The Opinion Congress long ago instituted a child quota of two per family. When the entire population of the planet is residing on a single continent roughly the size of China and Russia, resources must be carefully conserved for the welfare of all.

Abortions were obsolete in Opine because every pregnancy was planned. The very idea of terminating a pregnancy was nonsensical, unless it was a forced pregnancy, though there hadn't been a single rape in Opine for well over a century. Aborting a pregnancy as the product of two mutually consenting adults was considered violently unreasonable to the Opinions—provided the pregnancy presented no danger to the mother's health. In particular, debating the justification for aborting a planned pregnancy presented the conundrum that the individual raising the issue could have conceivably been aborted under the same argument, thus would not have existed to raise the issue in the first place. This was a contradiction. In a society where every pregnancy was planned, abortion was a logical absurdity.

As to those Ancients who believed a woman who is brutally raped and impregnated should be compelled by the State to carry the pregnancy to term, the Opinions were amazed individuals holding such views were permitted to remain full citizens.

The Opinions were also intent on not repeating the tragic consequences of their ancestor's indifference to Earth's ecosystems, namely, climate change launching a mass rise in sea levels, flooding the lands, helping along an already irreversible cascade of mass extinctions. Opine was a single gargantuan island. It was another fortuitous roll of the cosmic dice that once the rogue planet had been gravitationally captured by the blue dwarf star, the thawing of the vast frozen oceans did not entirely submerge what little land was left from billions of years of geological turmoil. So the small Bottlebrush family, like any other Opinion family, represented the embodiment of the Opinions' institutionalized practice of preserving and aligning their precious natural resources for present and future generations.

After vomiting in a recyclable canister and wiping away a few stray droplets, Gaura asked Aster if he enjoyed the Revelation.

"Yes, Mom, very much. It was the best surprise I ever got."

"Even a better surprise than your J.R.R. Tolkien book?" Kaffir asked his son.

"Yes," Aster nodded, "but I love my birthday present."

Opinions loved the arts, both the New Arts and the Ancient Arts. Their society was programmed to love culture. The Ancient Arts were particularly cherished. And such an astonishing spectrum of style and content! From the sublime to the Foolish. How such a people at one turn could be so productively brilliant, and then, at the next turn, so mind-bendingly Foolish was beyond comprehension.

"But Mom and Dad," Aster said, "how could a planet so long ago find its way to a completely new star, and how could everything, and everybody, happen a second time? What made it happen?"

"Nothing made it happen," Gaura smiled. "Nothing makes anything happen. Everything just happens."

"That's right," Aster concurred enthusiastically, his mother's words recalling an oft-repeated Opine axiom, "There is no reason that there is no reason."

"Ab-so-*lutely,*" his father Kaffir emphasized. "No gods, no fates, no reasons. The Ancients were always looking for a reason, when there never was one. Do you remember what the great Ray Bradbury said? That story about the Martians?"

"Tell me again," Aster said.

Kaffir then began to recite the book from memory. Adult Opinions had all memorized some of the most important passages in the Ancient Works. They memorized the passages not because they were required to, but because they wanted to, because they found it fulfilling, and profitable, and because they were cultivated in cultural awareness.

"Well," Kaffir began, "Bradbury said that 'the men of Mars realized that in order to survive they would have to forgo asking that one question any longer: *Why live?* Life was its own answer. Life was the propagation of more life and the living of as good a life as possible.'"

"And," Gaura said, "the Martians 'knew how to combine science and religion so the two worked side by side, neither denying the other, each enriching the other.'"

"Science is God," Aster said.

"And God is science," his mother said.

The Opinions were always fascinated with how "lies" can tell truths and "truths" can tell lies. Bradbury's fictional story, or "lie," teaches us fundamental truths about humanity, universal truths about life. Yet the others, the Fools, were just as good at manufacturing "truths" that were really lies, lies that inspired people to unknowingly destroy themselves precisely because they had been convinced those lies were truths. It was one of the many great paradoxes of Earth 1.0 that many of the accepted fictions promoted facts and many of the accepted facts promoted fictions.

Outside the Bottlebrush house there was a crash. The Bottlebrushes barely blinked. Car accidents occurred on Opine more often than on Earth. Opinion cars were made from magnesium instead of iron or steel, thus lighter and safer, lending perhaps a degree of blasé security among the drivers. Moreover, Opinions in general were known to be quite lacking in basic motor skills. They were always accidentally bumping into each other on streets, accidentally tripping, accidentally running their bicycles off the road. Public transportation, like buses and trains and airplanes, were very safe because Opinions were generally very caring and very responsible when it came to the safety and welfare of others. But sometimes they often got distracted looking after their own personal welfare.

There are very real sociocultural reasons for this. First of all, Opinions were utterly fascinated with the world around them. They worshipped nature. Their very names, not always gender-specific, were based on flowers, bushes, and trees, as the plant kingdom, in their view, contained the most perfect living things on Opine. They even tended to wear clothing decorated with colorful, variegated collages of flora. To Opinions, plants were perfect because they were the least aggressive, the least violent, the least judgmental, the most beautiful, the most innocent, the most tolerant living things on the planet. Opinions agreed with Ray Bradbury that animals knew better than people *why* to live, but they would add plants knew why to live even better than animals. This omnipresent adoration of nature infused into their upbringing often resulted in chronic distracted behavior. One Opinion years ago was so entranced with a double rainbow in the sky that he was struck by a train traveling seventy-five miles per hour. Witnesses noted that upon collision, his catapulted body followed the very beautiful arc of a rainbow.

There is another reason why Opinions could sometimes be careless drivers. There were no private sector insurance companies in Opine.

The people of Opine, and, by extension, the Opinion State, were the insurance companies.

The present scene in front of the Bottlebrush home would be so outlandish to the people of Earth, they would think the Opinions were completely out-of-their-mind-loo-loo-bonkers crazy. An indigo Arbutus had plowed into the passenger's side of a mint Sumac (the cars were also named after flora). The damage wasn't severe owing to the low speeds of each vehicle. A woman emerged from the mint Sumac with her young daughter, both sniffling and shaking. A young man emerged from the Arbutus, tears streaming down his cheeks, asking if the ladies were okay. They were. The woman asked if he was okay. He was. The lady of long pecan hair, still sniffling, introduced herself as Nolana Whitebeam, and her daughter of caramel hair, Dianella. The young man of amber hair introduced himself as Thymus Corkwood. The two shook hands and apologized to each other. Then they gave each other a hug. This was very common with the Opinions. When anything even slightly unpleasant occurred, a hug was always in order, regardless of whether or not the huggers knew one another. Thymus gave little Dianella a hug and the girl finally smiled.

By then, there were about ten neighbors upon the scene, including the Bottlebrushes, converging like a flock of seagulls spotting food.

"It's not bad," one man said to the accident victims. "I would say no more than a thousand."

"Blue Aria is just a few miles away," a woman added. "They'll do it. Here..." She thrust a few fifty-crassula bills (the Opinion currency) into Nolana's hand, who promptly thanked her.

"This'll do it," the first man said to Thymus, giving him about three hundred crassulas.

"Oh, no, it's too much," Thymus protested, wiping away his tears. It was the polite response, though Opinions always gave and they always received.

"Yarrow, you're going overboard," another lady said. "Give him back some of that. Here..." she poked a few fifties into Thymus's hand, a few more into Nolana's hand.

"Thank you, this is more than enough..." Nolana said, but other neighbors were handing her more. Both accident victims were now accruing more money than they really needed to repair the damage to their vehicles. This was also very common among the Opinions. Common decency did not have a price ceiling.

"No, take it," Yarrow Buckthorn insisted. "And Calla, you're one to talk. You gave two thousand crassulas to that roofing man who fell off the ladder into your blackberry bush."

"It wasn't two thousand. It was eighteen hundred something."

Another woman wormed her way to Nolana. *"I'm* Hebe, Hebe Hornbeam, and *I* just want to say—"

"Excuse me, Hebe, I was giving her—"

"—that we are so sorry for your accident and on behalf of the Hornbeam family..."

The bills were falling out of Nolana's hand. Thymus picked them up but Nolana told him to keep it.

"Would both of you like to see my house?" Hebe pressed on. "Have a refreshment? You just had an accident."

"Now Hebe," Gaura Bottlebrush stepped in, "we have to spread the joy. Let's be fair."

"That's right," her husband Kaffir said, turning to Nolana. "What is your name?"

"Nolana Whitebeam."

"And you, sir?"

"Thymus Corkwood."

"Thymus," Kaffir said, "why don't you go over to Hebe's, and Nolana, you and your lovely daughter will come over to our house, and then later you can all come over for dinner. I insist. And I'll call Blue Aria."

"No, I'll call them, Kaffir," somebody said. Their voices began to overlap.

"I'll do it."

"Hebe, that's enough! You've done enough!"

"Calla, what are you doing? You already gave your share."

"Oh, what's a few more crassulas?"

"You're all so wonderful," Nolena said, her eyes watery, "but I have to insist—"

"Here, take this."

"Stop that!"

"Wait, let's, let's—"

"Thymus, did you get enough?"

"Oh, plenty, plenty—"

"Calla, stop, I saw that! I saw that!"

Dr. Yarrow Buckthorn, a school psychologist who had abundant prior experience in these kinds of mounting goodwill disagreements, had already been fumbling for his smart phone to bring up a Fool Fact. Shouting above the clamor, he recited:

"Henry David Thoreau spent a night in jail for refusing to pay taxes that would finance a war against the Mexicans, a war predicated on the philosophy that the superior white culture is manifestly destined to supplant all other cultures."

"Ha ha! Ha ha ha ha ha!"

"Haaaaaaaa! Ha! Ha Ha!"

"That was a good one!"

They all bellowed in laughter. The air was now clear. Nolana and Thymus thanked everybody again and the crowd immediately dispersed, chuckling, sniggering, some muttering, "the Fools."

The Opinions did not spend inordinate amounts of time on social media, or surfing the Internet, or on most any other application common to the Ancient smart phone or tablet. They used phones primarily to make calls and to upload "Fool Facts." The Opine Congress blasted these amusing nuggets of Fool trivia to every citizen of Opine every single day. Their function was both to entertain and alleviate anxiety. The anxiety level in Opine was minimal, thanks to the government's well-established programs of regulated egalitarian income distribution, regulation of the economy, regulation of the mass media, regulation of the educational system, and certain conditioning techniques we have yet to discuss. Though in the same way it is impossible to achieve a temperature of absolute zero, it is equally impossible to achieve a perfectly stable, incorruptible, infallible social fabric. Opine was not perfect by any means. The Fool Facts were one form of "Contentment Culture," a stress reliever, a kind of healthy dose of gloating, or *Schadenfreude,* where citizens could feel some measure of relief from their current problems or stresses by laughing at the vast arsenal of ridiculous nonsense and obscenities cataloged in The Find's digital historical record. In the same way we on Earth laugh at and derive some sense of superiority and satisfaction from the mistakes dumb people make, the Opinions derived a similar sense of superiority and satisfaction from laughing at the dumb activities of an entire subclass of their ancestral species.

There was one Ancient social media analog to the Fool Facts. A typical Fool Fact received millions of "likes" per day.

Four

Like all Opinion homes, the Bottlebrush residence was decorated with a multitude of flowering plants. Kaffir Bottlebrush was named after one of them, a Kaffir lily. There were also anthuriums and gloxinias and cyclamens and begonias and bromeliads. Nolana Whitebeam and her daughter Dianella were staring at them as soon as they entered the front door, commenting on their "resplendent" beauty. The rest of the home furnishings were decent but unremarkable. We may marvel at a new tiled floor or sofa or countertop or paint job but the Opinions really didn't place much emphasis on home décor or appliances beyond their utilitarian functions.

Aster Bottlebrush and Dianella Whitebeam went to Aster's bedroom upstairs while the adults sat in the living room. Gaura Bottlebrush told Nolana she was welcome to invite her husband to dinner, if she had one. Nolana said thank you, but her husband had drowned in the ocean three years ago while trying to get a better look at a lovely spotted seatrout.

"My name is Dianella Whitebeam," the young girl introduced herself.

"I'm Aster Bottlebrush. You look content."

"Thank you. You do too."

This was a common Opinion greeting. Calling somebody "content" could mean "pleasure to meet you," or "good to see you," or "you look happy and healthy," or a combination of the three.

"Dianella, would you like to sit on my bed, or a chair?"

"The bed is fine."

They sat next to each other and smiled.

"My parents told me about the St. Bartholomew's Day Massacre," Dianella said.

"What's that?"

"It happened in the Ancient Year 1572 when a bunch of Catholics slaughtered thousands and thousands of French Protestants called the Huguenots."

"Why?" Aster asked.

"Because of a religious war."

"Ha ha ha! That's funny."

"Yes. They killed each other over God."

Aster thought about this for a moment, then with a smirk:

"You don't worship God the way I do. DIE!"

They both giggled. It was already obvious that Aster and Dianella would become good friends. Aster now felt obliged to continue the conversation by displaying his cultural knowledge, like two children sharing an appreciation of a popular smart phone app.

"That reminds me of the Jewish pogroms in the Middle Ages," he said.

"You mean the People's Crusade?" Dianella said.

"Yes, when all of those Catholic crusaders in Ancient Year 1096 were making the journey to take back the Holy Land from the Muslims—"

"Jerusalem."

"Yes, and on the way, they killed thousands and thousands of Jewish people because they were Jews instead of Christians."

"Because they thought the Christian god was the right god and the Jewish god was the wrong god. Even though they had no proof of that."

"My god is better than your god. DIE!" Aster laughed.

"I can't prove it but you're wrong anyway!" Dianella laughed.

"God is science and science is God," Aster said confidently, relieved he had just reviewed this with his parents.

"God is an *opinion,*" Dianella nodded, "and opinions always cause conflicts. I just learned that at my school, Lodgepole Elementary."

"Oh. I go to Crowberry Elementary," Aster said. "And I just got back from my Revelation!"

"You did? Congratulations! Wasn't it great?"

"Thank you. It was very great."

"I had my Revelation too," Dianella said. "I'll turned nine in April."

"I'll be nine next month," Aster said.

"Oh, that's good."

They stared at each other for several seconds with appreciative grins. Dianella looked over to the top of Aster's dresser, where there were assembled several plastic dinosaur figures.

"Oh, you have dinosaurs? What's that little four-legged one on the right?"

"It's Pakicetus. That's not a dinosaur. It's an old Ancient mammal that eventually developed into their whale, and our whale."

"Wow, into a *whale?* But I wish Opine had those big dinosaurs. The Ancient Earth was lucky to have them."

"Yes. At least we have whales."

"True . . ."

The conversation about dinosaurs and Ancient creatures continued, eventually veering towards other topics of common interest to young Opinion children. Opinions generally were not very good at engaging in small talk. They were not culturally conditioned to do so. Any substantive dialogue had to at best be intellectually enlightening, or, at the very least, informative or instructive to the extent that the participants would feel the expenditure of energy throughout the exchange was well worth the effort. The Opinions as individuals had different tastes and preferences, though paramount to them was not so much *that* something was liked, but *why* something was liked. To the Opinions, knowledge and truth were valuable above all else. An informal discussion about a favorite book had to elevate into what Earth may call an academic discussion. There was a synergistic thread in everything between "the truth" and "the beautiful," a thread central to their way of living, thinking, and communicating. It was not just "the truth" for them—it was Truth. Knowing Truth meant a better existence. Anything other than Truth was a tragic and comedic blunder, a laughable waste of human intelligence, and thus fodder for the kind of social satire upon which much of the Opinions' popular culture was based.

"I recently learned," Gaura Bottlebrush was saying as she, her husband, and Nolana munched on boysenberries and lingonberries, Schubert's *Eighteen German Dances and Ecossaises* playing lightly on overhead speakers, "that in the Ancient Year 1539 BCE, the Egyptian Pharoah Ahmose, after defeating the Hyksos people, decided to attack the Nubians down south—just because he could—and chopped off all the hands of the Nubians he killed!"

"Why?" Nolana asked.

"So that the scribe could count how many people were killed! Very easy—just cart the hands back north and count them!"

"Ha! A cart of severed hands!"

"But I have one better!" Kaffir said.

"Yes?"

"In the Ancient Year 1208 BCE, Ramses the Great's thirteenth son, Merneptah, had a similar campaign against the Libyans, and cut off all of their penises!"

"Really? Why not the hands?"

"Because the Libyan penises were uncircumcised! That proves that they were really Libyans!"

"Wow, how clever they were!" Nolana giggled. "That's one way to leave a mark in history!" She had completely forgotten about her car accident.

"You bet!"

"Too bad Ahmose didn't think of the penises!" Nolana said to Gaura.

"Yes, poor Ahmose. It's a lot easier to cut off a penis than a hand, I imagine. Though I never tried."

"Sure, it's got to be easier. And you can fit a lot more penises in a cart than hands."

"Yes—one appendage instead of five," Kaffir observed.

"And penises weigh less than hands, I guess," Nolana added.

They all laughed at this.

An awkward silence of looming small talk melted their revelry.

"And, and . . . Nolana," Gaura began, "what, eh, exactly do you . . . like to do?"

"I like to do . . . my work," Nolana said.

The Bottlebrushes relaxed. "Your work!" Gaura said. "And that is . . ."

"I work at the Cockspur Coral County Congressional Committee."

"Oh!" Gaura brightened, and delighted in repeating: "The Cockspur Coral County Congressional Committee!" The Opinions were very fond of utilizing alliterations for naming schemes.

"I know Cockspur Coral County very well," Kaffir said.

"Do you?"

"Yes, yes. I used to work for the Cockspur Coral County Cultivation Commission. Now I work for the Catchfly County Culture Coalition Center, as a Literature Consultant. Daphne Sweetspire across the street also works there."

"Ooooh," Nolana nodded, "Contentment Culture!" And Kaffir proudly nodded back.

"Yes," he said, "we work to review and disseminate the arts."

"And Nolana," Gaura continued, "what exactly do you do at, um, at the Congressional Committee?"

"Well, we do what every county congressional committee does, and that is to consider congressional candidates for service."

"Oh, so—Nolana, you help with the entire democratic process!"

"I do."

"How honorable!"

The "democratic process" in Opine was truly a democracy, in that every able-bodied citizen eighteen years or older was expected to serve in the Opinion Central Congress for a full month, no more than once every three years. Ten citizens were selected each month from each of the fifty counties (the single continent of Opine was one nation-state, or one country). Think of it as paid jury duty for a month. The Opinion Congress was patterned very closely to the Athenian Council of five hundred developed in the sixth century BCE, where fifty Athenian citizens were selected from ten "tribes," though serving for one year.

There was a single Facilitator during congressional sessions, one of the five hundred appointed to the position according to his or her experience facilitating local congresses, not in any authoritative capacity, but for the sole function of administering the sessions. Just as Ancient Athens thought it better to have the people themselves, rather than representatives, participating in the legislative process, the Opinions likewise had long ago decided the best way to avoid social upheaval was to ensure citizens were actively involved in the policymaking of their own government.

There were no elections for representatives because citizens were their own representatives, and there were no elections for presidents or prime ministers because the Opinions had concluded that voters in Earth's democracies were not thinking enough when they were voting. They were shopping, and the candidates were competing for their business. This, in the end, backfired drastically. Opinions were much more partial to the true participatory democracy of Athens rather than the democratic republic of America. This philosophy was in line with great Ancient thinkers like Jean-Jacques Rousseau, who argued that unless a person is directly involved in the legislative process, there is no way to know whether a particular enacted policy or law is in accordance with that person's will. Most importantly, what the Opinions understood is that while representing oneself might seem, on the surface, to serve self-interest, it ultimately serves collective interest, a universal State of Contentment.

Similar congresses of varying sizes, its members also rotating every month, were also established on the county and town level, so that local issues could be discussed and reported to the Central Congress. But neither the county congresses, nor the town and villages, held local political autonomy. They were essentially independent advisory committees, tasked with developing agenda items relevant to issues within their particular jurisdictions for the Central Congress.

Opinions knew from volumes of Ancient research that it was very difficult for local and national political ideals to align. A local politician, for example, has no incentive to vote against a corrupt practice if it means losing his or her local seat. "Fiscal federalism," where national and local governments shared funding and administration, meant that funding and administration were decentralized, which meant policies could be subject to the whim of the selfish. Local politics was "retail" politics, politics for sale. It didn't take long for the Opinions to discard it. Once the Central Congress agreed to legislative action on a particular issue, the tasks were delegated to various departments in each of the fifty counties: agriculture, housing, education, energy, justice, labor, treasury, transportation, and so on.

As for political parties, the Opinions had no use for structures that eventually fragmented into representing activists, fringe groups, or single-issue platforms rather than the general population. Whether it was a two-party or multi-party system, Opinions found no evidence of either one maintaining a balanced, fair representation of the entire electorate. On the contrary, after decades of Earth historical study and analysis, and following Aristotle's lead (he referred to them as "clubs"), the Opinions concluded that political parties, and local political entities, and any political system invoking representative government, eventually promoted extremism, divisiveness, socioeconomic inequalities, corruption, civil unrest, and a decay of healthy values.

The Opinions did accept American anthropologist Joseph Tainter's theory that all civilizations eventually collapse when the level of bureaucratic complexity reaches its breaking point. Simplify, simplify, simplify, the Opinions would say, when molding a society. The more complexity, the more incentives to become more complex, hence the more opportunity for divisiveness to derail progress.

There was very little room for contentious debate in the Opinion Congress, and very little possibility of different citizen groupings falling into cross-purposes, because everybody was on the same page. Everybody was working towards the same objective: a solution that will help absolutely everybody. Their society conditioned them to do so. They simply discussed what needed to be done and discussed the best way to do it. Everybody was afforded a chance to speak. The main objective of the Congress was to collectively find the *truth,* the truth being the solution to the issue. Issues to be addressed were arrived by consensus, while the implementation of solutions was decided by vote. If the Congress reached a deadlock on how to implement a particular piece of legislation—a relatively infrequent occurrence—then the issue was placed before the Opinion people by plebiscite. Plato certainly would have been very pleased with the modern Opinion Congress. While there was no philosopher king in Opine, every citizen was, in a sense, a philosopher, indoctrinated with the values of truth and justice through their compulsory education system, from kindergarten up.

Opinions serving in the Congress were optimistic about positive legislative outcomes, because the outcomes, regardless of the specific issue at hand, were designed to maintain every citizen within an equitable threshold of basic security and happiness. Congressional debates were conducted in a civil manner and always focused on how best to implement a particular piece of legislation.

There were no special interest groups because the group was the Opinion society and the interests of the society were paramount. The Opinions did not subscribe to Ancient constructs like "social status" because implicit in such a construct is the notion that one sector of society may be more important, or more privileged, or more well-off than another. To the Opinions, the very concept of "social status" was, at best, egregiously farcical, and at worst, obscenely repellant to the natural order.

Dogs do not impose social stratification on themselves based on breed. The Opinions would say that is because dogs are both not intelligent enough, and not dumb enough, to do so.

There was very little cause for social dissent when every citizen was assured a State of Contentment. Fairness for income distribution.

Fairness in standard of living. Equality of healthcare. Equality of education. Every Opinion knew from The Find that oppression, and bigotry, and intolerance, and inequality, and baseless fear, all of it bred dissent, and violence, and resistance, and revolution. The Fools had spoken. The Opinions had listened.

If a parent has five children, the parent does not decide that only one of them will eat healthy and the other four will suffer from malnutrition. Or that only one of them will enjoy parental care while the other four will be neglected. Parents never reason that some of their children must suffer for the sake of all their collective progress. For the Opinions, the family unit was exactly equal to the community, to the entire population. Just as parents do not deliberate on equality or welfare between their children, the Opinions did not deliberate on equality between all citizens.

Everything was laid out for them on The Find's quantum drive. The Fools had spoken. The Opinions had listened.

Yet mass acceptance of these radically progressive political philosophies was by no means a given. After all, the Opinions were only people—a reboot of Homo Sapiens. They needed some help, a push in the right direction. A conditioning, if you will.

Not so much a psychological conditioning, but a scientific one, a conditioning of their very humanity...

Five

Part 1

Three houses across the street, Hebe Hornbeam was treating Thymus Corkwood to her very best gluten free vegan gingerbread cake with white chocolate vegan buttercream frosting, and a cup of her very best insect poop tea. The Opinions were all on vegan diets. Hundreds of nutritional studies from The Find had made it more than clear that vegan diets were the healthiest of all diets, and, regardless, Opinions were completely against the idea of slaughtering animals for food, or even eating animal products. They surmised that your average animal, like your average person, does not enjoy being killed, for any reason. It's bad enough animals had to kill other animals for survival. Why do humans, the supposedly most intelligent creatures on the planet, have to make it worse for them, when it had been proven over and over that vegan diets were much more effective in extending life expectancy than carnitarian or selectarian or pollotarian diets? Only a fool would voluntarily lower his or her own life expectancy. Again, it was black and white: what was right, was right. As for insect poop tea, the health benefits were widely known both by the Ancients and the Opinions.

Hebe's unmarried sister, Daphne Sweetspire, was dancing around the living room while the other two sat on Hebe's floral linen sofa. She worked as a Music Consultant at the Catchfly County Culture Coalition Center, the same facility where Kaffir Bottlebrush worked.

Daphne loved to dance, but she was also re-enacting one of her favorite characters from Frank Capra's classic film, *You Can't Take It With You.* In that film, Ann Miller played the quirky Essie Carmichael, a free spirit constantly dancing in a haven for free self-expression established by Martin Vanderhof (played by Lionel Barrymore). Besides this one, Frank Capra's films, particularly *It's A Wonderful Life* and *Mr. Smith Goes To Washington,* and Henry Koster's *The Bishop's Wife,* were among the Opinions' favorites from Ancient Hollywood (only 1,463 full-length films were salvaged from The Find, most of them American). Any film that was optimistic, taught healthy life lessons, was profound and meaningful without resorting to profanity or violence, and ultimately made them feel good, was "profitable." If a form of entertainment was simply innocent clean fun, that was acceptable—as long as the general underlying theme was positive and there was no inclination to glamorize or promote decadence, cynicism, nihilism, pessimism or moral turpitude of any sort. Fantasy, science fiction, adventure, and fairy tales were all fair game. Goofball comedies like *His Girl Friday, Arsensic and Old Lace,* and *Bringing Up Baby* were adored (Opinions were huge Cary Grant fans, along with Jimmy Stewart, Spencer Tracy, and Sidney Poitier). Even the madcap silliness of a Mel Brooks film was appreciated, though the Opinions felt the advent of Vulgarian Culture, as they dubbed it, was as inanely frivolous as it was academically amusing (Ancient Slang Studies was a popular secondary school elective). Light situation comedy, such as *I Love Lucy, The Honeymooners, Mary Tyler Moore, All In The Family, Cheers,* and *Seinfeld,* were very much enjoyed.

Gratuitous content, however, was not tolerated, and, in fact, the Opinion Congress had permanently deleted digital files containing these elements long ago. The only violence permitted in art was that which served to illuminate a truth, or enhance a comic book effect—or a darkly satirical effect, as, for example, was expected and appreciated when depicting the pathetic plight of the Fools in elementary school morality plays. The Find provided the Opinions with more than enough historical data to study, critique, and condemn the shortcomings and atrocities perpetrated by the Fools on Earth. They didn't need it in their culture.

In short, negativity in art was only constructive when it was instructive.

"My sister loves to dance," Hebe said, as a grinning Daphne pranced about the room with leaps and arabesques and pirouettes, her long, tawny hair springing and flapping.

"Yes," Thymus agreed. "And dancing is very good for you."

"Yes, very healthy."

"Very healthy."

"Yes."

"And I can dance about *any*thing," Daphne said. The ends of her sentences rose in tone, peaked, and gently pinched off, like a sweet sonic spire. "I can dance about spring willows, or dappled Dalmatians, or I can even dance about architecture!"

"Well," Thymus nodded, "Daphne dances about dappled Dalmatians!"

"Definitely," Hebe laughed. "Do you like your poop tea, Thymus?"

"Yes, very much, thank you. I love poop tea."

"And . . . what else do you like?"

"Oh, I like spelunking, reading about genetics, and I'm also an amateur coloeopterologist."

Hebe gasped. "That's very fascinating! Did you hear that, Daphne? Thymus is a coloeopterologist!"

"Wonderful!" Daphne was whirling.

"I'm not a coleopterologist by trade," Thymus corrected. "I just like beetles."

"I once wrote a limerick about beetles!" Daphne suddenly stood erect to recite:

"There once was an Ashy Gray Lady,
Who loved a figeater named Brady.
They wanted to mate
But just couldn't wait
To look for a place that was shady."

She immediately resumed cavorting.

"That was very very good!" Thymus said. But Hebe's gaze remained fixed.

"And Thymus, your trade is . . ."

"Gene inhibition."

"Oh! Gene inhibition!" Hebe's orifices gaped. "Did you hear that, Daphne. *Gene* inhibition."

Daphne froze in a mid-spin. "How resplendent! I can dance about that too!"

"What kind of gene inhibition?" Hebe asked.

"Really the most important kind," Thymus smiled proudly. "What is commonly known as the Self Suppressor."

Hebe gasped again. "Thymus! You work on the Self Suppressor!"

"Beautiful!" Daphne crooned. "The resplendence!" She launched into a series of *fouettés*.

"Yes," Thymus said. "We synthesize it, at Geranium Genome Gentrification."

"You synthesize it!"

"Yes. Specifically, we alter the arginine-vasopressin receptor 1a on chromosome 12q14-15, and the sixth chromosome estrogen receptor ESR1 genes in the ventrolateral subdivision of the hypothalamus."

"Do you?"

"Yes, we certainly do."

Part 2

Herein lies the crux of how the Opinions were eventually able to foster such a peaceful, altruistic social dynamic throughout their entire society—though at a considerable cost.

The Opinion variety of the early human, the hominid, evolved in much the same way as they did the first time around on Earth, in the old solar system with the white sun. The Opinion human genome arose from the same kind of chemical and biological processes governing evolutionary "accidents," beginning with microbes, developing into aquatic creatures, developing into primates, developing into us. Different hominid groups banded together, competed for resources, cooperated, fought over resources, cooperated, fought over territory. The interplay of selfish and altruistic behavior was a consequence of genetic evolution, as described in seminal Ancient theoretical works such as George C. Williams's *Adaption and Natural Selection.* These behaviors were built into the new Homo Sapiens DNA, as before.

How was this seemingly improbable chain of events repeated? Just as stars with similar temperatures, masses, and chemical compositions blaze throughout the entire universe, many inhabiting different solar systems, in different galaxies, in different galaxy clusters, often separated by hundreds of thousands, if not millions of light years of empty void, so too does life blaze in far-reaching corners of the universe, comprised of the very same elements and forged by the very same chemical reactions that originate in those stars. It is very unlikely two intelligent life forms will ever be able to communicate, due to physical and temporal factors, not the least compelling of which are the limitations of space travel and the speed of light. Transient civilizations like Homo Sapiens will certainly never conquer the speed of light.

Though if another intelligent civilization *had* discovered Homo Sapiens 2.0 on what would become the planet Opine, they would have discovered a noticeable difference from Homo Sapiens 1.0. The new beings circling the blue star were given The Find. As discussed previously, once the quantum computer was discovered and solar energy powered it back up, the early humans were presented with language primers, in the form of digital dictionaries and encyclopedias, each word and phrase accompanied with a digital picture and accompanying audio pronunciation. There was barely any time for the Ur-Speech to develop. It was supplanted quickly by modern English. There were about another hundred language primers imbedded in the quantum memory, but they would be discovered later, stored in nested directories. English became the universal mode of communication thousands of years before it had on Earth. And once they could read English, they could read about, and learn about, *anything* in The Find.

However, this miraculous head start in language and civilization did nothing to tame the selfish and aggressive behaviors encoded in their genetic makeup. Once the Opinions were sufficiently evolved to apply scientific knowledge contained in The Find to actual practice, they decided to do something about their inherently selfish natures. A coalition of scientists from different counties throughout Opine developed a gene therapy targeting the VMHvl part of the brain, the ventrolateral subdivision of the hypothalamus. As Thymus Corkwood had briefly outlined, the scientists had targeted the arginine-vasopressin receptor 1a and ESR1 estrogen receptor genes. Studies dating back to the early twenty-first century on Earth had confirmed that these genes, and their role in the hypothalamus, were likely linked to selfish behavior in lab mammals. After experimenting with mice, it was eventually found that altering these genes in newly born infants would make human beings much more placid . . . much more altruistic . . . much more selfless. For Shakespeare, the "shrew" in *The Taming of the Shrew* may have been a woman, but for the Opinions, the "shrew" was a monkey. Namely, our evolutionary lineage.

What scientists found most interesting, and most exhilarating, was that the therapy helped to suppress violent behavior, as an extension of selfishness. Belligerence, as a character trait, was smothered. Opinions could still get upset, or irritated, or angry. Stress was a necessary component of the natural temperament. With this genetic alteration, the chances of an individual projecting that anger onto others, especially in the realm of physical harm, were vastly reduced.

Why this should be so had been extrapolated from documents within The Find. Opinions had determined through careful sociological and scientific research that selfishness as a character trait was essentially a form of violence. All modes of violence, be they physical or psychological, can be traced back to selfishness. This concept will be explored more fully in a later chapter.

Many on Earth would argue that altering the nature of human behavior was like "playing God." The Opinions would counter that it was not God who gave humans their selfishness. It was nature itself. It was the evolutionary process. Are we playing God when we develop technologies to treat illnesses, or cure diseases defying our natural immune systems? No, Earth says, that is not going against God, that is simply using scientific ingenuity to improve the quality of life. Precisely, the Opinions would say. We too are using scientific ingenuity to improve the quality of life. We have evolved to cure the disease of selfish instinct.

The Opinions surmised that even if Earth scientists had endeavored to develop a similar therapy, the social and political blowback would have made its implementation impossible. That is because Homo Sapiens 1.0 did not have the benefit of hindsight afforded by The Find.

Side effects are always a possibility. One side effect was not entirely unforeseen. Similar studies in the twenty-first century had also indicated a possible link between the ESR1 gene and sex drive. The coalition of scientists had not anticipated to what degree altering the ESR1 gene in this way would affect libido. In preliminary trials, there didn't seem to be much of a remarkable reaction. But after three generations of administering the therapy, it became clearly apparent that normal libido levels were drastically lowered in all subjects, in tandem with the equally dramatic success rate of lowering selfish behavior among the subjects.

This "taming" of the human genome was not viewed as a "crutch." Opinions had read Huxley's *Brave New World* and knew about the fictitious drug "soma," designed to take away the sting of any negativity with a drug-induced "high." The Opinions knew negativity in the human experience could never be eradicated. They knew it was neither practical nor healthy to eradicate negativity in the human experience. Rather, they were eradicating the negativity in human nature that could destroy civilizations. This was not eugenics, or controlled selective breeding. This was simply a branch of medicine, the Corrective Biological Sciences.

Owing partly to the gradual onset of the side effects across several generations, public resistance was not as vociferous as one might imagine. People, for the most part, were willing to sacrifice normal sex drives if it meant engendering a peaceful, tranquil, philanthropic civilization, where many domestic, sociocultural, or demographic conflicts stemming from the selfish instinct could be virtually annihilated, once and for all. It was found that people could still engage in loving relationships, and be physically affectionate, even with little to no libido. Due to the powerful effects of the gene therapy, most of the population eventually lost interest and forgot what they were missing. Sperm would now be obtained through microscopic testicular extraction, and fertilization would be administered in vitro.

While the idea of mass sexual dysfunction is abhorrent to us, it was, in time, embraced by the Opinions, who were determined to avoid the horrible fate of the Fools, a fate revealed so glaringly within the quantum drive of The Find. Opinion horror stories were the horror stories of their ancestors. Fear of what they *could* become drove the impetus behind their sacrifices.

Another side effect was completely unforeseen. After two generations of application, the therapy mysteriously began to induce vomiting, particularly among women. Opinion scientists were not quite sure why this was so, though the effect appeared to be more physiological than psychosomatic. The suppression of selfish and sexual instincts did not produce tension and anxiety—it actually had a soothing, calming effect, like a genetic tranquilizer. Yet somehow, the suppression "rebounded" or "deflected" as a kind of physiological feedback rejection, manifested through the gastrointestinal tract. At first it was quite alarming that such a large percentage of the population was throwing up with a frequency approaching two to three times a week. Though in time, as with other mainstream therapeutic medications, people learned to deal with the inconvenience and messiness, accepting it as just another sacrifice their society had to endure for the common benefit of all. Within a couple of decades, the vomiting became so assimilated into the normal course of daily life that people treated it as nothing more than a cough, or a sneeze.

The development of such a therapy was universally considered to be a monumental scientific achievement, to say the least, a milestone in the ongoing progress of the Human Gentrification Project, an Opinewide collaborative effort to "gentrify" Home Sapiens 2.0, or flush out the undesirable contaminants of the human genome. The Opinions really did view the venture as a decontamination. Just as there were undesirable microscopic organisms within the human body that needed to be flushed out, there were likewise undesirable elements in the human genome that needed to be flushed out.

Part 3

Nobody took for granted the historical significance of this achievement, so we can appreciate why Thymus Corkwood's revelation that he synthesized the Self Suppressor at the well-known lab, Germanium Genome Gentrification, elicited quite a stir from Hebe Hornbeam, and her sister, Daphne Sweetspire, who, upon hearing it, became so exultant in her gratitude for Mr. Corkwood's singular contribution to the betterment of society that her swinging raised foot knocked over a replica of a Tang Dynasty orange porcelain horse, which, after promptly ending its tenure sitting upon Hebe's coffee table, shattered into three angrily jagged pieces on the floral ceramic tiles.

Hebe stood up, froze, gaped at her mutilated horse. With clenched teeth, furrowed brow, and arms rigid at her sides, her upper body began a minuscule shiver, like a teacup rattling from a train blocks away. A sustained, muted whir of "mmmmm," occupying an unfrequented octave, pinched out the back of her throat. Daphne and Thymus rushed up to her.

"Oh, Hebe, Hebe," Daphne cried, but the woman was unresponsive. The horse was decapitated. One leg was severed. "I'm so sorry! I'll make it up to you!"

"Here," Thymus hastily shoved teal-green bills (for teal-green was the color of leaves) into Hebe's stricken hands. They fluttered to the tile floor. "You can buy a new one, on me."

"No, no, no, no Thymus," Daphne waved a hand. "You need that for your car repair."

"I've got plenty."

"No, no, this is my responsibility. I did this." She scooped up the bills, handed them back to Thymus. "Hebe, listen to me..."

The woman was still mewling and shivering.

"I'll buy you one just like it, and two more, to add to your collection."

"No, no it's okay," Hebe sniffled, and slowly lowered herself to sit.

"I'm going to do it," Daphne said. "What kind of sister would I be if I didn't?"

"It was an accident," Hebe said shakily, swiping a knuckle across an eyelid.

"Yes, but I'm buying you a horse. That's final."

"All right, all right," Hebe smiled wanly. "Oh..." She gingerly picked up the pieces, eyed them nervously. "We should go to the Bottlebrushes and tell them, and that young lady Nolana, about Mr. Corkwood. They invited us, remember?"

"Yes!" Daphne brightened. "Yes, let's do that! Mr. Corkwood . . ."

"Yes, of course, if you'd like . . ." Thymus was happy to distract Mrs. Hornbeam.

It was rather common for an Opinion's composed demeanor to quickly deteriorate into mini panic attacks over relatively minor mishaps. Mrs. Hornbeam's Tang Dynasty horse was a replica, easily replaced. Artistic replicas from the Ancients were popular and easily accessible to any citizen. But when a society takes great pains to lower the anxiety level of its citizens by emphasizing, first and foremost, egalitarian welfare through its laws, educational system, and cultural values, a tiny ripple in an otherwise undisturbed State of Contentment can possibly result in disproportionate waves. Of course, Opinions were not clones, so the intensity of Mrs. Hebe Hornbeam's reaction was in part peculiar to her character.

When they arrived at the Bottlebrush home, Hebe commenced triumphantly as the bearer of celebrity news.

"Gaura and Kaffir, I must tell you that this young woman, Nolana, had a most fortuitous car accident! The luckiest car accident imaginable!"

They all stared eagerly.

"This man," Hebe jabbed out a thumb, "Mr. Thymus Corkwood, is a scientist who works to synthesize the *Self Suppressor!*"

The three of them were astonished.

"The Self Suppressor!" Kaffir echoed.

Nolana's mouth hung open.

"Yes," Hebe said proudly. Her sister Daphne joyfully shook her fists with a broad grin. "And," Hebe continued, squinting in thought, "if I remember correctly, he alters genes in a subdivision of the hypophallus."

"The *hypothalamus,"* Thymus corrected.

"Oh yes, what a wack-a-noodle I am! The hypothalamus."

"The ventrolateral subdivision, to be exact," Thymus added.

"Of the hypothalamus," Gaura gestured to her own head, grinning.

"What resplendence!" Daphne said with clasped fingers.

"Yes, very resplendent, your work," Kaffir agreed.

"Oh, thank you, thank you. I didn't invent it, you know!"

"Oh, but you . . ." Nolana began. "Are you married?"

Thymus hesitated, all eyes on him. "No . . . no . . . I . . ." He glanced at Mrs. Hornbeam, who seemed to be urging him on with her nods. ". . . I haven't really thought of it . . . really."

"You're a busy man," Gaura said. "Making the most important therapy in the Corrective Sciences."

"A busy, *brilliant* man, of marriageable age," Mrs. Hornbeam winked.

"Dianella!" Nolana suddenly shouted, and Daphne yelped. *"Dianella!* Come down here please!"

"You too, Aster!" Gaura yelled.

"Dianella!"

"Coming! We're coming!"

The two children bounded down the stairs and stopped behind their parents.

"Come here," Nolana fluttered her fingers, and they stepped forward. "This man," she said, "Mr. Thymus Corkwood, the gentleman I hit, is a scientist. He works on the Self Suppressor!"

The two children goggled him.

"You do?" Dianella said.

"Yes, I do," Thymus smiled. "We synthesize it at the lab, at Geranium Genome Gentrification."

Momentarily grasping for something impressive, Dianella finally said, "Mr. Corkwood, I know a lot about Fool selfishness. Like... between Ancient 1846 and 1873, the California State Government authorized both the enslavement and murder of thousands of Native Americans, just so settlers could get the gold!"

The adults laughed approvingly.

"A California governor apologized for it—one hundred and fifty years later!"

They laughed again.

Aster excitedly added, "And at the Battle of the Somme in 1916, over three hundred thousand British, French, and German people died, and the British only gained six worthless miles!"

"You two know your Fool history!" Thymus laughed.

"And we're not like them," Dianella stated.

"Because of people like Mr. Corkwood," her mother nodded.

"Nolana," Hebe winked, "isn't your accident with Mr. Corkwood a happy one?"

"Oh yes, very happy!" Nolana gazed at Thymus.

They shared gladness for the happy car accident during the Bottlebrush's vegan dinner of coconut millet with berbere spiced squash, shallots, and chickpeas, with a delicious lemon panna cotta to top it off. Nobody vomited.

Six

Part 1

Nolana Whitebeam and Thymus Corkwood were married one year later at the Rock Rose Reception Rotunda in Cockspur Coral County. Ceremonies and receptions were always held in the same building. There were no places of religious worship in Opine. After decades of studying the relevant documents in The Find, the Opinions had come to the conclusion that if God was the most benevolent being in the universe, and His followers on Earth solemnly vowed to emulate His benevolence, then His worship by those religious institutions claiming a hegemonic legitimacy over that worship (which in itself was nonsense) certainly resulted in some of the most heinous, malevolent acts ever to be perpetrated against innocent people, in the name of the very benevolent being these institutions solemnly vowed to emulate in the first place. This, to the Opinions, was a violent contradiction in the very foundation of these belief systems, rendering those belief systems invalid, and, by extension, the formal organizations supporting them. Opinions saw God everywhere they looked. They didn't need buildings or icons or religious authorities.

The Opinion marriage rate was very high, due to a variety of socioeconomic factors. With the absence of sexual tension, the benchmark for lifelong compatibility rested solely on mutual love, respect, admiration, and emotional connection. This included homosexual partnerships, widespread in Opine. The Find had taught the Opinions the evils of bigotry and the blessings of tolerance all too well. Couples could always have children through a simple medical procedure. As long as the two-child quota was followed, resources would be distributed fairly. Opinion culture had always stressed the importance of familial bonds and family values as a crucial element in fostering a universal State of Contentment.

A factor even more critical to the high marriage rate, alluded to previously, was the manner in which the Opinion economy was organized. If there was one key element to the success of their economy, it was the establishment of a centralized social program instilling a particular cultural value in every citizen's upbringing: selflessness. The implementation of the Self Suppressor through the Human Gentrification Project made this possible. The Opinions were very clever in imbedding a philosophy of individual welfare within a larger framework of social welfare. Opinions could only bring about their own general happiness and welfare by first looking out for the happiness and welfare of the society as a whole. This socioeconomic idea was nothing new, of course. Similar theories had been bandied about by the Ancients. But it worked for the Opinions. Gene therapy, and the benefit of hindsight, made it work.

Over the centuries, the Opinions had studied assiduously the economic systems espoused by the Ancients.

They understood how capitalism, in its most insidious incarnation, had developed from an industrial economic system producing an inordinate accumulation of wealth for a small group of people—the dominant powers—the main consequence of which was to needlessly lower the standard of living, comfort level, and accessibility of health and security benefits for the majority of the population.

They also understood various concepts like diminishing marginal utility, which helped to explain why wealthy people generally needed to continually accumulate a lot more wealth to compensate for the diminishing pleasure of the wealth they continued to accumulate.

They understood how this phenomenon was related to social vices such as drug addiction, illicit sex, or gluttony—the more one "consumed," the more one needed to consume to offset the diminishing "utility," or usefulness.

They understood how despite several commendable efforts to close the widening gap of income disparity, the overall historical trend remained constant: the rich and powerful continued to doggedly pursue more power and more wealth, resulting in more income disparity, more class conflict, and a degradation of the systems and structures that had been designed to ensure a fair, comfortable standard of living commensurate with the yields of honest labor.

Yet the Opinions also appreciated, in a nod to John Locke, the reality of natural ability and talent, knowing full well that a select few were endowed with extraordinary motivation, extraordinary ambition, extraordinary aptitudes for innovation, extraordinary creative minds, such that these individuals had every right to be compensated more than those whose intellectual powers did not rise quite as high. Thus the entrepreneurs, the celebrities, the executives, and all the rest who, through the rigor of their ingenuity and ambition, were able to acquire more assets and wealth than the majority of the population, were never opposed by the people of Opine. Every citizen was free to pursue the highest level of professional attainment their abilities would allow. It wasn't the accumulation of wealth the Opinions were against. In fact, they encouraged it. It was its distribution that most concerned them. If the "invisible hand" was to govern the flow of a market economy, then such a hand would be under the watchful eye of the Opinion people, who knew the dangers of selfishness.

The Opinions were not even against a "winner-take-all" market, where fortuitous circumstances allowed individuals in high profile professions, like entertainment or sports, to earn gargantuan incomes. Opinions had their share of celebrities like the Ancients. The key was to inculcate cultural values into every citizen that defined who the "winner" must always be. The "winner" must be the entire society, so that in the end, the winner was each individual. And who enforced such cultural values? It was the centralized government, the Opinion Congress—in other words, the people themselves. This was more of a nod to the other great philosopher "John," John Rawls.

But exactly how could they do this? Essentially, they were following the historical trajectory of all progress. "Looking back in order to move forward." This was one of their mantras. For the Opinions, looking back provided them with the necessary knowledge, and just as importantly, the necessary *fear,* to move forward.

Fear of what? Fear of what brought down societies for Homo Sapiens 1.0. Fear that it could happen to them.

Part 2

It had long been known, from hundreds of years of sociological research, that in a capitalist system, people generally expect to have what others have in a similar economic situation. This is only fair. But some people have a lot more than others, and some people have so little they are not living comfortably, or securely, because they do not have access to the same basic resources allowing them to be as healthy as they *should* be, or as secure as they *should* be, or as comfortable as they *should* be. Once the social construct of "class" is eliminated, people expect to have the fundamentals of what *everybody* should have, and what everybody *should* have then becomes the basic necessities of life that will ensure security, comfort, and happiness, or, in a word, the Opinions' idea of "contentment." Yet this is not possible if a disproportionately small amount of people owns most of the wealth in a society. It is not possible, in other words, to reconcile selfishness with any fair economic system.

After poring over thousands of pages of Ancient economic theory, one of the many quotes that caught the Opinions' attention, and one that formed the basis of their present economic philosophy, was the following by Jeremy Benthem:

> "The greatest enemies of public peace are the selfish and dissocial passions... Society is held together only by the sacrifices that men can be induced to make of the gratifications they demand: to obtain these sacrifices is the greatest difficulty, the great task of government."

And, in response to Benthem's dilemma, this one by John Stuart Mill:

> "...The sole end for which mankind are warranted,
> individually or collectively, in interfering with
> the liberty of action of any of their number, is
> self-protection. That the only purpose for which
> power can be rightfully exercised over any
> member of a civilized community, against his
> will, is to prevent harm from others."

These two quotes encapsulated what the Opinions eventually concluded must be done to establish and maintain collective happiness and well-being: the people must interfere with their *own* liberty of action, and exercise power over their *own* will, by eradicating selfishness. By eradicating selfishness, one may not prevent all types of harm in the legal sense (for example, negligence or strict liability), but at least one can avoid harm from others via an unbalanced economic system.

How can an economic system avoid harming its citizens? Opinion law dictated that every person's income must be reported by the employer to the Congress electronically. Computer algorithms either approved the salary, or adjusted the salary so that it met the requirements for the highest possible standard of living commensurate with the fair compensation value of the individual's occupation and status within that occupation, all in accordance with the present state of the economy. In other words, computer algorithms were established to approve and/or adjust the highest possible salary for an individual based on his or her occupation, experience, and present economic conditions. This decision was ultimately not up to the employers. It was all processed by computer.

The "highest possible standard of living" didn't mean opulence. It meant the highest amount of gratification and comfort one could attain from work and private life. The Opinion standard guaranteed that every adult be able to own property in the form of full ownership or common interest developments (such as a condominium or cooperative housing). Rentals were deemed to be exploitive of the tenant, and thus banned. Every individual was given the opportunity to build home equity. Homelessness was forbidden, under law. Poverty was illegal. Inadequate living conditions were illegal. The physical size of the property depended on the specific needs of the owner or owners; whether it was a single person, or a married couple, or a married couple with children. If one was in a position to afford more property, or even multiple properties, one could always invest in such ventures. Everybody was entitled to the basic amenities of a comfortable living, including a front lawn, a back yard, and a garden, as it had been proven many times that people surrounded by nature always lived happier, healthier lives. Reading books by ecopsychologists like Theodore Roszak supported what they knew instinctively, namely the mental health benefits of stressing a communal bond with the natural world. The cold, impersonal, congested, mechanistic, cutthroat, unmerciful menace of urban steel and concrete and high-rises was abandoned. Urban areas, in general, were viewed by Opinions to be congested infestations of wealth juxtaposed with poverty, and thus magnets for class conflict, segregation, unfair discrepancies in standards of living, cynicism, and cultural and moral decadence. Opine was a suburban world without the urban, a land of towns and villages. Even large industrial buildings and complexes were given a homely, cozy ambiance. When people went to work, they were meant to think they were going to work at their second home. Nature was everywhere. You couldn't escape it. And nobody disrespected nature.

If John Locke wrote in his Second Treatise of Government that every hard-working, industrious citizen should have the right to private property, the Opinions surmised he was not referring to the squalid living conditions of a hovel.

Besides ownership of property, every citizen in every one of the fifty counties was guaranteed the same quality healthcare. Health insurance was socialized in Opine. One of the more ludicrous ideas on Earth, and one of the cruelest ramifications of unfair distribution of wealth in a capitalist system, was gauging the quality of healthcare, and accessibility of health insurance, on conditions outside an individual's intrinsic worth as a member of the human race. If universal healthcare was anathema to some back on Earth, it meant that, according to their view, not every individual was entitled to the same level of care. What it came down to was, of course, a selfish sense of superiority among those who saw themselves as privileged. If you're wealthy, you have nothing to worry about. If you're not wealthy, watch out . . . there's no guarantee you can afford to be healthy. To the Opinions, this was utterly absurd, another form of bigotry hiding behind the euphemism of "freedom of choice."

If John Locke warned that domination in politics is taking advantage of other's necessities, the Opinions definitely listened.

Part 3

In the areas of standard of living and healthcare, then, the Opinions granted every citizen the right to be comfortable, secure, and healthy. And any economic activity diminishing that right for others was considered a *harm.* It was a state-imposed universal welfare, not unlike what occurred, on a much smaller scale, during the Ukrainian Euromaidan protests, in Earth's year 2014. The Ukrainians, during this infinitesimally brief snapshot of Ancient history, were heroes to the Opinions, selflessly caring for one another in the midst of this, and other humanitarian crises, including the subsequent Russian invasion of Ukraine in the 2020s.

How to pay for all of this? It is not easy if the wealthiest sector of society does not care if the wealth of the economic system in which they benefit is not distributed fairly.

But modern Opinions were conditioned to be equally fair to all.

They were conditioned genetically, and it was reinforced into their cultural upbringing, just as surely as children are brought up to obey their elders. Because if they don't, they will get punished. The Opinions knew what the punishment was for being selfish. The punishment was becoming like their Earth ancestors.

The same central computer system that calibrated income levels for different sectors of the economy, and forwarded those to the county congresses, who in turn enforced them in each county, likewise calculated the amount of yearly income "taxes" each citizen contributed to both the Central Congress and county congresses. Although these payments were, in effect, taxes, the unselfish Opinion really regarded them as donations for the benefit of all, to maintain the

State of Contentment. Taxes were calculated based on individual or collective income levels in conjunction with the current state of the economy. Citizens were notified by the first of February the amount of their expected donation. If the first of May deadline was missed, not to worry. The amount was automatically debited electronically from both personal and business accounts into the central and local treasuries. No questions asked. Accountants abound in Opine, but their services are not required for filing tax returns.

One of the most beautifully symbiotic aspects of this system is that it followed very naturally from the Opinions' mentality as a selfless people. As we saw in the car accident between Nolana and Thymus, citizens were always more than willing to compensate their fellow citizens for unexpected loss. Had the neighborly local residents not been able to offer Nolana and Thymus enough compensation for their repairs, or if they simply had not been present to witness the accident, the local government administrations would have stepped in to cover the costs. Private insurance companies did not exist in Opine. They were evaluated long ago to be exploitive and inequitable in nature—selfish. The risks outweighed the benefits. Not to be trusted.

To be sure, this "coerced" tax rate would appear outrageous, and unrealistic, to many on Earth. A few examples will suffice.

A person earning a median income is not expected to donate much—less than ten percent of their gross earnings. But a person earning, say, a million crassulas a year, automatically donated around forty percent of those earnings, subject to fluctuating economic conditions. A person earning ten million crassulas donated about sixty percent of those earnings. A person earning 100 million crassulas donated about eighty percent of those earnings. And a person earning one billion crassulas donated at least ninety-five percent of their income. Corporate taxes were calculated on a similar "order of magnitude" system, always considering a particular company's profile, capital expenses, and expected fair profit margin.

The Opine Congress then uses its revenues to maintain its social programs and subsidize whatever industry or business needs it, be it housing, agriculture, education, the solar electric car market (fossil fuels are completely banned), infrastructure, healthcare, research and development, corporate subsidies, arts and culture, space exploration, unemployment insurance, disability insurance, social security, or any other social program. The market and financial economies are free to run, as in a capitalist system, though strictly tempered with regulatory computer algorithms.

Delving into the intricacies of how the Opinions achieve their balance between *laissez-faire* and regulatory policies within an interdependent market and financial framework would require a rather dry, unappealing interruption to our narrative. In response to any questions or objections corralled by a battery of Ancient political scientists, the Opinions would simply point out that any social, political, or economic theory cited as a potential challenge to the Opinion model would be rendered invalid without first assuming the initial sociobiological condition of the Self Suppressor. The behavioral patterns of Homo Sapiens 1.0 would simply not match up with those of a genetically modified species like the Opinions. In the absence of a shared genomic experience, the Opinions would reassure Ancient experts that the people and businesses of Opine eventually get back what they put into their society—in spades. And if Adam Smith, in *The Theory of Moral Sentiments,* claimed that the impetus behind our actions is largely based on earning the esteem of others, the Opinions certainly reaped the rewards of such sentiments.

Part 4

The Opine government is a true democracy, not a democratic republic, because the people represent themselves, like the Athenian democracy. But even if the people are representing themselves, do they have a right to impose such a tax rate on the wealthy? Will not the wealthy be opposed to this? Don't people have different values? Won't people in different sectors of society have different self-interests?

The Opinion government—the people—would respond in three ways:

(1) "We, the democratic representatives of ourselves, are the dominant protective association. We are here to protect everybody from harm, including harm from selfishness."

(2) "The freedom of the individual to keep his earnings with as little interference from the people as possible is *not* valid compared to the freedom of the people not to be harmed by the selfishness of the individual."

(3) "There cannot be a pluralism of values when it comes to rights and freedom, because that would imply there is a debatable gray area between universal right and universal wrong. There is no gray area for us, because within that gray area there is no moral

standard, but only selfishness, and therefore, unfairness. Within that gray area is the proven failure of Homo Sapiens 1.0. Within that gray area is the *opinion,* and the opinion cannot be relied upon to reveal the truth of human values, since the opinion itself is selfish."

For the Opinions, a book like *Community And Society* by the German sociologist Ferdinand Tönnies, propounding that the local and non-local entities of the title would always confront mutual conflicts of interest, would demonstrably be recast as *Community Is Society.*

In connection to these points, the Opinions would also cite the aforementioned Ancient political philosopher, John Rawls, who, following the lead of the Ancient Greek philosopher Diogenes, would say that an individual's inherited station in life is determined not by choice, but by chance. One person's inherited disadvantage could easily have been the next person's disadvantage, so that the standard for justice becomes the elimination of any one individual's unnecessary disadvantage. As long as the disadvantage is an *honest* disadvantage—not due to sloth, or cheating.

Opinion public education always emphasized a healthy work ethic. They couldn't abide laziness. Upon completion of secondary school, the Opinion State continued to subsidize vocational, undergraduate, and graduate study. If a person was having difficulty finding employment, the Bureau of Occupational Placement ensured a position for every able-bodied individual. Nobody was left out. If a working-aged individual refused to work, he or she could be confined to a home incarceration unit, a penal practice we shall explore more fully in due time. The Opinion work ethic did not tolerate a physically and mentally functional citizen sitting home watching TV or embarking on perpetual vacations while every other citizen contributed to the State, the State of Contentment. Independently wealthy citizens were also expected to contribute, even if through a voluntary or philanthropic capacity.

In Opine, a roll of the dice granted you a station in life, and as long as you did your part, you would enjoy the maximum contentment possible and an equal opportunity to prosper. This was essentially a utilitarian philosophy, in that a social policy enacted by the people will always be right if it promotes universal happiness. No longer would there be an occasion for what Kathy Cramer calls "the politics of resentment." A common Opinion proverb: "Why *resent* when you're *content?*" This was utilitarian free market capitalism with a social safety net, regulated by the people themselves.

Hence the Opinion tax code, and their general view of equitable levels of living standards, a nod to the two great "Johns," Locke and Rawls. The very wealthy did not have to worry about buying off the rest of society's discontent if everybody was made to be content. And business did not have to worry about supporting a welfare state because everybody's welfare was the state's business. And labor unions did not have to exist because the entire state was one and the same with a labor union.

The Opinions had successfully conquered the Divide-The-Dollar Game, which posits that there is no distribution principle that won't be upset by some new majority. In Opine, any justification for upsetting the distribution principle would have to be predicated on undue selfishness, a human trait that has been quashed by the Self Suppressor. Recall that an Opinion earning a yearly income of one billion crassulas still gets to keep 50 million crassulas. Asking such an Opinion how a person could possibly be content with a net income so much lower than their earnings would be answered with an incredulous stare. "You're asking me how I can possibly be content with 50 million crassulas when so many others have so much less?"

And yet, these tax codes were not set in stone. Opinions can make a case for why they are unable to meet the rate required by the algorithm. In that case, their grievance would have to be settled in court. This does not happen often, and is usually due to unusual personal circumstances.

More often, and amazingly—at least for us—Opinions have the option of donating *more* than what is automatically extracted from their accounts. Do they? Yes, sometimes they do, again, depending on their personal circumstances and the current economic conditions.

Many would find the idea of voluntary tax burden unrealistic, or at least aberrant. That is understandable. Because Earth is the first try. The Opinions were representatives of the second try. They refused to mess up the second try. The moral narrative for the Opinions became the lessons of Earth's moral narrative. The collective proximate goal was to avoid the fate of Homo Sapiens 1.0. Do not repeat their mistakes, at all costs!

This was the soothing, happy State of Contentment indoctrinated into the minds of couples like Nolana Whitebeam and Thymus Corkwood as they celebrated embarking on a new life of Opine matrimony at the Rock Rose Reception Rotunda.

Seven

An outsider may be very surprised to walk into an Opinion social gathering, such as a wedding reception, and witness culture dating back to over nine billion years. Nolana and Thymus requested the wedding band play not only popular selections from Opinion composers, but also familiar hits from the heydays of Homo Sapiens 1.0 popular entertainment. Walking into the Rotunda you would hear Glenn Miller (such as *You and I),* and Stevie Wonder (*You Are The Sunshine Of My Life),* and The Monkees (*I'm A Believer),* and Frankie Valli (*Can't Take My Eyes Off You),* and The Beatles (*Twist and Shout),* and Louis Armstrong (*When You're Smiling),* and James Brown (*I feel Good),* and Ray Charles (*Georgia On My Mind),* and Earth Wind and Fire (*September).* (Yes, the Opinions adopted the names of all twelve calendar months, but each month was nineteen days long.) While Nolana and Thymus preferred popular music from roughly Ancient 1930 to 1980, another wedding reception may include selections from the Ancient 1990s, or the 2030s, though the popular music of these later periods generally did not spark as much enthusiasm as earlier periods. Most of the popular culture recovered from The Find derived from the United States, so while it was always assumed an American buried the quantum computer, it was very much appreciated that this particular American at least possessed a broad appreciation of the arts, including works from the great masters of music, art, and literature throughout the world, thereby gifting Opine with a generous portion of its present high culture.

The Opinions, however, were generally not proficient dancers. They often stepped on each other's feet, bumped into each other, or even lost their balance in a tumble. Always with a laugh, to be sure.

Any wedding reception was incomplete without some comic cathartic entertainment, and Thymus Corkwood was lucky enough to have a friend and colleague, Dr. Lupin Hollyhock, who happened to know the famous satirical author, Clover Watsonia. Once the Cockspur Coral County Justice of the Peace administered the marriage oaths, and once the newlyweds had their first dance and cut the vegan vanilla banana carrot cake, Mr. Watsonia and his sidekick Shasta Leadwort mounted the stage to the utter amazement and delight of all one hundred twenty-one guests. Sitting across from each other, they launched into one of Mr. Watsonia's acclaimed satirical Fool Dialogues, beginning with Mr. Leadwort. Their delivery was rapid-fire.

"Hello, I am interested in buying some misinformation."

"Of course, you came to the right place! May I ask what kind of misinformation you are interested in spreading?"

"Well, I am running for public office, and I am against purple eggs. Specifically, I am interested in keeping the green eggs as the dominant eggs in our society, whereas my opponent is pushing for equal rights between the purple eggs and the green eggs. I am interested in spreading some misinformation about not only my opponent, but purple eggs in general, so I can get more green eggs to agree with me that it is in their best interest to keep greenness superior to purpleness, and to keep purple eggs from attaining positions of leadership or influence. But I must accomplish this in such a way that the purple eggs do not believe me to be anti-purple, as I surreptitiously work against them while acting as if I am working *for* them and simultaneously benefiting from the misinformation that garners me enough votes to win a position of leadership that will allow me to pursue my real agenda, green egg kickbacks and misappropriation of government funds at the expense of purple eggs."

"Ah, a true kleptocrat! Well, well, we can certainly help you with attaining your political goals. May I suggest you also add some alternative facts to your misinformation package? We have a special this week: buy two alternative facts and get one for free."

"Hey, that's a good deal! Do you think the alternative facts are worth it?"

"Oh, yes, there's nothing like a few alternative facts to dress up a juicy misinformation campaign. Keep in mind that while misinformation can be deliberately inaccurate, alternative facts are unmitigated unadulterated undeniable falsehoods, guaranteed, or you get your money back."

"That sounds like a good idea. I'll take those three alternative facts for the price of two!"

"Spectacular! A wise decision! And may I interest you in some gaslighting?"

"Gaslighting? Is it effective?"

"Effective? It's explosive!"

"Explosive?"

"Absolutely. If you light a flammable vapor it will explode. Imagine if you light the vapors of a false reality? It too explodes, ready to be devoured by any Fool in its blast radius."

"But will they really accept it? I'm a little hesitant to spend so much money unless I'm guaranteed results."

"You're worried about results? You can't seriously doubt the results when history has shown it works every time!"

"Every time?"

"Sure! Listen, there are two types of Fools, each a victim of ignorance. There is the Fool who is not yet a Fool and doesn't know he is a Fool when he becomes a Fool, and then there is the Fool who is a Fool to begin with who openly embraces becoming more of a Fool but still doesn't know he's a Fool. The first type of Fool is initially not a Fool but his ignorance makes him susceptible to the wily false rhetoric of the Gaslighting Monster such that he, the Fool-In-Waiting, is tricked into believing a reality he *thinks* concords with what he *should* know but in actuality what he *doesn't* know is being exploited and twisted and warped to mold him into a future compliant Fool. The second type of Fool was a Fool and is still a Fool because he believes the Gaslighting Monster is confirming what he thinks he already knows but in actuality the false reality that he is looking to validate is both validated and exploited to further embolden the Foolness that made him a Fool ever since he endeavored to become a Fool. In both cases your Gaslighting Monster is pandering to either a present Fool or a Fool-In-Waiting, so that in the end you will end up with more Fools, which in turn helps your Gaslighting Monster to recruit even more Fools."

"I'm not sure I understand but somehow it makes sense!"

"Of course it makes sense! It makes sense because all that matters is that it makes sense to the Fools because as long is it makes sense to them it doesn't have to make sense to you or make sense at all."

"Oh, that's very reassuring!"

"Yes, and that is exactly what we work to ingrain into your victims, the reassurance that they are free to bask in whatever doubts you tell them to doubt until they doubt everything except the comfort zone of a false reality where facts become fiction and fiction becomes fact and history is rewritten and uncertainty is bliss. May I also interest you in a conspiracy theory?"

"Does it cost a lot?"

"Yes, but believe me, it costs a lot more to everyone else!"

The entire reception hall roared.

"But what if..." Mr. Leadwort continued, waiting for the laughter to subside. "...what if it works out that I eventually can oppress and suppress and repress the purple eggs. Don't I have to worry about them rebelling?"

"It won't make a difference if you use our misinformation package! Even if they *do* rebel, it can be to your advantage!"

"Really?"

"Sure! If the purple eggs rebel, then they will all be aggregating and coordinating and conglomerating, gathering their resources together, and this will work to your advantage if the purple eggs put all their eggs in one basket because then all you have to do is destroy the basket."

"Destroy the basket?"

"Yes, destroy the basket."

"Isn't that illegal?"

"It's not illegal if you get people to believe it's justice instead! You can say that the basket was really destroyed by a purple egg who thought that the basket was full of green eggs. Or you can say that the purple eggs in the basket were about to attack the green eggs and the green eggs were acting in self-defense. Or you can say that it wasn't really a green egg who destroyed the basket but a purple egg who painted himself green so that green eggs would be blamed, thereby giving the purple eggs an excuse to start a war with the green eggs. As long as you keep repeating untruths, people will mix up truths with untruths, until the untruths will become truths and false reality becomes reality and the Gaslighting Monster feeds itself and smiles and winks at the end!"

Then, a prearranged entrance: one of the band members, a trombonist, approaches the stage.

"Excuse me," he says, "I object to this entire exchange! It shows a complete contempt and disregard for basic human decency; a cynical and shameful perversion of ethics; and a blatant desecration of what any law-abiding citizen values as a moral compass."

Clover pulls out a toy pistol. "Fuck you," he says, pointing it at the trombonist, "and die!"

Snap, and prior rehearsals had polished the trombonist's adept arched twist of his upper body, the concealed squib jetting an intense arced spray of fake blood onto the tables closest to the stage. The extended tongues of the cackling guests were greeted with a refreshing delightful sampling of naturally flavored cherry lemonade.

A twelve-year-old girl sitting at a far table had been tugging at her mother's sleeve.

"Mom?"

Mom was too busy laughing and applauding.

"Mom?"

"Yes, Aussie?"

"Would the Earth people call a Fool like that a mothersucking cockfucker?"

Aussie's mother tilted her head in thought, then turned to her husband.

"Filbert, is that right?"

"Ummm... I think it's 'motherfucking cocksucker,' Aussie."

"Yes, that's it," the mother said to her daughter, "I think your father's right. Motherfucking cocksucker." Then, with a grin, to her husband: "Been a while since I took Ancient Slang Studies!"

The laughter and applause was subsiding when one of the guests towards the back chanted:

"Children!"

Clover Watsonia and Shasta Leadwort stood up. "Who's that?" Clover said with exaggerated interest. All the guests turned their heads.

"Children!" the man called again.

It was Mr. Figgle! Everyone loved Mr. Figgle! He always seemed to randomly turn up at large gatherings where the discussion turned to good old clean Fool-bashing, although his presence here was again prearranged, through a connection with his longtime friend, Clover Watsonia. Mr. Figgle was retired Professor Emeritus of Comparative

Sapiens Social Anthropology at Mangrove University (although he held the academic title of "doctor," the informal "mister" served as an affectionate sobriquet). Bald with ash grey tufts on his temples, a bit more rotund than the average Opinion, his globular eyes, cheery grin, and jolly demeanor were infectious. He was like a Professor Santa. His first name, Jonquil, had long passed out of common usage. The guests greeted him with a round of applause.

"Hello Mr. Figgle!" Clover waved. "Do you mean the destroyer of egg baskets are children?"

"Of course!" Mr. Figgle replied. "Any so-called adult whose mind is not yet developed enough to comprehend the civilized basis of a civilization really is a child entrapped inside the body of an adult. Your average child is not mature enough to understand the natural balance inherent in any society, regardless of that society's place in history or cultural norms, so that like the immature child, the adult child will resort to deceit and violence to realize his own selfish values."

Clover Watsonia looked down at the "dead" trombonist, his autumn leaf embroidered linen dress shirt dappled with fake blood. "What do you think of that, Mr. Trombone?"

Lifting his head, the trombonist said, "From now on, I'm keeping my mouth shut."

"Shut up!" Clover barked, and *snap,* shot him again. The squib had already expended the blood reserve, but the audience appreciated the gesture.

Mr. Figgle's grin was perpetual as he spoke.

"Do you mean to say, Mr. Figgle," Mr. Watsonia's scripted response continued, "that those individuals who claim their God-given gift of power justifies their violent acts and brutal dominance are really *children?"*

"Precisely," Mr. Figgle nodded emphatically, as heads of guests swiveled like a tennis match. "Only a civilized adult with a sufficiently developed mind grasps the natural balance of cooperation, compromise, and comradery. A brutish, selfish child only knows bullying and lying as the instruments by which he gets what he wants. The despot or tyrant is a child with resources and henchmen to enact his bullying, adept only at taking the 'civil' out of 'civilization,' an egregiously adulterated shell of an adult. His distorted worldview is self-worship, in the same way a brutish, selfish child craves power. He must flout the laws getting in his way to secure this power in the same way a child will flout the rules of good behavior."

The guests clapped. Thymus Corkwood sat with his new wife sparkling with pride. Nobody could have asked for a better wedding reception.

"What about Alexander the Great? Caesar? Napoleon?"

"Chilllldren!" Mr. Figgle crowed. "Talented children who sought to conquer the world, their arrogant self-worship occulting the sanctity of innocent life! Children whose crimes against humanity hide behind reverent historical epithets like 'the Great' and 'the Mighty' and 'the Conquerer!' The very idea that 'greatness' can be accredited to the subjugation of humanity! The massacred are the collateral footnote to the great conqueror, but the worm's great feast is always the detritus of his empire!"

"What about Mao Zedong, Hitler, Stalin? Ivan the Terrible? Genghis Khan? Leopold II?"

"Children, all children, children, *children!* The adult-child is not civilized enough to see the common thread binding all humanity! He cowers, he cringes, he recoils from our differences; he fears the open embrace of tolerance; he weaponizes his national ideologies, or his ethnic ideologies, or his racial ideologies, or his cultural ideologies, with hateful propaganda, for bullying is the only defense mechanism a child imprisoned in an adult body can use to hide his childish fear and weakness! Yes, *weakness,* because deep down, the bully child *fears.* He fears the differences in people, the differences that others embrace yet he fears to embrace, and convinces himself these differences are harmful, giving him the justification, even the moral imperative, to compensate for these fears by striking out with malevolence, bigotry, and violence, and preying upon the weaknesses of his followers by instilling these fears into them, so that they too can be relied upon to strike out with malevolence, bigotry, and violence. But—the child tyrant fails to look back to inform what lies ahead, and it is this shortsightedness that ultimately destroys him."

"And what of emotivism, subjectivism, triumph of the will? Maybe there's no universal moral standard!"

"Bunk! Gunk! Junk!" Mr. Figgle jabbed. "Subsume a moral standard to the whim of the individual, to emotion, to *taste?* Oh, foolish Enlightenment, what were you thinking? So there's no scientific standard to human decency? Then, why not let people just sort out their differences, like this: One says 'I don't like *your* values, and *I* am stronger than *you,* so I will conquer you!' The other says, 'But now *I* am stronger, and I don't like *your* values, so *I* will conquer *you!*' And they go back and forth, back and forth, a nonsense seesaw game of

King of the Hill, one set of values measured on one yardstick, another set of values measured on another yardstick, until we have so many yardsticks for human worth that the only humans deemed worth anything are the ones who happen to be holding the yardstick until somebody else grabs it! And so goes the scale of history, tilting this way and that way: a few million dead here, a few million dead there; a sham democracy here, an unjustly overturned election there; a bit of ethnic cleansing here, a little political purging there; with Objectivism crying out the whole time, 'What about humanity?' and Subjectivism crying out, 'Genuflect before me, Humanity, for *I* am the triumph of the individual will!'"

"Mr. Figgle, is there no hope for those young aspiring tyrants? What advice would you give them?"

"I would say to all of those tyrant hopefuls: If you're trying to oppress your people or start a war and those annoying animal kingdom universalities are getting in your way, such as the instinct to live and be happy... don't worry—you can always claim personal *taste!*"

"But not us!" somebody shouted. "We have the Self Suppressor!"

Appreciative laughter and applause.

"We salute Mr. Thymus Corkwood," somebody else shouted, "and his beautiful new bride!"

The rotunda erupted in cheers.

"And the Hollyhocks!" a woman called out. "Lupin and his dad, Mistol!"

More cheers.

Lupin and the elderly Mistol smiled and waved.

Mr. Figgle chortled, though it was lost in the clamor.

Thymus's colleague, Lupin Hollyhock, and Lupin's retired father, Mistol Hollyhock, specialized in gene therapy. It was Mistol's great-grandfather, Nalca Hollyhock, who was renowned as one of the pioneering genetic scientists behind the Self Suppressor.

Everybody was most pleased with these surprise attractions. Of course the general agenda of all Opinion public events was to ensure the participants felt better off, in that the proceedings were intentionally fashioned for each and everybody's *profit*—not just entertainment. Opinions always felt they needed to "get something" out of a social gathering, and that "something" was most beneficial if it took some form of emotional or intellectual enhancement. If Opinions didn't feel they were constantly improving themselves, they were wasting their very valuable time on Opine.

Following the prepared dialogue between Clover Watsonia and Mr. Figgle, several guests approached Thymus Corkwood to express not as much their congratulations on his marriage (though the volume of monetary gifts was certainly not lacking), as their appreciation of both his vocational contribution to the State of Contentment and the ceremony's celebratory acknowledgment of his vocation's *raison d'être*.

"Thymus, we can't thank you enough!" Daphne Sweetspire smiled sweetly, clasping her hands with his. "Such a blessing what you've done!"

"Oh, so wonderful of you! Congratulations Thymus!" Daphne's older sister Hebe Hornbeam beamed. "And I really hope we'll be seeing much of you from now on!"

"Yes, thank you, thank you," Thymus bowed and grinned.

"Salvia," Hebe said to her husband, flicking her head toward Thymus, "a Self Suppressor scientist! What an honor!"

"Thank you for all you've done, Mr. Corkwood," Salvia said. He had played the string bass in the band, and was also the Principal Bassist for the Ox Eye County Symphony Orchestra. "A very profitable ceremony. And the both of you look very content."

"Thank you," Thymus said.

"Thank you," his wife Nolana said, "and you as well."

Peering over Nolana's shoulder, Thymus spotted the silver-haired Mistol Hollyhock leaning into Mr. Figgle's left ear. Mr. Figgle listened, and laughed. Mistol was one of Thymus's heroes. He, along with his son Lupin, had done some pathbreaking work with Chimeric Antigen Receptor T-cells at their facility, Thunbergia Therapy Thresholds, especially in the area of immunosuppressive microenvironments. And, of course, to know the Hollyhocks was to know the legendary Dr. Nalca Hollyhock, whose therapeutic innovations formed the basis of Thymus's work with the Self Suppressor. Thymus's company had in fact financially supported research and development in Lupin's company several times, and Lupin's company had returned the favor. They also owned each other's stock. Indeed, there was an Opinion stock market, though it was heavily regulated by the Central Congress. No exploitive dealings permitted. They were not going to permit a repeat performance of economic catastrophes like Ancient 1929, 1987, 2008, and 2043.

"A toast to my good friend and colleague, Thymus Corkwood!" Lupin shouted with a glass of champagne, a few gulps worth. The Opinions drank very moderately, as fearful of alcoholism as they were of any disease. "Had it not been for his company's very generous contributions," Lupin said, "the T-cell program would never be what it is today!"

Thymus was just as gratified when Mr. Figgle later walked over offering a warm handshake, a business card, and his trademark squinty smile. "All the best, and keep me apprised on the latest."

The card simply said "Figgle," with a phone number and email address. Curious, Thymus thought, but Lupin did mention once that Mr. Figgle was always very interested in keeping current with the genetic sciences.

On the way out of the rotunda, several guests noticed a middle-aged woman staring up at the foliage of a red oak. The mid-October leaves were an iridescent coalescing of yellow, green, orange, red, and brown, mirroring the floral pastels decorating many of guests' attire. One leaf in particular was dangling off its stem, a final clinging goodbye flutter before it's seasonal descent. Several guests hurried up to her, including Kaffir and Gaura and Aster Bottlebrush, Hebe, Daphne, and Nolana's daughter, Dianella.

"What is it?" someone said.

"It's the leaf. The hanging leaf."

They followed the gaze of the middle-aged woman.

"They don't fall off by themselves," the woman said. "The tree pushes them off. Little cells called abscission cells cut the leaf off by the stem, little by little, until the leaf drops. The tree can't sustain frozen leaves in the colder months when food production slows. So they let them go."

The people stared at the leaf.

"It's a little sad, somehow," somebody said.

A man passing by on a scooter saw the people looking up. He too looked, his eyes finding the leaf. Seconds later the scooter swerved, hit a guardrail, and the man blasted into the air, shrieked, somersaulted before diving into a thick hawthorn bush. Several people rushed over, bills flapping in outstretched hands.

A faint gust, and the little leaf was finally cut off from its parents. It took a good ten seconds to find its resting place.

"What resplendence," somebody murmured, and somebody else agreed, and Gaura smiled, and Aster stared, and Dianella contemplated, and Hebe sighed, and Daphne threw up.

Eight

Seven years later, Aster Bottlebrush was sitting in the Boxwood Borough Brainery along with fifty other students, taking his Academic Contentment Assessment.

All Opinion children were required to take this assessment at the age of sixteen. The purpose of the assessment was twofold: first, to evaluate where the child's natural abilities lie; and second, to evaluate exactly what line of work the child would be interested in pursuing. Essentially, the educational philosophy sought to determine midway through secondary school what the student was good at and what made the student happy. Students were enrolled in either the Academic Track, which encompassed all the liberal arts and sciences, or the Vocational Track, exploring fields ranging from carpentry, construction, and plumbing to law enforcement, paralegals, paramedics, and the culinary arts. All students must take courses in civics, history, and ethics, regardless of their track.

A true State of Contentment could only be achieved if every working citizen felt the years they devoted to their livelihood fulfilled their passions. Money was only as valuable as the meaning attached to it, as that value ultimately would be imparted onto not just themselves, but to the whole of society. Contributing to society should be a happy, rewarding affair. The educational system was tailored to this end.

Opinions understood that when Thomas Jefferson wrote the phrase, "the pursuit of Happiness," he was not referring to the pursuit of recreational activities, or a family vacation. He was referring to the freedom to pursue truth, the freedom to pursue knowledge. If philosophers like Tocqueville warned that citizens of a democracy would constantly be plagued by restlessness, condemned to "distracting themselves from their own happiness," Opinions made sure the educational experience instilled sufficiently "profitable" values to preclude any tendency towards restlessness.

At the secondary level, the curriculum was derived mostly from knowledge acquired from The Find, as the fundamentals of all Opinion knowledge were based upon millennia of Ancient research, culture, and innovation. Scholarship by independent Opinions in every discipline was well-represented in undergraduate and graduate studies—though again, it was impossible for any Opinion's work not to be indebted in some way to the foundational knowledge bequeathed by Homo Sapiens 1.0.

Aster was brilliant, though he found himself distracted by the presence of Dianella Whitebeam, now Dianella Corkwood, with her caramel hair and gentle visage, sitting to his left, two rows back. He occasionally glanced over his left shoulder to watch her take the assessment. He didn't really know why he kept looking at her. She was pretty, but every girl was pretty, in their own unique way. It really didn't make sense for him to be looking specifically at Dianella more than any other girl. It's true he had gotten to know her over the years at their secondary school, the Boxwood Borough Brainery. But he had gotten to know lots of people. There wasn't anything unusually remarkable about Dianella. Every girl was, again, in some unique way, remarkable. She was one of many who he could potentially marry in the future.

The questions were not very difficult. He should be able to concentrate and get through this easily. Following are some samples from Aster's Academic Track Assessment:

Question: How is the gambler's fallacy related to radioactive decay?

Aster: Gamblers believe that if the same event happens many times in a row, like getting heads on multiple coin tosses, then tossing another heads is less likely. But the chances will always be 50%. For radioactive half-life, there is always a 50% chance that half a radioactive nucleus will decay.

Follow-up: Do you find physics interesting?

Aster: Yes.

Follow-up2: Do you often think about being a physicist?

Aster: No.

Question: Describe one of the earliest examples in Earth's literature addressing the inequality between men and women.

Aster: *Medea,* by Euripedes. Medea is famous for saying that after all the hardships and abuse women experience in a male-dominated society, she would rather be dead if she is not appreciated by her husband, and that she would rather go to war three times than give birth once.

Follow-up: Do you enjoy reading books like this?

Aster: Yes.

Follow-up2: Do you often think about historical literature?

Aster: No.

Question: Can different infinities produce a negative energy?

Aster: Yes. In the Casimir Effect, two uncharged metallic plates can be drawn together by one infinity of the virtual particle field outside the plates being larger than that of the field between the plates (similar to the infinity of irrational numbers being larger than that of the rational numbers). This creates a negative energy density between the plates.

Follow-up: Do you find mathematics interesting?

Aster: Yes.

Follow-up2: Do you often think about pursuing a career involving mathematics?

Aster: No.

Question: What are three important Earth twentieth-century works of literature focusing on social injustice, and what oppressed groups are depicted in each?

Aster: John Steinbeck's *Grapes of Wrath* depicts the oppression of poor tenant farmers during the Great Depression; Upton Sinclair's *The Jungle* depicts the oppression of poor immigrant workers in early twentieth-century Chicago; and Harper Lee's *To Kill A Mockingbird* depicts racial inequality and the oppression of African Americans in the early twentieth-century American South.

Follow-up: Did you find these books illuminating and meaningful?

Aster: Yes.

Follow-up2: Do you ever think about writing a work of literature?

Aster: No.

Question: What is the most common misconception concerning Machiavelli's political philosophies?

Aster: Many Ancients believed Machiavelli's concept of "the end justifies the means" espoused a despotic philosophy of rule. In fact, in works such as *Discourses on Livy,* Machiavelli recommended a strong republican state over monarchies, though warned that even in a peaceful democracy, peace and prosperity often leads to restless ambition, and men, essentially evil in nature, will always look for an opportunity to act upon these selfish ambitions.

Follow-up: Do you find political philosophy interesting?

Aster: Yes.

Follow-up2: Do you often think about a career in public service?

Aster: No.

Question: Can a single musical chord express unfulfilled longing?

Aster: Yes. For example, a chord associated with tension, like the dominant triad on the fifth scale degree, can be prolonged and represent unfulfilled longing. Music of the Ancient Romanic era explored delaying the resolution of the dominant chord in this way.

Follow-up: Do you enjoy listening to music?

Aster: Yes.

Follow-up2: Do you often think about being a musician?

Aster: No.

Question: What is one of the most influential works of political art in Earth's history?

Aster: *Guernica,* by Pablo Picasso, painted in 1937. It depicts the brutal bombing of the Basque town of Guernica by the Nazis.

Follow-up: Do you find it interesting how the beauty of art can portray the ugliness of humanity?

Aster: Yes.

Follow-up2: Do you ever think about being an artist?

Aster: No.

Question: What is one of the first Earth examples of a nation using misinformation to start a war?

Aster: In 1870, Prussian chancellor Otto Von Bismarck had fabricated a story about the Prussian king insulting a French envoy during a meeting about Spanish affairs. This "Ems Dispatch" spread by Bismarck resulted in the Franco-Prussian War, France's subsequent defeat, and the birth of the German Empire, which eventually contributed to European international tensions that led to World War I and World War II.

Follow-up: Do you find the lessons of history interesting and inspiring?

Aster: Yes.

Follow-up2: Do you often think about being a historian?

Aster: No.

Students had two hours to complete the entire assessment (Opinion days were 27.8 Earth hours). Aster would have completed the questions a half-hour ahead of time, had it not been for Dianella sitting within viewing distance. He couldn't help looking at her every two or three questions. And she definitely noticed several times.

The assessment ended with a "preliminary diagnostic question."

Question: Please state at least one occupational field you may see yourself pursuing in the future.

Aster thought for a moment, then wrote: "Ancient Sexuality Studies."

Later, a smiling Dianella approached Aster and immediately asked why he had kept looking at her during the assessment. She didn't feel there was anything inherently wrong with his glances. His behavior left her curious.

"I like looking at you," Aster said. "I think you're pretty."

"Thank you. You're pretty too."

"Thank you."

"But you can look at me any time, Aster," Dianella said. "Why did you need to look at me during the test?"

"I don't really know. You were there, so I looked at you."

"But you were taking a test."

"I know. I took the test."

Dianella smirked, not satisfied.

"Aster," she said, "are you thinking you and I are a good match?"

Aster shrugged.

"I'm not sure."

"We have plenty of time to decide if we're a good match. In the meantime, you can give me a kiss."

"Okay."

Aster didn't hesitate. They, like many boys and girls, had exchanged quick pecks several times over several years. It was no big deal. This one was on the lips, his slightly parted.

"Blech," Dianella said, wiping her lips with a finger. Opinions were generally not hypochondriacs, but were careful about maintaining proper hygiene and actively followed healthy sanitation practices.

"Oh, sorry," Aster frowned.

"No, it's okay. Be content."

"Thanks. You too."

They both smiled and began walking to their next history class, The Amoral Foundations of Political Misanthropy.

Nine

LIKE MOST OPINION OFFICE BUILDINGS, the Catchfly County Culture Coalition Center was decorated with floral carpets, floral murals, potted flowers and plants and vines, and illuminated waterfalls. Speakers dispersed throughout the building intoned the quiet forest murmurs of avian wildlife, alternating with variegated styles of music drawn from both Earth and Opinion culture. Employees were tasked with continuing the ongoing task of sifting through and evaluating hundreds of thousands of artistic works recovered from The Find's quantum drive. This monumental effort was shared between various publicly funded organizations throughout all fifty counties of Opine.

The importance of the arts and culture in Opine cannot be overstated. Cultural Gentrification was not a system of politically centralized censorship. Content incorporating sexuality, violence, or profanity was permitted, as long as these elements were "profitable" to the intellect, in that they served to reveal, through the beauty of artistic representation, universal truths about humanity, and how the human race has learned to weather the hazards and corruptions engraved on its biological blueprint. As discussed earlier, gratuitous content served no real value, and was thus expunged rather than censored. Any work that promoted cynical or hateful ideologies was also useless, and unhealthy. A disease is not censored, or corrected. It is eliminated. Some creative works were diseases, and likewise must be eliminated. This was not censorship. It was preventative cultural decay. The challenge was to determine whether an objectively fine work of art could potentially be subjectively corrosive to the State of Contentment. It was not always easy to detect whether a malicious hidden germ was infecting an ostensibly beautiful turn of phrase.

Today, the literary work under consideration by Literature Consultant Kaffir Bottlebrush and his colleagues was the Ancient late eighteenth-century novel, *Jacque the Fatalist,* written by the French philosopher and critic, Denis Diderot. This work had been reviewed by the Literary Board once before, but was tabled after a consensus of "truth" was not reached by the allotted time. Literary Boards could not forward a work to the Central Congress until the members succeeded in discovering whether its value rose to the level of a universal profitable truth. Such a discovery could take time, especially if the subject matter was controversial. The quality of writing was not as crucial as the message it aimed to reveal.

The members were impressed with the banter between Jacque and his master, the spirited conversations ricocheting between comic romantic anecdotes and self-referential philosophical discussions about whether individual actions mean anything when our fate is already written on a "great scroll" high above. What the Board found fascinating is that Diderot, in some sense, was wrestling with whether the apparent "imprisonment of the body," in what we now understand as genetics, could ever attain any degree of freedom within a universe where "Destiny is in charge of us." Happily, the author comes to the conclusion that we do have the freedom to take responsibility for our actions and make the most out of what cards nature has dealt us, regardless of the fact we have absolutely no say on what cards we are in fact dealt. The Board thought this was truthful, and thus profitable. But Mr. Didoret often peppered his narrative with bawdy stories, often inviting the "Reader" to weigh in on his critical comparisons with other authors.

"I would like to point out this passage," Mr. Rubus Cliffbush was saying. "This is towards the end. He refers to his own book and writes:

> 'If my book is any good, you'll like it; if it's bad, it won't do you any harm. There is no book more innocent than a bad book. I rather enjoy—pausing only to change the names—writing down the stupid things you do. Your follies make me laugh, but what I write offends you. To be perfectly frank, Reader, I'd say that of the two of us the more unkind is not me. I'd be only too happy if it were as easy for me to defend myself against your aspersions as it is for you to defend yourself against being bored or imperiled by my book. Just leave me alone, you miserable hypocrites. Carry on fucking like rabbits, but you've got to let me say fuck. I grant you the actions and you let me have the word.'"

"Bold!" another consultant, Mrs. Heather Smilax, raised her eyebrows.

"Yes," Mr. Cliffbush nodded, "and then, later in the passage, he writes, speaking again to the Reader:

'What harm were you ever done by something as natural, necessary, and right as genital activity, that you should wish to exclude all mention of it in your conversation and imagine that your mouth and eyes and ears would be polluted if it weren't?'"

"If I may," Mr. Crocus Sophora interjected, "the author has a point there. The genitalia are natural and necessary, and no harm can be done by speaking about them."

"Yes," Mrs. Smilax said, "as long as the motivation behind speaking about the genitalia is not to objectify, or cheapen human worth."

"Truth," several consultants nodded.

"Yes, truth," Kaffir Bottlebrush said, "yet I think we still have not determined whether the belligerent tone derails the *primary* truth, which is that we all must make the best out of what nature has given us."

Everybody nodded in agreement.

"Remember," Kaffir continued, "he does call his audience 'stupid,' and 'miserable hypocrites.'"

"And, as Rubus indicated," Crocus said, "he told the Reader to keep fucking like rabbits."

"And that in return, he should be allowed to say 'fuck,'" another consultant added.

"Which is natural," Crocus said, "but *why* should he be allowed to say it?"

"I think," said Mrs. Sugi Blackthorn, "he is emphasizing the point that the imperfections of an individual are reflected in the imperfections of the society, so that when judging the imperfections of the individual it should always be done in light of the imperfect society of which he is a constituent, so that in the end we arrive at a universal moral code that succeeds in helping us all, despite these imperfections, mitigate on an equitable level the choices and value judgments we are confronted with as we navigate the vagaries of an uncertain future."

Nobody fully understood what Mrs. Blackthorn had just said, and neither did Mrs. Blackthorn, but it seemed to ring of truth.

"Yes," Rubus said. "I believe Mrs. Blackthorn has something there."

"And... this means... that Mr. Diderot's book is... sufficiently profitable?" Kaffir posed.

The Board members all looked at each other expectantly. Nobody spoke. Silences like this were always awkward. They may be hitting another impasse.

"His writing is admittedly first rate," Mrs. Smilax finally said, answered with nods and affirmations of "truth, truth."

"There is plenty of evidence in The Find to suggest he is a widely acclaimed author of French literature," another consultant said.

"Truth, truth," several of them said.

"He is a learned scholar," Crocus said. "His philosophical ideas are well-thought-out, and articulated with the very finest of prose..."

"Truth, truth."

"...and his original, refreshingly conversational tone helps to engage the reader."

More nods.

"Fucking like rabbits," Heather Smilax cut in, "is the kind of language that definitely engages the reader."

The nods were tentative, though still unanimous.

More silence. And then *bing,* a few phones chimed. Kaffir pulled his out.

"Today's Fool Fact," he announced, and the group leaned forward. "During Stalin's forced collectivization of agriculture in 1933, one of the many thousands of peasants who died of starvation, Petro Veldii, noticed that somebody had died in the grave Petro had dug for himself. So he dug another one, laid down, and died!"

The entire Board laughed heartily, a much needed release.

"Save your people by killing them! Good one!" somebody giggled.

"That man Petro did a lot more for himself than a tyrant does for an entire country," somebody else said.

"Truth, heh heh heh, truth."

The sniggering subsided into another silence. Again, the members eyed each other.

"Dr. Garva!" Kaffir suddenly brightened. "We can consult Dr. Garva!"

"Yes, yes, do that, Kaffir. Consult Dr. Garva," they unanimously agreed. Kaffir promptly stood up and exited the conference room.

Dr. Mallow Garva was a celebrated veteran of the Catchfly County Culture Coalition Center, and as such, was sometimes consulted when the Board found themselves unable to discover whether a particular work of art was profitable enough to reveal a universal truth. Years ago, Dr. Garva had been promoted to a Senior Truth Arbiter. Besides serving as one of The Find's Senior Data Administrators—a very exclusive, prestigious post—as Truth Arbiter he served as a literary consultant to the literary consultants. Just as the Roman Senate during the Republic functioned mainly as an advisory assembly, so too did the Truth Arbiters within the general area of Culture Gentrification. As this was the second discussion considering Diderot's *Jacque the Fatalist,* it might be prudent to solicit Dr. Garva's advice on what direction to proceed.

Looking left and right on his walk down the hallway, Kaffir eyed the lovely fish swimming in the recessed wall aquariums, very exotic fish, from Elephantnose to Zebra Plescostomus to Snakeheads to Dwarf Puffers. The vast Opinion Ocean, which covered 96% of the planet surface (as opposed to 71% of the Ancient Earth), was home to over 65,000 known species of aquatic life. It was such a pleasure to walk pretty much anywhere in Opine, indoors and outdoors, knowing that at any given moment you could immerse yourself in the plethora of wonders offered by the natural world. Kaffir smiled at this truth as he ran into Daphne Sweetspire, who worked on another floor as a Music Consultant.

"Kaffir! Where are you off to?"

"Hi Daphne! I'm off to consult with Dr. Garva about a French novel being considered for truth clearance."

"Oh, wow, a Truth Arbiter! Well, I hope it works out. We're sifting through some Bud Powell recordings, and a pop artist from the Ancient seventies named David Gates. Also we're reviewing Fauré's archive."

"Wonderful. I hope more of Fauré surfaces."

"Instrumental music of this type is never harmful. It's really a pleasure to clear. And to hear!"

"Absolutely. Truth in beauty!" Kaffir playfully pointed to Daphne's face, returned with a playful simper.

"Yes, truth! I'll let you get back to your work, Kaffir."

"Okay, see you soon, Daphne. Be content."

Daphne stood on her toes and gave Kaffir a quick peck on the lips before walking. Again, this was considered normal social etiquette. One of the effects of the Self Suppressor was to dramatically subdue any pangs of jealousy that may otherwise flare from superficial or unreasonable grounds for objection. Without the sexual tension of libido, Opinions did not feel compelled to interpret innocent gestures of physical affection as a threat to the strictures of loyalty established by the marriage bond. Loyalty was demonstrated by long-term devotion, love and mutual trust—a trust that could not be sullied by a little kiss here and there when the catalyst for sexual antagonism had been biochemically stifled.

When Kaffir entered Mr. Mallow Garva's office, the ivory-haired Truth Arbiter was at his computer terminal, selecting with his mouse a particular blue folder in a very long list of blue folders against the desktop's shamrock-colored background. The man quickly toggled a screen saver upon Kaffir's announcement.

"Dr. Garva, I'm sorry to interrupt, but the Board needs some direction on a Diderot clearance."

"Yes, Kaffir. I was just compiling relevance data from The Find."

"Oh, yes. I'm sorry for interrupting."

"That's quite all right." He stood up and took a penetrating, level look at Kaffir. "Which Diderot work are you evaluating?"

"Jacque the Fatalist."

"Ah. Of course, it's not under my purview."

"Yes. We just would appreciate some direction. This is the second deliberation."

"That's natural for a great author. What is the nature of the impasse?"

Kaffir blinked. Every deliberative impasse was identical in nature. "The . . . truth of the work's thematic profitability."

"As it pertains to . . ."

Kaffir hesitated. "As it pertains to . . . whether the author is artistically justified in directing hostility toward the reader."

"Well, Mr. Bottlebrush, again, it is ultimately up to the Board. But I would consider whether the hostility directed at the reader arises naturally from a truth the work aims to reveal."

"Yes," Kaffir agreed, though this didn't help.

"If that truth, for example, is to strive to make the best kind of choices that will navigate us as successfully as possible through a potentially hostile world, then that hostile world may be represented as the book itself, so that the reader, in a sense, becomes the author himself—or the main character, Jacque, if you prefer."

"Ah, yes. Yes, yes, I see."

"So that in writing the book, Mr. Diderot is navigating through his own philosophical dilemmas through a vicarious experience with not just *the* reader but *all* readers, including himself. His hostility is thus not malevolent but a reconciliation with acceptance of humanity's imperfect knowledge about existence. If the Board feels that reconciliation is sufficiently profitable, then the work is profitable."

Kaffir thought about this for a few seconds, briefly wondering if it was close to what Sugi Blackthorn had said, and immediately arrived at the irrefutable conclusion that Diderot's *Jacque the Fatalist* was, in truth, a sufficiently profitable work of art, and that its merits to that effect rose so high as to have temporarily eluded a fully penetrative appreciation by the esteemed Board of Literary Consultants.

"Thank you, Dr. Garva. That was extremely helpful."

"You're most welcome," Dr. Garva bowed. "Be content."

"You as well. And again, I apologize for disturbing you."

"That's quite all right."

Kaffir's eyes flicked to the computer screen's screen saver display of floating moray eels. "I... didn't see anything before," he said.

Dr. Garva walked a few paces forward, broadened his grin. "Kaffir," he said, "I would not have thought to ask if you had seen anything."

"Yes, of course."

Kaffir turned and hurriedly left.

Ten

Ms. Carnellia Gayfeather, a guidance counselor at the Boxwood Borough Brainery, was one of those rare citizens whose cider hair complemented to a perfect match her cider complexion, a fortuitous genetic handshake with standard Opinion skin tone. Opine's single land mass, covering about four percent of the Opinion surface, had originally been fragmented into nine continents, all of which drifted together through the action of plate tectonics into what the Ancients would have termed "Pangaea," though a considerably smaller one than the supercontinent of their Permian Period. Happily, the final agglomeration, replete with lakes and rivers, occurred in the temperate zone of the planet's twenty-seven-degree obliquity, or axis tilt, catalyzing the evolution of a mammalian species whose melanocyte-stimulating hormones would select the present cider-like skin pigmentation. Simply stated, the average Opinion was brown-skinned, with various shadings, depending on latitude. Of course, in Opine, skin tone was not viewed racially, but embraced as just another characteristic making each individual unique.

As always, when Aster entered Ms. Gayfeather's office, he marveled at how the epidermal hue of her humanity had seemingly soaked into the waves of her lovely tresses.

"Aster Bottlebrush! Take a seat. Have you been content?"

"I have, Ms. Gayfeather. And you as well?"

"Yes, thank you. I have here your Academic Contentment Assessment. You did very well, as we all expected!" Her smile was as effervescent as a blazing star.

"Thank you, Ms. Gayfeather. I tried my best."

"You are doing very well. Everybody is proud of you. I did want to speak to you about your potential occupational contentment prospects."

"Okay."

"You have an impressive range of knowledge throughout the full gamut of disciplines. The humanities, vocational, social and natural sciences . . . you have a healthy mind, young man!"

"Thank you."

"Now, your preference metrics reveal that you are not at this time particularly inclined towards any one area, despite consistently high achievement."

"Well, I'm interested in everything," Aster shifted uncomfortably. "I just have trouble making a decision."

"There's no rush right now," Ms. Gayfeather's eyelids fluttered. "Though you did indicate a preliminary interest in Ancient Sexuality Studies."

Aster took a moment.

"Well, that was just, like you said, a preliminary interest. I haven't decided on anything yet."

Ms. Gayfeather smiled pleasantly.

"I'm sure you know that Ancient Sexuality Studies is not an

available concentration in higher education, per se. There will be opportunities to touch upon ancient sexuality within a rich assortment of curriculums offered by ancient sociological or anthropological courses of study."

"Yes. Yes, that sounds fine. Very fine."

"Do you think you may be interested in pursuing something along the lines of ancient sociological or anthropological courses of study?"

"Yes. Yes, I may consider that."

"Aster, what do you think it is about the prospect of pursuing ancient sexuality that piqued your interest enough to cite it as your primary preliminary preference for career contentment?"

Aster had to think carefully, lest he furnish the kind of unsatisfactory answer that would needlessly prolong the discussion, or worse, end up in a referral.

"I really was thinking about the subject . . . scientifically."

"Oh? Scientifically?"

"Yes. And a scientific exploration of ancient sexuality conflates very naturally with your suggestion about ancient sociological or anthropological courses of study."

"Yes, yes that is truth," Ms. Gayfeather nodded, her eyelids fluttering again. "And what is it exactly about the scientific basis for ancient sexuality that interests you?"

Aster had to think again.

"I . . . am interested in . . . the scientific basis of ancient sexuality as it relates to . . . a power complex."

"Oh? A power complex?"

"Yes. Yes. A power complex."

"How so?"

"Well . . . the Ancients, as individuals, or communities, or nations, were constantly seeking out ways to assert their . . . respective identities, using power play tactics to compensate for underlying insecurities or inadequacies . . . and . . . sexuality was a mechanism of stressing a sense of superiority, or power, where other desirable attributes were lacking."

Aster breathed, thankful that jumbled catchphrases from prior sociological studies had coalesced somewhat intelligibly. Ms. Gayfeather nodded, seeming to confer with his thesis.

"Yes, Aster, that is very insightful. And what about the physical component of this power complex?"

"The physical component?"

"Yes. How the Ancients asserted this power play physically. For example, the physical act itself?"

"Oh, the physical act itself?"

"Yes."

"Do you mean . . ."

"The physical act of sex."

"I didn't think about that," Aster said quickly.

"Well, the physical act does come into play with this power complex, does it not?"

"Sure. Sure it does."

"Like the Ancient fixation on the power of the male genitalia."

"The . . ."

"I'm sure you recall from your first-year studies that the Ancient tendency to establish male-dominated societies was justified through a sociopolitical projection of the power of the penis."

"The puh . . . Yes, of course. Yes. I do."

"And the degree to which, and the way in which, this power dynamic is embraced within a social unit—that is, to what capacity the penis itself dominates affairs in a social unit—is reflected in the overall power distribution practiced throughout that unit."

"Yes. That's right, Ms. Gayfeather. That's right."

"Well, Aster, I am willing to bet that your interest in Ancient Sexuality Studies is really part and parcel of your overall interest in Ancient Sociological Power Dynamics."

"Yes," Aster nodded. "Yes. Thank you for clearing that up for me, Ms. Gayfeather."

Carnellia Gayfeather smiled and fluttered her eyelids.

"You're welcome, but I am only clarifying what you already know."

Eleven

It is certainly true that Homo Sapiens 2.0 had several advantages over Homo Sapiens 1.0 in jumpstarting their civilization. Besides the obvious quantum head start in all the branches of knowledge afforded by The Find, and the incalculably valuable hindsight of historical perspective granted by the same, the evolution of advanced civilization on Opine occurred on a single continent surrounded by one enormous ocean. All of the geopolitical and demographic complexities of a six-continent social, economic, and political network (excluding Antarctica) were reduced to ten million square miles, roughly the size of present day China and Russia. There was no threat of foreign enemies beyond Opinion shores. They had ample natural resources to provide for their society, the technical know-how from The Find to utilize those resources, and, again, the wealth of historical precedents to ensure every collective decision benefited the whole.

Yet we must remember that in the one hundred years before 2046, when Home Sapiens 1.0 civilization collapsed forever, the benefit of historical hindsight was just as glaringly available for them to take notice. There was more than enough opportunity to inaugurate proactive, cooperative, international measures designed to avoid the looming cataclysm staring every sentient observer in the eye. Unfortunately for Homo Sapiens 1.0, when there are enough Fools in the ruling class minority pursuing their own selfish agendas, while simultaneously misdirecting the majority's values to help fulfill those agendas, the false securities of a warm beach where a civilization rests become the quicksands of ruin . . . and oblivion.

All the debilitating factors were set in place long before 2046, each metastasizing concurrently, progressing symbiotically like a community of viruses. It is well beyond the scope of this volume to chronicle the course of events and historical currents as they transpired, though the Opinions reported six pivotal generalities, summarized below:

(1) Political Overreach. When a powerful nation exploits its own influence on the world stage, it becomes very difficult to manage the complexity of problems, and resentment, that inevitably arise. Just as ancient Rome stretched its influence beyond manageable limits, twentieth-century world powers were seduced by the same erroneous conviction that campaigns to spread their political ideologies throughout the world, whether through invasion or "rollback" (forced regime change), would be embraced with open arms. It is one thing to interfere in a sovereign state perpetrating crimes against humanity. It is quite another thing when one state's "social engineering" suppresses another state's national self-determination. Beginning with the Treaty of Versailles after World War I, empires drawing arbitrary borders without regard to the sensitive intricacies of deep-rooted cultural heritages resulted in a boiling pot of resentment

and animosity that only gained fuel with time. The world was horrified at the unthinkable atrocities committed by savage, bestial tyrants like Hitler and Stalin—millions upon millions of innocent souls wiped out. Those tyrants cared nothing for the self-determination of nations, and even less for the sanctity of a human life. Yet other nations needed to learn lessons from countless imperialist and regime-changing debacles throughout the nineteenth, twentieth, and twenty-first centuries. They never did. A community of nations is a community of shared values, and such a community has no right to encroach itself upon others without invitation. Just as importantly, promises and pacts made in good faith should be kept, or the repercussions could be disastrous. Civilizations may rise, but empires always fall. If nationalism and exceptionalism make other peoples suffer, an entire world will suffer.

(2) Income Inequality. World powers unfortunately tended to sow discontent among their societies through unequal distribution of wealth. Those in the top few percentiles of the wealth bracket also tended to deflect the blame onto anybody but themselves. For the Opinions, the argument that one cannot have a true free market economy without avoiding poverty was absurd. Equality in wealth distribution didn't mean there couldn't be any wealthy people. It just meant there shouldn't be anybody needlessly suffering. If a small power class, or oligarchy, can manufacture false narratives to maintain divisiveness and discord among the majority, then focus is shifted away from the

instigators, and the income gap can widen. The erosion of community associations exacerbated this effect. Analyzing the Ancient data, Opinions found that, for example, the more membership in trade unions went down, the more income inequality went up, and the more political parties fragmented. Inevitably, the masses reacted to these trends with shaken faith in democratic principles; solidarity decaying into factionalism; and a desperate resort to xenophobia, racism, and bigotry as scapegoat mechanisms.

(3) Political Favors. Ancient Rome's example is once again instructive. As the Roman Republic matured, the political landscape was soiled by corruption seeded in the patron/client relationship, where the client performed favors for a wealthy patron in exchange for influence in some capacity, whether it be a business venture, a court case, or securing a position. It wasn't long before the favors became monetary payments. Political bribery became the mainstay of modern world powers, so that representatives of the people would not necessarily be working for the benefit of the people, but instead working to receive payments in return for influencing the narrow agendas of their wealthy clients. As in the Roman example, this kind of quid pro quo arrangement made those holding political power beholden to the wealthy individuals of influence working to selfishly benefit themselves at the expense of those who the leaders had pledged to represent. And when money becomes the power broker of a political system, those with the power can buy elections, sow divisiveness,

reap more benefits, gain more power, until resentment and discontent splits the binding seams of society.

(4) Privatization. Dovetailing with the previous factor, the Opinions found that privatization of public services became exploitive, and destructive, whenever such privatization worked to misalign public interests with private interests. For example, let's say a state hires a private military company to fight a war, thereby saving on its military expenditures and risk of casualties. While it may not be in the public interest to continue that war, it is certainly in the company's interest, since war is the business of a military company. The private military company has every incentive to keep the war going, regardless of whether or not it is benefiting the interests of the state. This in turn provides a political incentive to accept bribes for securing private contracts. Taking this a step further, if people occupying high positions in defense or national security are susceptible to bribery by foreign private companies, the misalignment of interests will again serve only to erode that security. When basic public services and programs like water, health, education, and social insurance are privatized, the emphasis on community and solidarity may be replaced with the tensions and inequalities of a competitive market, where the business interests of those holding the reins blot out the universal principles upon which these programs were originally founded. Opinions understood very clearly that it wasn't the private nature of privatization that was the issue. The issue was when unregulated industry tempts self-serving

intrigue. Regulation may be viewed as loss of freedom, but if an unregulated child can be a menace, an unregulated industry can be destructive.

(5) Health Crisis. During the period between 2010 and 2040, the Opinions also saw the erosion of community-based social programs, such as healthcare. A society's healthcare is a kind of union, where every individual participates in a system that will ensure they are provided with equal opportunity to physical and mental health benefits. A healthcare system strapped by the commercialization pressures imposed by the private pharmaceutical and insurance industries reinforces economic inequality, and the ensuing numb acceptance of that inequality by a population increasingly wracked with economic despair. Desperate people suffocating under the weight of a dysfunctional health system may turn to self-destructive behaviors. The opioid crisis of the early twenty-first century was a direct symptom of this behavior. Just as utter despair with the economic status quo drove people to abandon hope and point fingers, utter despair with obtaining access to basic medical treatment likewise drove people to plunge into the deadly spiral of drug addiction—including legal prescription pain killers. When the prevailing powers enforce a mentality that things will never get better than the status quo, it leads irrevocably to the disintegration of the community, and the disintegration of the individual. If the world is being destroyed one can at least take blissful refuge in self-destruction. The health crisis eventually reached epidemic

proportions, mostly because health was engulfed by selfish politics.

(6) False Realities. One of the many disturbing quotes that caught Opinion attention was by a political consultant named Karl Rove during the administration of President George W. Bush. According to the reporter Mr. Ron Suskind, Rove stated: "We're an empire now, and when we act, we make our own reality. And while you're studying that reality—judiciously, as you will—we'll act again, creating other new realities, which you can study too, and that's how things will sort out. We're history's actors . . . and you, all of you, will be left to study what we do." For the Opinions, arrogant statements like this smacked too much of Orwell's dystopian classic, *1984*. This kind of rhetoric could potentially lead a state slipping into what the historian Timothy Snyder (a favorite Opinion Ancient scholar) termed the "politics of eternity." If a population is so disillusioned with the status quo, and if the ruling powers then propagate a fabricated narrative deflecting attention away from campaigns for progress or social reform, the only tenable course becomes defeating the "enemy"—whomever that enemy might be. The new status quo becomes "eternal," where history becomes an open template to be rewritten; uncomfortable past transgressions and atrocities are stamped irrelevant, and forgotten; and the future becomes a constant struggle to overcome hostile forces looming about every corner, while the small power classes sit comfortably retaining their power, wealth, and suppression of the majority.

> This was the operative pattern when democracies began to collapse in the 2030s. As in the case of income inequality, alternate realities and "alternate facts" became the psychological tactics brandished by unscrupulous members of the power base, cajoling the population into believing the current state of affairs could never be improved until the "enemy" is defeated, the enemy being the "fake" media, or the "other" political party, or the "other" race, or the "other" ethnic group, or the "other" country, or the "other" religion, all of them conspiring to trample on your rights, or take away your jobs, or invade your country, and as long as you believe there *is* an enemy your attention will be diverted away from the truth, which is crucial, because the real truth threatens the lies that selfish power clings to. A people's discontent can be refocused when fear manipulates them against themselves, until "otherness" wipes out "togetherness," divisiveness wipes out solidarity, and confusing contradictory gales of misinformation sweep away a sense of striving for a common cooperative purpose. Antagonism is a bitter comfort when the right path is lost. That is when the human spirit ossifies—when it forfeits the values of truth and goodness to the expediency of surrender.

According to the Opinions, if there was one word that characterized the pathology infecting all six of the above factors, it would be "divisiveness."

With divisiveness is born tyranny's father, the demagogue.

Twelve

So who exactly was the enemy in this one-hundred-year precursor to the cataclysmic events of 2044–2046? What did the Opinions identify as the common degenerative thread running through this preamble to the final plunge?

It was not the business leaders, by virtue of the leadership positions they occupy, who were enemies. Business leaders can be benevolent.

It was not a particular political system, by virtue of its ideologies and philosophies, that was the enemy. A dictator can be benevolent. An oligarchy can be benevolent. A government holding central control of the entire economy and the distribution of wealth can be benevolent. The pejorative is not built a priori into a system's ideals or structures.

It was not a particular nation's people, by virtue of their particular customs, or culture, or ideologies, or belief systems who were the enemy. All peoples are equally great because the majority of citizens in any particular nation are good, decent people, and all decent, good people can be benevolent.

It was not the rich and powerful, by virtue of their wealth and power, who were the enemies. The rich and powerful can be benevolent.

It was not power and money that caused corruption.

It was power and money *in the wrong hands.* It was the leader of base character *knowingly* wielding power and money for personal gain who was the enemy. These were the Fools. And those who willingly believed their lies and absurdities were Fools by one degree of separation.

They were Fools not only because of their own misguided principles, but because their myopic worldview and ignorance of history would not allow them to see that by making others worse off, they were also paving the path to making themselves worse off. In the words of Voltaire, as fools, they could not free themselves from the "chains they revere."

Hateful people following the lead of hateful people makes humanity hateful, and hate never survives.

When the new SARS-CoV-3 virus hit in 2044, one hundred years of social magma finally burst through the spidering cracks of the status quo, a magma brewed by many such Fools.

The timing could not have been worse, as the first cases were discovered in Pennsylvania five months before the 2044 presidential election, right in the midst of one of the worst worldwide financial crises in history. The world economy was failing once again from financial and housing market speculation. This was compounded by the worsening global warming crisis, a crisis that, despite being overwhelmingly confirmed by the scientific community, many "educated" leaders in a position to correct still chose to ignore, driving refugees from flooded coastal regions into areas already too overpopulated to accommodate them. People were already losing their life savings and their homes, and now they were about to lose their minds.

It wouldn't have mattered if the virus had been discovered in another democratic country, for by this time the general skepticism, uncertainty, and loss of confidence unfurled by the forces of misdirection had already made steady progress chipping away at democracy's pillars.

Warning signs of this ubiquitous social deterioration had been abundant and glaring. Many prescient scholars and pundits had chronicled the waves of social distress flooding free nations. One such author, Howard Zinn, writing as a concerned American citizen speaking to a worldwide readership directly affected by the alarming trend, described in blatant terms the widening gulf systematically instilled on the populace by the elite Establishment. With the reader's indulgence, we quote here a relevant passage from *A People's History of the United States:*

> "...With such continuing malaise, it is very important for the Establishment—that uneasy club of business executives, generals, and politicos—to maintain the historic pretension of national unity, in which the government represents all the people, and the common enemy is overseas, not at home, where disasters of economics or war are unfortunate errors or tragic accidents, to be corrected by the members of the same club that brought the disasters. It is important for them also to make sure this artificial unity of highly privileged is the only unity—that the ninety-nine percent remain split in countless ways, and turn against one another to vent their anger.
>
> "How skillful to tax the middle class to pay for the relief of the

> poor, building resentment on top of humiliation! How adroit to bus poor black youngsters into poor white neighborhoods, in a violent exchange of impoverished schools, while the schools of the rich remain untouched and the wealth of the nation, doled out carefully where people need free milk, is drained for billion-dollar aircraft carriers. How ingenious to meet the demands of blacks and women for equality by giving them small special benefits, and setting them in competition with everyone else for jobs made scarce by an irrational, wasteful system. How wise to turn the fear and anger of the majority toward a class of criminals bred—by economic inequality—faster than they could be put away, deflecting attention from the huge thefts of national resources carried out within the law by men in executive offices."

Zinn goes on to observe that despite the Establishment's machinations of sowing controlled public discontent, despite their "controls of power and punishment, enticement and concessions, diversions and decoys," they were ultimately unsuccessful at staving off revolts. For the time being, the pinions of society held. But the SARS-CoV-3 outbreak in 2044 taught society its breaking point.

When the first cases were detected among forty-two people at one political party's rally, the other political party immediately hurled accusations of political terrorism. Decades of mounting divisiveness could not temper suspicions. The rift had been planted decades ago, and it was widening.

This was an especially aggressive and virulent strain of the SARS virus, one that seemed to have learned from its predecessor's shortcomings back in 2020. It also seemed to have anticipated the continued unraveling of social cohesion within and between world powers. The diseases of human civilization, both societal and pathogenic, were now working as cohorts.

It could have been contained, had the trajectory of modern history been different. But political overreach had eroded trust across borders; income inequality had eroded trust within borders; the dispensing of political favors had eroded trust in government; privatization had further widened the social gap; the health crisis eroded confidence in basic security and plunged people into greater despair; and the dissemination of false realities anesthetized people into blind acceptance of what they believed to be their only recourse, an eternal war against a fabricated enemy.

There had been bioterrorism at play, but it had not been committed by a political party. It was meant to look like political bioterrorism. In fact, the mastermind had been Mr. Vatzim Botkin, a formerly dispossessed refugee from Belarus working at the biotech company Axion Industries in Luxembourg. Mr. Botkin had been studying pathogens at Axion, and had engineered the SARS-CoV-3 virus genome. Normally, biotechnicians synthesize viral genomes for research and development. Mr. Botkin's research activities were anything but noble. He had devised a treacherous scheme to exploit the fragile state of affairs in democracies like the United States, where long-standing class, racial, and ethnic conflicts were feeding the kind of divisiveness that further emboldened political entities working to promote those very conflicts. Teaming with two other corrupt biotechnicians, one from the United States and one from the Russian

Federation, Mr. Botkin plotted to release the virus at an American political rally, while he and his co-conspirators, with access to the genome, were secretly synthesizing a vaccine well in advance of the competition, so that each could divide the spoils of what could potentially turn out to be the most lucrative medical treatment in the modern era. Back in 2020, the SARS-CoV-2 virus had been traced back to a lab in Wuhan, China. This time, it would appear out of nowhere, and the blame could rest on whomever the people chose. Certainly, there might be some fatalities, but the vaccine would save the day and the wealth would keep pouring in.

However, neither Mr. Botkin nor his co-conspirators ever anticipated how aggressive the virus would be, nor to what degree it would mutate. They also never anticipated the reactionary avalanche that would ultimately render their vaccine first marginally effective, then virtually impotent.

Conspiracy theories ran rampant through a mass media flooded with misinformation campaigns targeting susceptible members of a bitterly divided population. Even before a working vaccine could be distributed, citizens were perpetrating local acts of bioterrorism onto fellow citizens, as a form of political retribution. They were like suicide bombers, except they were suicide carriers, carriers of a virus deadlier than they imagined. The virus did not need to be the enemy. It could become a weapon, a weapon to be used against the enemy.

The spread of the virus was ghastly. Travel restrictions were enforced too late. By the time the vaccine was ready, a whirlwind of conspiracy theories placed almost every major world power at the center of blame. American websites and blogs blamed the Chinese, with no evidence other than citing the 2020 precedent of Wuhan. Social media blindly followed. The Chinese blamed the Americans, citing no evidence other than the fact that the first known cases had surfaced during a political rally. Social media blindly followed. Some began implicating the Russians, claiming that decades of attacks on democratic institutions must mean their campaigns had progressed to biological warfare. Social media blindly followed. When it was discovered that several Middle Eastern people had attended the political rally, that they had hailed from places like Afghanistan, Syria, and Palestine, some blamed them with no evidence whatsoever. Social media blindly followed. No democratic nation could assume a leadership role in fighting the new plague, for a deep distrust of government and dwindling faith in the democratic process had by this time dismantled the buttress of solidarity needed to support such a role. International cooperation between the world powers was also unrealistic, as the fear of ideological infringement bred freely through pervasive, violent nationalism.

As the conspiracy theories went viral, so did the virus. Thorns of betrayal and bitterness jabbing at a nameless foe, growing upon a precarious social foundation, were now conveyed through the virus onto the same nameless foe, the foe being whomever happened to match the current biased targets. Local acts of bioterrorism became international. Vaccines had been rolled out, but as with the Covid-19 pandemic, too many people were skeptical about its safety or effectiveness. Many people believed that the vaccines from the first SARS-CoV-2 virus had played a considerable role in conditioning the new strain's virulence and resistance to therapies. There was no scientific evidence for this. Social media blindly followed. Vast swaths of the world's population were too used to gobbling up the wrong information and arriving at uninformed decisions. Ironically, none of the most prevalent conspiracy theories maintained that some of the scientists who had manufactured the vaccine were the bioterrorists themselves.

When this truth was laid bare, and by the time Mr. Vatzim Botkin and his co-conspirators were apprehended, mass panic had already set in. People now had even less cause to trust the integrity of the vaccines, even the ones synthesized outside of Mr. Botkin's sphere of influence. More transmissible variants of the virus were now surging through every known corner of the world. Both the vaccines and therapies were only moderately effective, and could not keep up with the pace of mutation. The virus was learning, and it had help from its victims.

Nineteen months after the first cases were reported, over two-thirds of the world population was wiped out.

Then, inexplicably, after March of 2046, everything went dark. The digital record had abruptly ceased.

There was no documentary evidence on The Find to indicate what might have happened.

Given that only about forty percent of The Find's data had been recovered, the Opinions speculated that post-2046 records had simply been lost. Though it seemed peculiar the historical record had been disrupted in the middle of the worst plague in human history.

It was possible that some kind of major electromagnetic disturbance had completely erased digital data. But only a catastrophic event, unlike anything ever encountered, would have obliterated the world's digital records so quickly. Perhaps a local astronomical event? A fatal pulse of cosmic rays? Or was the electromagnetic pulse induced by humans?

Or, perhaps, the quantum computer was simply buried in 2046, affording no opportunity to record later events. Given the recent tragic turn of history... hastily buried?

There was no way of knowing. Billions of years had disintegrated the preservation of any clues. A small quantum computer within the vacuum seal of an AM-III glass box had been the only remnant of that ancient epoch.

A small quantum computer that would reset the parameters of human evolution.

Thirteen

Kaffir Bottlebrush was always very excited to relate his correspondences with the esteemed Senior Data Administrator and Truth Arbiter, Dr. Mallow Garva. Mrs. Gaura Bottlebrush was especially interested in Kaffir's sneak peak at the archives on Dr. Garva's computer. Only Senior Data Administrators were privy to the contents of The Find. Once an Ancient work in a particular field passed the first round of review by the Data Administrators, it was passed on to the appropriate consulting group for peer review. Once it passed peer review, it was then passed on to the local congresses, who approved it for submission to the Central Opinion Congress. Upon ratification by the Central Opinion Congress, it could be safely distributed to the general public. Once again, the Opinions did not regard this as censorship. It was preventative cultural decay.

"Were you able to read anything on the screen?" a wide-eyed Gaura inquired.

"No, but I saw the links," Kaffir said. "It was very exciting to get a glimpse of that."

"Yes, very exciting," his wife agreed. "Don't you think so, Aster?"

"Yes," Aster nodded. "Yes, I do. Very much."

But Aster wasn't really paying attention. Aster was very distracted this evening. He was thinking about Zeus, the Olympian king of the gods, and the power of the penis.

Zeus had five wives: Metis, Themis, Eurynome, Mnemosyne, and finally, Hera. From these unions sprang many important gods and goddesses. With Metis came Athena; with Themis came the Seasons: Eirene, Eunomia and Dike, and the Fates: Cotho, Lachesis and Antropos; with Eurynome came the Graces: Aglaia, Euphrosyne, and Thaleia; with Mnemosyne came the Nine Muses; and with Hera came Hebe, Ares, and Hephaestus.

Zeus also had many extramarital liaisons. He violated his own sister Demeter, resulting in the birth of Persephone (who he pursued twice). He cheated on his wife Hera with Maia, and with Dione, and with Leto. His affair with the mortal woman Semele proved to be her demise, for when Hera suggested to Semele that Zeus appear to her in his true form, Semele was instantly vaporized—but not before Dionysus was born. Zeus's affair with the mortal Io, disguised as a heifer, resulted in her condemned to torment by a gadfly sent by Hera. Zeus also disguised himself as a bull to seduce the princess Europa, yielding Rhadamanthus and Minos (and centuries of associated Cretan mythology), Europa's namesake of course surviving as a continent. And this is just the short list.

Aster thought about Ms. Gayfeather's words, when she stated the degree to which, and the way in which, the "power of the penis" is embraced within a social unit is reflected in the overall power distribution practiced throughout that unit. Quite a sweeping statement. Aster wondered how often this theory was examined by the Ancients.

Zeus takes the paradigm to the extreme. Although he is a mythological character, he certainly represents the ultimate example of an authority figure—the king of gods—exercising his dominant male role through sexual exploitation.

Essentially, Ms. Carnellia Gayfeather was asserting (and who was Aster to question the undeniable truthfulness of that commonly held Opinion assertion) that whether or not a male projects the dominance of his sexuality within a social unit determines whether or not the power dynamic in that social unit is balanced. It then followed that if the instrument of male sexuality was emasculated, there was less of a chance of an unbalanced power dynamic.

Of course, Aster was working out what had already been well established as common social philosophical knowledge among the Opinions. With the Self Suppressor came the suppression of the instinct to reproduce (libido), thus the suppression of self-gratification, thus the suppression of sexual dominance, thus the suppression of a general instinct to dominate, hence the maintenance of a balanced power dynamic. The study of Ancient sexuality was the study of the will to dominate.

It seemed to Aster that if the biological tendency to oppress, to dominant, to subjugate, was extracted from the human genome, then any similar tendency manifested in the realm of sexuality would be rendered nil. If the will to unjustly dominate has been removed, then the sexual expression of that will must by default be neutral. There is no ulterior motive to the sexual act. The sexual act is, in and of itself, an act, wiped clean, immune to contamination.

Hypothetically, then, if Aster ever manifested a desire, an *instinctual* desire, to perform a sex act—physically—then, since he, like all Opinions, had been treated with the Self Suppressor, there can be no instinctual tendency to unjustly dominate through such an act, as that would violate the biochemical properties on which the Self Suppressor was constructed.

So, if one of the side effects of the Self Suppressor was to suppress the instinct to perform a sex act, then why was Aster thinking about it at all? Why had he been looking at Dianella in *that* way? Why did he want to see more of Dianella in *that* way? Was it possible that many of his friends were feeling those same Ancient coming-of-age cravings and simply hadn't spoken about it? But Aster's friends were very open with him. They spoke of girls in terms of their beauty, femininity, wit, intelligence, talent, warmth . . . and there was always the normative hug or peck on the lips here and there . . . but never any discussions about the *act.* After all, everybody could have children. Just inseminate the egg. The *act* was frivolous. It was kind of like writing letters. Nobody was interested anymore in writing letters. It was much easier to make a phone call or send an email. The act of writing letters was abandoned. It was frivolous.

From a purely biochemical perspective, there couldn't be anything wrong with Aster's growing desires to explore the sex act. That had to be the truth. The Self Suppressor would not allow any imbalances in the fine-tuned climate of Opinion power dynamics.

Aster was fairly confident that once he explained this line of reasoning to Dianella, she would understand and embrace it. What he was unable to anticipate was the approach he would use to express this reasoning. He had initially imagined a diplomatic description of what he was feeling, supported with a plea for its psychologically neutral basis. What actually transpired in his bedroom that evening was a rude interruption to Dianella's recitation of how pressure and volume are related to temperature in the ideal gas law. He asked her if he could please see her breasts.

Dianella wrinkled her brow. Why on Opine would he want to see her breasts? What an odd request.

"Aster, only my doctor has seen my breasts. Why do you ask?"

"For . . . the artistry," Aster blurted.

"The artistry?"

"Yes."

"You want to paint me? But you don't paint."

"For the beauty of the artistry. Beauty is an artistic truth of nature, and I would like to . . . experience that truth."

"But why?"

"Because . . . I think it would be a good thing."

"Why?"

"Because truth is always good."

"But why is it a truth?"

"Because the human body is a truth."

"But Aster, indiscriminate nudity leads to objectification of the body. You know that. The sanctity of the naked body is preserved for partners who have proclaimed a bond of love for each other. We learned that long ago."

"Yes, but maybe you and I have that bond."

"Maybe," Dianella smiled, "but not the marriage bond."

Aster took a moment to reflect on this truth.

"Dianella, I can't objectify your body. Any more than I can objectify a flower."

"But the Ancients didn't objectify flowers. They objectified people."

"I see you exactly as I see a flower."

"But flowers do not know people see them. People do."

"Dianella, do you think I will objectify your breasts?"

"No, Aster," she smirked.

"Then . . . can I look?"

Dianella stared. She was bemused, and amused.

"Why?" she finally said, the corners of her lips creeping up.

"Because . . . I am not indiscriminately objectifying. I am discriminately admiring."

This seemed to have a different effect. Probing his eyes, Dianella capitulated to their innocent charm. After a dismissive giggle, she pulled off her sweater and unclasped her bra.

"There."

Aster's focus locked. She quickly began to dress.

"Wait," Aster said.

"What?"

"I'd like to touch it."

"Aster!"

"I touch you as I would a flower."

She drew in a breath, transfixed. He raised a hand. She never looked at his hand. His eyes rendered her unresponsive. She continued looking at his eyes as he rested his right hand over her left breast.

His palm brushed something like a tiny marshmallow nib in a satin swell. She was trembling.

Then, only five seconds later, he withdrew his hand. Her gaze lowered, flicked down to his sweat pants, flicked back up. It was that flick of the eyes that alerted Aster to his betraying protuberance. His eyes did their own flicking.

Dianella quickly got dressed, and distractedly resumed reviewing how pressure affects temperature.

Fourteen

The reader may have already surmised one serious issue arising from the Self Suppressor therapy. A side effect, eradication of libido, posed the very imminent danger of the species becoming disincentivized to reproducing itself. When a drug loses its potency, there is little incentive to keep taking the drug. Likewise, if the self-gratification of libido is missing, there is little to no incentive to perform an act that ceases to deliver the gratification. Apparently, and fortuitously, the therapy did not affect testosterone and estrogen levels the way it did other hormones associated with libido, such as progesterone, dehydroepiandrosterone (DHEA), dopamine, and oxytocin. Testosterone and estrogen, stimulated by luteinizing hormones (LH) and follicle stimulating hormones (FSH), are crucial for the production of sperm and eggs. So while the human genome was deprived of the *instinct* to reproduce, the *mechanisms* to reproduce were left intact. The Opinion scientists who created the therapy, like Dr. Nalca Hollyhock, breathed a collective sigh of relief upon confirmation that the basic processes governing the reproductive system remained functional. It would have been quite a calamity if the preservation of selfishness in the human genome was necessitated by irksome technicalities such as the production of sperm and eggs.

The Opinions also had to deal with a sociocultural issue. After several generations of administering the therapy, people grew to tacitly accept the loss of their biological instinct to copulate. But the problem still remained of shielding them from reminders. Knowledge of loss always arouses resentment. Imagine a person is told he has won a hundred dollars, and then told there was a mistake and the prize was really fifty dollars. He will register this as a loss, and resent it, even though he has gained fifty dollars. The idea was to impress upon the Opinion people that they had gained one hundred dollars—the Self Suppressor—while omitting the conditional that they had also lost fifty dollars—their libido. Any reminder of this conditional could ignite a conflagration of resentment. One of the tasks of a Culture Consultant was to identify and eliminate any explicit artistic depictions of sexual intercourse in the areas of literature, art, or film, especially if the depiction was in the least bit gratuitous. Yet it was the realistic, tasteful, erotically charged depictions in The Find's library posing the most concern, as these represented most faithfully the emotional fulfillment of the depicted acts. Only sexual themes for the purpose of comic effect were tolerated, as long as the depiction was tasteful. The Opinions must remain content that the "drug" of libido has lost its potency, and they must simultaneously forget the fifty dollars they paid for its loss.

Over time, this kind of sociological conditioning began to dissociate the biological imperative for sexual intercourse—the perpetuation of the species—from the mutual physical and emotional gratification it granted. The self-gratification from sex began to be viewed as just another manifestation of selfishness inherent in the human genome. It seemed natural and right that an ancillary benefit of the Self Suppressor would be to stifle the selfish predispositions of sexual gratification. After all, were there not plenty examples of Home Sapiens 1.0 wielding sexuality as a weapon to fulfill self-seeking goals? As a weapon to oppress, to exploit, to extort? To objectify? To prostitute? To enslave? Had not countless depraved acts defiled the instinctual imperative to perpetuate the species to the extent that, by comparison, the dog in heat becomes ennobled? This was the line of reasoning ameliorating the loss of a basic biological instinct. Again, the supporting evidence was provided by The Find. The formulas for committing atrocities has been laid out for the Opinions.

The sex act, then, was not considered a crime, but an aberration. It was imperative the Opinions never be given an opportunity to question that norm. Dianella Corkwood was thus obliged to report the aberration she witnessed with Aster Bottlebrush. Perhaps she was mistaken, but it seemed as if Aster had touched her breast for the sole purpose of sexual gratification. That he found the act sexually gratifying called into question the norm. It had to be addressed. Even though she found it amusing, it had to be addressed.

Dianella's stepfather, Thymus Corkwood, was of course exactly the right person to learn of this development. Being one of the genetic scientists synthesizing the Self Suppressor, he would certainly be interested in attending Aster's interview with the school psychologist, Dr. Yarrow Buckthorn—the same Yarrow Buckthorn who had offered the mollifying Fool Fact at the car accident between Thymus and Nolana.

Aster never failed to notice the thick, tiny black curls of Dr.

Buckthorn's hair, engineered synthetically, it seemed, like nubs of Styrofoam. His face was long and narrow, his searching eyes punctuating a dark amber skin tone. It could be an intimidating visage, especially in sober meetings like this, the usual Opinion brightness shrouded with the grey cloud of formality. Aster was glad to have the very familiar face of Thymus Corkwood as a buffer.

"Mr. Aster Bottlebrush," Dr. Buckthorn said.

"Yes."

"Are you content?"

"I am, thank you. And you?"

"Yes, thank you. You know Dr. Corkwood very well?"

"Yes."

"And his stepdaughter Dianella?"

"Y-yes. We have been friends for years."

Dr. Buckthorn flashed a grin.

"Do you know why we have called you to this meeting, Aster?"

"Yes."

"Good. Would you like to tell us about it?"

"About . . . you mean the . . ."

The man nodded solemnly. Thymus was behind him in a corner, grinning pleasantly.

"I explained to Dianella . . . that I wanted to feel the artistry of the human figure," Aster proceeded carefully, "because the human figure is truth."

"You wanted to feel the artistry of the human figure," the doctor repeated.

"Yes."

"And the human figure," Yarrow repeated again, shooting a glance back at Thymus, "is a truth."

"Yes."

"That's true," Thymus nodded along. "The human figure is a truth."

"A beautiful truth," Aster ventured.

"Yes, well, beauty is truth," the doctor agreed.

"Yes. That was why I wanted to experience it."

"Yes. Of course, naturally, we all want to experience the truth in beauty. But Aster, we're talking about a particular part of the human body, aren't we?"

"Yes. Yes, we are."

"We are talking about a young lady's breast."

"Yes. Yes, Dr. Buckthorn. But not because I was objectifying her."

Dr. Buckthorn waited.

"It was really just a kind of curiosity with . . . that aspect of her beauty."

"You were curious about a part of her body that is identified with sexuality."

Aster looked at Thymus, whose grin had receded. Thymus squeezed another one out.

"I wasn't thinking so much about sexuality," Aster said, "as I was artistry."

"So much?"

"What?"

"You said you weren't thinking 'so much' about sexuality."

"Yes. I was . . . I was . . ."

"Aster," the doctor said, leaning forward with clasped hands, "you don't have to worry about any disciplinary action. We are just probing into your line of thinking here. You didn't do anything wrong."

"Yes."

"A person can only act out his or her own natural inclinations, subject to his or her own inhibitions."

"Yes," Aster swallowed.

"Now, the fact that you just characterized your actions as not 'so much' sexually motivated, suggests to me that there indeed was something of a sexual component to your psychological leanings at the time."

"Well, I'm not . . . I'm not exactly sure about that."

"You're not exactly sure?" The doctor's eyebrows raised.

"Not exactly."

"But you must have at least an inkling of a notion even if you are not exactly sure."

"I might. I might have a notion."

"And what notion might that be?"

"It might be . . . it might be that I was curious."

"Curious about what?"

"Curious about that part of her body."

"The breasts?"

"Yes."

"Dianella's breasts? Or all breasts?"

"What?"

"Are you curious about all breasts in general, or just Dianella's breasts?"

"Well . . . I am thinking . . . yes, Dr. Buckthorn. I would say it was Dianella's breasts. At that time."

"And at other times?"

"What?"

"Aster, I am certain you have had plenty of occasions at the beach to see young ladies clad in very skimpy bathing suits, bikinis, et cetera. Some of that swimwear is very revealing. Are they not?"

"Oh, yes, they are, they . . . yes." Aster took a moment to subdue his tone.

"Furthermore, you must also have noticed we live in a culture where some women feel quite comfortable, and safe, visiting public beaches without even wearing the tops of their swimwear. A consequence of the inhibitors provided by the Self Suppressor."

Dr. Buckthorn acknowledged Dr. Corkwood with a twitch of the head. Aster dutifully nodded.

"And I imagine you have also had occasion to see Dianella in one of these . . . revealing swimwear outfits?"

Aster's nod was a spasm.

"But you felt compelled, Aster, to experience closer what you had many times had occasion to view."

"Yes. But . . . but not . . . not view entirely."

"Ah, not entirely. What do you mean by that?"

"Well, I suppose I felt—"

"You *knew,* Aster."

"Yes. Yes, I knew . . . that I felt compelled to experience . . . her whole breast."

"Ah, the whole breast. You are referring also to the nipple, Aster."

"Yes. Yes, that's right, Dr. Buckthorn. The nipple."

"And why the nipple, Aster? Why the nipple?"

"Um . . . why . . ." Aster's eyes flailed.

"It's okay," Thymus smiled. "Tell him, Aster."

"Because . . . I wanted to feel . . . what it was like."

"Because you found it stimulating?"

"Yes."

"You were sexually stimulated, Aster?"

"I was . . . the, the-uh, the truth is . . ."

"Yes, the truth, Aster! You wanted to experience the emotional truth of Dianella's beauty through the physical truth of sexual arousal? Isn't that so?"

"I . . . I think so, yes."

"You *know* so?"

"Yes."

Dr. Buckthorn slapped a triumphant palm on the desk, then turned to Thymus, whose nod confirmed his triumph.

"What do you think, Dr. Corkwood?"

"I think it's magnificent."

"Yes. Did you hear that, Aster?"

"What?"

"I don't think there has been anything quite like this since the trials," Thymus mused.

"What?" Aster blinked.

"Would you like to confirm?" Dr. Buckthorn asked Thymus.

"Certainly, yes," Thymus said, and approached Aster.

"There's nothing to worry about, Aster," the psychologist finally grinned. "Every anomaly can be corrected through the magic of genetics."

"What? Anomaly? What's wrong?"

"Nothing's wrong, Aster," Thymus smiled, holding out a small, circular plastic device. "May I please see your index finger?"

"Okay. Ow!" The medical lancet clicked.

"Thank you." Thymus placed the lancet in a small plastic bag. "A little blood sample, to test your DNA."

"What for?"

"You may be resistant to the libido component. Extremely rare. But there's no worry."

"The libido component?"

"Yes, the libidinal branch of the Suppressor."

"I . . . I didn't mean to harm Dianella. I just . . . I just like her a lot."

The two doctors smiled.

"We know you do," Thymus said, "and I can tell you she likes you just as well. That's why we can't have either one of you feeling any discontent. Can we?"

"No," Aster said, trembling. "No discontent."

Fifteen

IT WAS THE FALL EQUINOX, and the Opinions were celebrating Diawli, the Hindu Festival of Lights. Like the Ancient festival, Opinions spent a few days with family and friends reveling in great Indian food, while ghee lamps and fireworks staged the stellar sparkles and streaks of the distant cosmos.

When an emerging civilization inherits the rich, variegated palette of cultures and belief systems from an ancient world, there will be a strong compulsion to absorb facets of those cultures, just as the Opinions observed the inevitable influence of cultures across borders of that ancient world through conquest, trade, and globalization. Yet the historical underpinnings of these cultures and belief systems were detached from Opinion heritage. While holidays for the Ancients were celebrations of their own common heritage stretching back centuries, or even millennia, the Opinions had adopted these cultural memories essentially from a single digital text, The Find. For the Opinions, then, Ancient holiday celebrations were stripped of their original historical meanings and instead focused on the generic festive character of a holiday; that is, the celebration of community, family, and the interconnectedness of diverse peoples. This was one of many ways to honor the Ancients at their best:

celebrate what brought them together, and celebrate it without prejudice.

Thus the holiday calendar rotated from year to year. One year, the Opinions displayed Australian flags and celebrated Australia Day, Canberra Day, Anzac Day, and Boxing Day, as well as Christian holidays such as Christmas and Easter. Not because the Opinions favored the Australian holidays, and not because they favored the Christian religion, but because they were honoring Australian culture this particular year. The next year, they may celebrate a Coptic Christmas, a Coptic Easter Sunday, and Ramadan, in honor of Egypt. The next year, they may celebrate the Christian holidays with France's V-E Day, Bastille Day, and Armistice Day. The next year, they may celebrate the Spring Festival, the Qingming Festival, May Day, the Dragon Boat Festival, and the Mid-Autumn Festival of China. One year they may celebrate Shab e-miraj, another year the Fourth of July, another year St. Patrick's Day, another year Tet Nguyen Dan, another year Rosh Hashanah, another year Mawlid, another year Thanksgiving, depending on the honored country. There were more than enough opportunities for holiday celebration in Opine. One world's diversity became another world's integration.

As for the Opinions themselves, there was not so much as an official flag, but a symbol: a lavender freesia flower. The freesia symbolized trust and friendship—universal trust and friendship, as divisiveness was foreign to Opine. Every citizen displayed this symbol somewhere in their home, though it was not required by law. All of the tribal or national symbols of Opine prior to the Self Suppressor were discarded, and forgotten.

Daphne and Kaffir were celebrating with other consultants in the Aviary Lounge, enjoying the featured Festival of Lights lunch: lapsi halwa, aloo tikki, samosas, and some mithai for dessert. The topic of conversation between the two co-workers/neighbors was the music of Richard Wagner, always a tough nut to crack for the Culture Consultants. While Wagner's place among the pantheon of fin de siècle great Romantic composers was indisputable, his politics and personal views were rejected wholesale by the Opinions—and the majority of Ancients, the Opinions gathered. From a purely musical perspective, Wagner's works contain passages reaching the summits of the Romantic ideal. Privately, he was a violent German nationalist and a vociferous anti-Semite. How does one reconcile the beauty of the artwork with the ugliness of the artist? Decades ago, the Culture Consultants had arrived at a compromise. Wagner's music was to be available commercially in audio format. His writings, however, were completely deleted from the Find's database. And, following the lead of Israel, who the Opinions greatly admired, both live and broadcasted performances of Wagner's music were banned.

"It's very hard to ignore the love and passion in his music," Daphne was saying. "How could a man consumed with so many bigoted philosophies write music capturing the essence of love?"

"Yes. It is a mystery," Kaffir said.

"Oh, the emotion is so free, so uninhibited," Daphne began to sway a bit in her chair, as if in the throes of a blissful dance. "Do you hear it, Kaffir? Do you hear the passion in his music?"

"I do," Kaffir smiled, captivated more with Daphne than what she was saying. "Though I'm unfamiliar with most of his operas. I do enjoy the Ring cycle, and its connections to German myth."

She took a moment to reflect. "Kaffir, do you think listening to music like that . . . is harmful to the mind?"

"Harmful? Music about love?"

"Music that can excite the passions. You know all those stories about Ancient rock concerts, how the music inflamed their violent instincts? There were riots, and even deaths."

"I don't think Wagner's music would do that. And some of those people were taking illegal drugs."

"But music could act like a drug. I remember during one of our sessions reading Thomas Mann's *The Blood of the Walsungs.* Do you know that one?"

"No, not that one."

"It depicts a brother and sister attending a Wagner opera. The eroticism in the music is so seductive, they are incited into an incestuous relationship."

"Incited? I don't see how music can force a brother and sister into an inappropriate relationship."

"But the brother and sister were watching the scene from *Die Walküre* when Siegmund and Sielginde fall in love, realizing they are brother and sister. Remember that?"

"Oh, yes. I do remember that scene."

"Kaffir, are you surprised that opera was cleared?"

"Well, that opera is only the second part of a four-opera cycle, so I imagine they didn't want to ban the entire cycle. And, at any rate, we have the Self Suppressor to protect us."

"Yes," Daphne's smile receded, in deference of the genetic miracle. "Yes, we have the Self Suppressor."

"It... it is an extraordinary achievement. The Ring cycle, I mean," Kaffir said.

"Yes! Extraordinary."

Her eyes rolled away in another daze. Kaffir was eyeing her so intently, neither noticed Mr. Figgle quietly pulling up a chair on the opposite side.

"Kaffir," Daphne said, her eyes returning to him, "do you ever wonder what it feels like? To feel that passion?"

"Oh... I think we can all feel the passion in music like that, no?"

"I mean the erotic passion. To *feel* that eroticism. To *feel* it swarming through you." She had leaned forward, a renewed luminescence to her eyes.

"Well... I... don't think..."

Daphne waited, unblinking.

"... Like I said... the Self Suppressor... protects us from our passions from running too high."

"I know. But sometimes I just wonder... all the poetic descriptions of erotic passion in the literature... do you ever... wonder?"

The two of them still didn't notice Mr. Figgle. He was listening in, appearing charmed.

"Well, Daphne, I'm sure everybody is, to some extent... at least at some point of time... curious as to the biochemical and neurological effects of a... of an instinct that evolution had selected to be, you know, pleasurable."

"So that the species can reproduce."

"Sure. But, Daphne, we can just as well be curious about the pleasurable effects of something else, like a drug. You can think of libido as a drug, which can potentially be harmful."

"Oh yes! I know! Of course . . . libido is not a drug."

"No, no, but it could be thought of as a drug, in that it could be abused."

"Yes, it can. It can be abused, for sure."

Daphne drifted off once again.

"But . . ." she began, ". . . can passion be abusive?"

"Abuse is not of a thing itself; only in its agency."

Both colleagues started. It was Mr. Figgle! That Mr. Figgle, always turning up when you least expected it. They both chanted his name. The professor dragged his chair over to them.

"Mr. Figgle, I didn't know you were here today!" Daphne said.

"Just freelance consulting," Mr. Figgle smiled warmly, "on my spare time."

"What did you mean," Kaffir asked, "that abuse is in its agency?"

"Agency," Mr. Figgle said, "or the capacity to exert power, is the channel through which abuse thrives."

"So passion can be abused?"

"Oh yes, of course!"

"Erotic love?" Daphne asked, her tone a bit timid.

"Certainly! Who is the agent behind the erotic love, and what drives his or her impulse? Is it to cement a lifelong, meaningful emotional bond? Or a guise to exert dominance? The plight of erotic passion has always been the confusion of emotional compatibility with physical utility—and we all know how utility can run thin."

"The utility of passion?"

"The utility of desire," Mr. Figgle explained to Daphne. "A bond of love survives, while a bond of desire decays when its usefulness has expired. Desire can be love, desire can be abuse."

"You mean," Kaffir said, "that the human passions can be abused if they are used for insincere ends."

Mr. Figgle reached over to pat Kaffir's shoulder. "That's one way of putting it! My attempt at academic eloquence certainly gets the better of me!" He giggled.

"But Mr. Figgle," Daphne leaned over, "can Wagner's music be used for insincere ends?"

"Ah, abuse is not of the music itself, but in its agency."

"What do you mean?"

"Wagner's music, when taken solely as the *thing itself*—music—is undoubtedly a thing of beauty, although I must say I find some of his operas rather exhausting and ponderous. But that's just my taste, Daphne."

"Do you think when the Ancients listened to Wagner, the music might have incited them into immoral behavior, like Thomas Mann described in his story?"

"The power of music to move the passions is undeniable. It is most concerning when an artist like Wagner can be used to promote a dangerously warped worldview."

"Are you referring to Hitler's admiration of Wagner?" Kaffir asked.

"I am indeed. Hitler was not as much concerned with the music itself as he was for using its power to circulate his demented racial ideologies. Germany needed to spread its *Übermensch* purity throughout Europe, and Wagner's music was one vehicle for that scheme. For Hitler, Wagner's nationalism and anti-Semitism infused itself into the German psyche through his music. Again, abuse is not of a thing itself, but of its agency."

"It's not easy for me to stop listening to Wagner, Mr. Figgle," Daphne admitted. "I know he was a bigoted man, but still, his music just . . . warms my heart. Is it wrong for me to think that?"

"Daphne, have you ever seen Hitler's paintings?"

"Oh, no!" she gasped. "Hitler's paintings were deleted from the database over a hundred years ago. Have you seen them, Kaffir?"

"No, no, how could I? I just know they existed."

Mr. Figgle offered them a gentle grin. "Daphne," he said, "if you took a look at those paintings, and had no idea who produced them, you would think they are works displaying considerable talent. But as soon as you associate the art with the artist, in this case, the art becomes abhorrent. Can the art be separated from the artist? It *can* be. I would suggest that it is only the morally superior individual who is able to produce or experience art for art's sake without devolving it into an instrument of exploitation. Think about all the people who have interpreted religious texts to justify their acts of racism, bigotry, and violence. Think about all the people who have interpreted seminal works of philosophy to justify, again, their acts of racism, bigotry, and violence. Think about all the people who have interpreted the words or themes or paint strokes of a creative artist to do the same. You don't need a blatant manifesto like *Mein Kampf* to spread hate. All you need is an agent to soil the seed of a musical note, or a brush stroke, or a word, until it springs weeds of malice, and destruction."

With a parting tap on the table, he rose, then turned after several steps.

"That being said, while Hitler's works of art are—as works of art unto themselves—competent, I personally would rather look at turtle turd."

Daphne waited for him to leave the Aviary before speaking.

"What a smart man. And . . . kind of a peculiar one."

Waiting for Kaffir's acknowledgment, she noticed his distant stare.

"Kaffir? What?"

"Oh. Just thinking about what he said."

"Ha! Which part?"

"About the Hitler paintings."

"Yes?"

Kaffir finally looked at her.

"How on Opine could he have possibly seen them?"

Sixteen

A FEW DAYS LATER, outside the Geranium Genome Gentrification facility, a man in his mid-twenties was staggering down the street in a fevered rant. The words at first were unintelligible, until concerned citizens began to inch over, at which time his agitation intensified. "Mass death is God's eternal orgasm!" he screamed, over and over again. Then: "Everybody should die! Kill everybody!" And then: "Everybody! Two hundred million people should die!"

The population of Opine was approximately two hundred million people.

In short order he was surrounded by around twenty citizens with black stun guns. The man appeared to lunge at a few of them. From the facility window, genetic scientists could hear a series of crackling pops. The man's body shuddered, stiffened, and he fell. A few citizens pulled out their cell phones to call the police. One woman knelt by the unconscious man and tenderly stroked his hair for minutes. A few other citizens stuffed some bills in his pockets.

A block away, a red Pomeranian on a leash was yapping. The entire crowd turned, waved and smiled, some of them blowing kisses.

Every Opinion citizen in good standing was provided with a registered stun gun. The stun gun was only to be used for self defense, and to incapacitate any mentally ill individual who may pose a physical threat, whether voluntary or not. It was calibrated to render the victim unconscious for about five minutes, followed by a longer period of grogginess and disorientation. No permanent damage was ever inflicted by these citizen stun guns. People rarely used them, and carrying them added a further dimension of security and well-being to an already reliable State of Contentment. Law enforcement officers carried similar stun guns, though with greater firing ranges.

A sustained utopia is impossible because the universe is mutable. The cosmos is wired to evolve according to the laws of thermodynamics, and the biological world is wired to develop itself through natural selection. Neither the cosmos nor the biological world can ever achieve a perfect stasis, as the law of entropy commands everything to tend towards disorder, and for the biological world, disorder means evolving, or changing. While the Opinions attained great strides in overcoming disorder through their political system, educational philosophy, and employment of the Self Suppressor, there will always be anomalies, or ripples in the fabric of Contentment. Anomalies, in the form of mental illness, and crime.

When a citizen's social and economic needs are met, he or she normally has no incentive to challenge the established order, whether that challenge takes the form of lawful protest or criminal action. This is the norm in Opine. The vast majority of Opinion citizens are content. When an Opinion citizen feels compelled to commit a crime, it is usually due to either mental illness or a genetic "glitch." These glitches are corrected with a "booster" therapy, designed to correct the ineffective viral vector, carrier of the CRISPR-Cas9 therapy, in the original treatment (the non-viral vectors were found to be even less effective in clinical trials). Since the inception of the Self Suppressor, the vast majority of Opinion crimes involve different degrees of larceny, from petty theft to embezzlement. Violent crimes are exclusively committed by those suffering from mental illness. The last recorded cases of murder or rape in Opine were well before the administration of the Self Suppressor. Another triumphant consequence of Opinion genetic engineering.

As in any other society, when a criminal act is found to be perpetrated by an individual clinically evaluated to be in complete control of his or her mental faculties, the state must exact punishment. This is regardless of whether or not the infraction was induced by the aforementioned genetic glitch. An example must always be set for the rest of society. The Opinions did not want to set a precedent for legal defense deferring to "the glitch made me do it." Further complicating the issue was the relatively few number of cases where the determination as to whether the DNA of the test subjects contained a glitch was inconclusive. Thus the Opinions had to decide on a suitable, humane penal code for those relatively rare cases.

Rather than needlessly burdening the Opinion tax payers with outdated, abandoned correctional facilities, the Central Congress finally decided to adopt the house arrest program of various Ancient nations. Every citizen in Opine is required by law to have keyless electronic locks installed on all residential doors. Owners gain entry by scanning their RFID (Radio Frequency Identification) cards on the sensor. Multiple sources of renewable energy such as solar, hydropower, and wind ensure the system will never fail, though a proper official can always perform an override if necessary. Similar to the systems adopted by schools beginning in the Ancient twenty-first century in response to school shootings, the doors are all networked to the Home Security Administration, part of the Department of Housing, in conjunction with its county agencies. The central and local computer networks keep track of whenever a door is locked or opened. In addition, all residential windows are equipped with identical electronic locks, although these normally remain inert, giving residents freedom to open and close windows without electronic surveillance. Administrators can lock any door or window from the central computer, just as school officials in Ancient times could lock any classroom door. In most cases, this is never necessary.

The conditions change when a citizen is placed under house arrest. When a court issues this sentence, the subject will be confined to his or her residence, isolated from other occupants, for its duration. The basic necessities of life are provided to the subject, but the Home Security computer locks all access to the incarceration quarters, windows and doors. Alternately, the prisoner may be relocated to a vacant small one-bedroom residence. Throughout the duration of the sentence, the prisoner may watch television or read, but all communication devices are forbidden, including, but not limited to, phones and computers. Any attempted breach of a window or door immediately alerts the local police. If the prisoner attempts to escape, the penalty is an automatic doubling of the sentence duration.

At this point in our narrative, no Opinion had ever attempted to escape house arrest. Though it should be stressed this was solely due to the unthinkable prospect of serving a double sentence. Having been conditioned both culturally and genetically to crave social interaction, the thought of being confined to a single room or residence without any opportunity to communicate was absolutely abhorrent to Opinions. The worst kind of punishment one could impose on an Opinion was solitary confinement. It didn't matter that the conditions of the confinement were relatively comfortable compared to an Ancient prison cell. The sentenced offender was absolutely miserable being cut off from the rest of the world. Solitary home confinement was a very effective crime deterrent in Opinion society. Those mentally unstable individuals who were unlucky enough to serve a sentence could at least look forward to corrective therapeutic treatment upon release.

Thymus Corkwood gazed blankly out his office window as a mentally unstable young man was being stunned three floors below. He was too preoccupied with Aster Bottlebrush's case to notice. What would happen, he thought, if somebody *didn't* respond to corrective therapeutic treatment? Would a convicted criminal have to be confined to house arrest for life? But, no, no, that's impossible. Everybody responds to corrective treatment.

Still, it had happened.

Aster Bottlebrush was certainly not a criminal. He had acted on a biological impulse. But it had happened.

Upon examining Aster's DNA, Thymus had determined the original CRISPR-cas9 vector had failed to edit the arginine-vasopressin receptor 1a and estrogen receptor genes. And Aster's immune system seemed to be resistant to any corrective therapy. Thymus had been monitoring Aster for the last eight months after administering a booster vector. Aster's condition had remained the same. Complete biochemical resistance to the vector. Absolutely magnificent. The first recorded case of neutralizing antibodies causing complete immunity to the Self Suppressor.

The potential repercussions arising from this phenomenon were too dizzying to contemplate. What would this mean for Opinion society? Should Aster be permitted to pass on his genetic resistance to his children? Would his condition be detected in other subjects? And if it is detected, should *those* individuals be permitted to reproduce? What kind of society would decree that certain people were permitted to have children while others could not? How could a universal moral code be maintained in this scenario without lapsing into self-contradictory precepts? No individual could possibly *choose* to be resistant to the therapy. A person cannot *choose* his or her own biochemistry or immune system. By what justification, then, may a society compel such an individual to refrain from having children? What possible law, argument, or body of evidence could ever support the arbitrary conclusion that a person resistant to the therapy will more than likely not develop into a law-abiding, productive member of society?

Yes, it is possible that somebody like Aster could develop character traits tending towards selfishness, or hostility, or duplicity, or even brutal violence. He could turn out to be an imminent threat to the status quo. But he could just as well turn out to be a warm, caring, selfless, industrious Opinion citizen, never prone to disrupting the balanced State of Contentment despite occasional urges to consummate his involuntary libidinous impulses. Who is to say that

Aster Bottlebrush's natural biochemistry is a threat to society at large? On what reasonable or legal grounds can such an argument be supported?

Thymus thought about this at length. Being a geneticist experienced in the rigors of scientific trial and error, navigating through such thorny philosophical issues was unfamiliar territory. A scientific hurdle, however, he was ready and willing to tackle. There was one possibility, however remote, that might untangle these potentially adverse philosophical complications. Perhaps he could even the playing field. What if the resistant antibodies in Aster's system could be used to turn on *only* the estrogen receptor ESR1 gene, thereby enabling the genetic expression of libido while sustaining the altruistic component of the therapy? It had been determined that the libido side effect was associated specifically with the estrogen receptor gene. Perhaps selfishness in the genome could be suppressed to an acceptable level while safely expressing the libido component?

This had never been attempted before, but of course no Opinion had ever resisted the therapy before. There was no evidence as of yet to suggest that a new pathway enabling the expression of libido would necessarily turn off the genetic expression of altruism. Perhaps Aster's biology could offer a new, enhanced modification to the original therapy?

Thymus Corkwood would keep this hypothesis to himself, for now. But he would be getting to work immediately.

Seventeen

As Kaffir, Gaura, and Aster Bottlebrush sat at the dining room table waiting for the Needle Palm County (NPC) News Team to arrive, their cheery chatter accomplished little in the way of smoothing out wrinkles of discontent muddling their minds. The Bottlebrushes, like millions of Opinion families, were used to minor kinks in life's road here and there, but never an unexpected detour like this. Out of all the millions of Opinion boys out there, how was it that Kaffir and Gaura's son was the only one whose immune system had managed to resist the most successful genetic therapy in history, the Self Suppressor? It didn't make sense. He was by all measurable standards a completely normal seventeen-tear-old Opinion boy. Not once did he exhibit any signs that the therapy was ineffective. Yes, there was that one unusual incident with Dianella sparking the whole controversy. Unusual, but not criminal. Genetic anomalies of this sort had to be reported immediately to the Opinion Congress. That was the law. It didn't mean the person was necessarily in trouble. It just meant the subject needed to be monitored, and hopefully treated. There were no grounds for concern. Aster was a sweet, selfless, unassuming boy, always giving of himself, always attentive to his responsibilities both at home and at school, a self-motivated and ambitious student, a high achiever in almost all academic disciplines—really a model Opinion adolescent in all respects.

All right, it was true he was biochemically given to libidinous cravings. But all he did was touch a girl's breast. He wasn't some kind of mentally warped fiend. It didn't necessarily mean the *entire* therapy was ineffective. Even Thymus had admitted more genetic testing had to be performed on the target alleles in Aster's DNA to determine exactly the extent of the immune response. It may be the therapy was manifesting itself in hitherto unexplored novel genetic pathways. There was no cause for alarm at this point, Thymus had stressed. Aster didn't do anything wrong. It wasn't *his* fault the therapy apparently hadn't been effective.

Still, such assurances did not smooth out the wrinkles of discontent. The Bottlebrushes were not used to this. An interview on national television was always an exciting event. To be in the national spotlight was usually an honor. Why else would an Opinion be interviewed, other than for fostering or supporting or strengthening the current State of Contentment? Accomplishing extraordinary strides in the bestowal of happiness and good will and beneficence to all—*that* represented the apogee of Opinion honor. Aster's case was quite different. Aster was . . . different. A curiosity to be examined and evaluated. An aberration to the calm. An open question. Opinions could not rest on open questions. They needed to be resolved.

"Aster, you have nothing to worry about," Aster's mother attempted an unwavering smile. "You just answer truthfully like you did with Dr. Buckthorn."

"It's embarrassing," Aster stated, as he had stated several times.

"Aster," Kaffir said, "remember you don't have to talk about Dianella. That whole episode was between you, Dianella's parents, and Dr. Buckthorn. News reporters always respect privacy."

"Of course! They always respect privacy," Gaura reaffirmed. "We don't have smutty sensationalist tabloids like the Ancients did. Journalists are honest and respectable, like their Walter Cronkite or Edward R. Murrow or Woodward and Bernstein. They are not out to damage your reputation or circulate false rumors."

"I know, Mom. I'm just nervous."

"Oh, that's because you've never been interviewed like this. You just be yourself and everything will be fine."

Gaura shared an uneasy grin with her husband.

Aster wasn't sure it would be fine. He had been having more and more thoughts over the last year. More and more visions. More and more urges. He didn't want to feel like that now. Not in front of a reporter. Not in front of a camera. What fueled his apprehensions was not so much the interview itself, but the lady who would be conducting it. Ms. Bellis Jewelwood of Channel 9, NPC News, was one of the most attractive news anchors on TV. Her hair was like streams of caramel drapery. Her gaze could dazzle you. When she was reporting a story you never wanted her to leave, in the same way one could stare indefinitely at a wonder of nature. A beautiful person was a wonder of nature for an Opinion. For Aster as well, except now it appeared he was the only Opinion on Opine who regarded a woman as much of a titillation as a wonder.

Twenty minutes later, there she was, Ms. Bellis Jewelwood, right in front of him, her glittering reality blotting out the backlighting and cameraman. She was wearing a tawny skirt and a hunter green sleeveless crew neck, more low-cut than Aster had both hoped for and dreaded. Most Opinion women felt very comfortable dressing liberally. They had nothing to worry about. Men were harmless these days.

"Aster, again, NPC News is so, so thankful you agreed to this interview. Your viewership will be very happy. I can promise you that."

"Thank you, Ms. Jewelwood."

"Please, Bellis."

"Bellis. Okay."

"Now we're already recording, so we're just going to continue talking, like there was no camera. Why don't you start by telling us about yourself? You go to Boxwood Borough Brainery?"

"Yes. Yes, that's right."

"And your parents tell me you are doing sensationally well! You participated in the Illicium Fool Initiative?"

"Yes. Yes, I . . . that was last year."

"And why don't you tell us about that?"

"Well, the Fool Initiatives are inter-county, publicly funded educational initiatives that promote Fool Awareness by examining a number of Ancient socioeconomic tragedies."

"I see, and what study did you submit for the Initiative?"

Aster immediately felt more relaxed. The topic was well-removed from sex drive.

"I decided to investigate the privatization of rainwater."

"Really? The Ancients privatized rain water?"

"Yes. They did, at least on one occasion, at the end of the twentieth century."

"Where did it happen?"

"In Bolivia, a poor country in South America. The World Bank was set up during that time to provide loans and grants to low-income countries to help reduce poverty. The Bolivian city of Cochabamba needed help financing its water service, so they turned to the World Bank, who required that the water service be privatized. A private company in San Francisco called the Bechtel Corporation took over."

"And what happened?'

"Bechtel was charging so much money for water that it made the poverty worse. People in Cochabamba were paying as much as a quarter of their entire income for water, and if they didn't pay their bills, the corporation could seize and auction off their homes. They weren't even allowed to collect rainwater."

"Rainwater? How could a corporation own rainwater? That's like privatizing thunder or lightning."

"I don't know," Aster's shrugged, "but I guess they were following the Washington Consensus."

"The Washington Consensus—that was the set of economic policies established by Washington D.C. to help countries like Bolivia experiencing an economic crisis."

"Yes, that's right."

"Ha, what Fools!" Bellis laughed. "I guess that's how you help a poverty-stricken country. Own their rainwater and make them pay for it!"

"Yes, that's right, ha ha," Aster chuckled along. He was feeling better now. It was pleasant talking about his academic accomplishments with this very beautiful news lady.

"Well, Aster, you certainly are a credit to your community. Your parents must be so proud of you." She flashed a warm glance at Kaffir and Gaura sitting off to the side.

"Yes, well, they say they are proud of me."

"I'm sure. Now, turning to the Self Suppressor therapy..."

Aster's smile wilted.

"... As is commonly known, it is not entirely unprecedented that an individual be resistant to the therapy, including just the side effects. There have been isolated cases in the past—very isolated cases."

"Mmm."

"But you, Aster, are the only person who has been resistant even to the booster therapies. That's extraordinary. That's something your neighbor Dr. Thymus Corkwood, who synthesizes the therapy, calls 'miraculous.' Do you agree that it's miraculous?"

"Miraculous? Well, Ms.—um, Bellis, Opinions don't believe in miracles."

His parents and the news crew tittered.

"You are right about that, Aster. But you have to admit your condition is completely unusual."

"Yes. I was told that it *is* very unusual."

"And that is the truth. What I think many people will find just as astounding is that as a consequence of your natural resistance to the therapy, the Ancient instinct of libido has been reactivated in your biochemistry. Can you tell us a little bit about what that's like?"

As in Dr. Buckthorn's office, Aster looked for help, this time from his parents, knowing full well he would receive none.

"I think it's like... being interested in something."

"Being interested? I see. You mean like being interested in pursuing a hobby?"

"No. No. More like, being interested in experiencing something."

"Oh, experiencing something. Like what, Aster? What would you like to experience?"

The flicker of a smile playing upon Bellis Jewelwood's lips was making Aster not want to experience this interview.

"It's like . . . you know those Ancient works of nude art, like Goya's *The Nude Maja* or Manet's *Olympia?* It's like wanting to see those."

"Anybody can view a work of art and appreciate its beauty. What you have is different. You have a craving inside you, don't you, Aster? A yearning, a longing, a desire, a *compulsion.* Those words are closer to a psychological portrait of libido, aren't they?"

"Um . . . yes."

"And what do you crave?"

"I . . . it's . . . it's the instinct, you know, to perpetuate the species."

"Right, but our medical procedures can easily perpetuate the species. The therapy has suppressed our natural cravings. But you feel it."

He didn't answer.

"You feel it, Aster?"

"Yes. I can't help it."

"Oh, we know you can't. Nobody is blaming you. Let me ask you something, Aster. And this is not meant to make you feel uncomfortable. If you look at somebody like me, let's say you see an attractive woman. A beautiful woman."

She waited for the acknowledgment, which came as a quick nod.

"But you see . . . something else in me? Sexuality, perhaps. A person who you might find sexually desirable?"

"No," he said quickly.

"No?"

"No. I mean you are . . . very pretty. But that doesn't mean I find every pretty woman sexually desirable."

"But you feel the libido, and libido is sex drive."

"Okay."

"And the sex drive is triggered by sexual desirability."

"Okay."

"Aster, you can tell us the truth. Feeling sexually attracted to somebody is an expression of your natural libido, escaping through an impotent genetic therapy."

"O . . . kay."

"If I took off my top right now, right in front of you, you would have a reaction, wouldn't you? Wouldn't you have a natural reaction to such a stimulus?"

"I . . ."

Where were his parents? He couldn't move his eyeballs.

"Well, let's say it wasn't me. Let's say it was any attractive woman. Would you have a reaction? Possibly?"

"I . . . would . . . yes, possibly."

"What kind of reaction? Describe it to us."

Bellis Jewelwood was leaning forward enough for him to smell her scent. Briefly lowering his gaze, it snapped back up when he saw the curve of her breasts smiling at him.

Aster took a breath. He was trying his very best not picture Bellis

Jewelwood without her top as she had directed. He was monumentally unsuccessful at this endeavor. Even worse, how on Opine could he ever offer a characterization of the energy that percolates, that scintillates, that intoxicates throughout him at even the slightest carnal prompt? And what of his *physical* reaction? That would involve very unseemly words, like "erection." Opinions did not generally mention the word "erection" in public. It was a faux pas, akin to pointing out a beautiful sunset to a blind man. He would have to rely on vague metaphors.

"It feels like . . ." he groped, ". . . like opening a birthday present."

"Oh? A birthday present?" Bellis blinked.

"Yes. A birthday present. Except in this case, the birthday present is a person, a person . . . wrapped up. There's this excitement welling up inside you, and you really want to see your present unwrapped. You can't wait to see it unwrapped. And when you finally do . . . it's, it's, um . . ."

"Fulfilling?"

"Yes," Aster breathed. "That's exactly right. Fulfilling."

Bellis Jewelwood nodded, smiled sweetly, as did Aster's approving parents. It was a very fitting answer to a very fitting young man.

Eighteen

"MY DAUGHTER," said Mrs. Vanda Cottonwood, addressing Mr. Shumard Shadbush of the Boxwood Borough Brainery Board of Education, "is not a birthday present."

Everybody attending the meeting chuckled, partly in reaction to Mrs. Cottonwood's bite of sarcasm, but also in nervous acknowledgment of the underlying unsavory flavor threatening to spoil the usual savory proceedings. The Bottlebrushes, seated in the front row, smiled politely but were in fact not very pleased.

"Mrs. Cottonwood," Mr. Shadbush said, "we all appreciate your jab of good humor, but you must of course know that our friend Aster, a most upstanding member of the Boxwood Borough Community, as we have just outlined, did not mean to imply that any human being's worth can be relegated to the secular value of a mere birthday present."

"Of course, that is the truth," the Superintendent, Mr. Larch Spekboom, nodded emphatically.

Mrs. Hedera Blackthorn, sister-in-law to Sugi Blackthorn, was acknowledged, and stood up.

"I think we should all remember," she said, "that Aster's condition is not abnormal, strictly speaking. Libido is a natural instinct common to the animal kingdom. It is only the Self Suppressor, synthetically engineered in the laboratory, stifling that instinct."

"Through a side effect," Thymus Corkwood added. "The original therapy does not specifically target libido."

"Yes," Mrs. Blackthorn concurred, "but all the same, I would like to suggest that it is the therapy itself that imposes an abnormality in human behavior."

"Not so much an abnormality," Thymus said, "but a consequence of a necessary genetic correction."

"That's true, yes, very true," the Superintendent nodded. Many in the room murmured in agreement.

Mrs. Blackthorn turned to face Thymus. "I'm sorry, Dr. Corkwood. I didn't mean to suggest that the therapy itself is abnormal. It is indeed necessary, and right. Perhaps I should have said it imposes an artificiality in human behavior?"

"A beneficial artificiality," a man said.

"Yes, beneficial," Thymus said, "and I would also like to point out that the science of genetic editing is imitating, in a sense, the genetic editing that is executed naturally throughout the biosphere, in the form of mutation."

"That's a good point," Mr. Shadbush said.

"True, true," Superintendent Spekboom nodded, echoed by several community members.

"What may not be natural," Vanda Cottonwood indicated with a raised finger, "is the inadvertent unleashing of a natural instinct resulting in a person mentally... *unwrapping* other people to satisfy a rampant salacious appetite."

A smattering of giggles erupted, promptly waved off by Mr. Shadbush.

"Now, Mrs. Cottonwood," he said, "there is no scientific basis supporting a conclusion that Aster's condition induces him to mentally 'unwrap' people . . . and even if he does mentally unwrap people, there is no reason to conclude that the intrinsic nature of that unwrapping is salacious."

"That's very true, Mt. Shadbush," Superintendent Spekboom nodded.

"But Aster has the libido," a man said, "which could plausibly indicate a sexual unwrapping."

"Yes, plausibly, truth," Mr. Spekboom nodded again.

Thymus stood up, "Ladies and gentleman," he said, "I can assure you that the Ancients were not so shackled by their libidinal impulse as to be rendered powerless to resist mentally unwrapping their fellow citizens."

Everybody found this agreeable and profitable, in keeping with the good-hearted cheer of a typical board meeting.

"Aster," Mr. Shadbush said, "maybe you, being the subject of this discourse, can shed some reassuring light. Do you find yourself mentally unwrapping people?"

"No, sir, I do not mentally unwrap anybody," asserted Aster, who had mentally unwrapped NPC News reporter Ms. Bellis Jewelwood four days earlier and had previously asked his friend Dianella to physically unwrap herself.

"I do that," a man volunteered. "Just out of sheer curiosity." The entire crowd laughed.

"I think we're missing the real issue," a lovely Mrs. Myrtle Frangipani stated. "It is not so much whether or not Aster mentally unwraps people, but whether a purely sexual prompting of such an unwrapping could compromise his capacity to maintain social interactions in accordance with community norms."

"Ah, yes, well said, Mrs. Frangipani," the Superintendent said. He was still nodding.

"Thank you, Mr. Spekboom," Mrs. Frangipani bowed.

"I would just like to say," Guara Bottlebrush said, turning to face the assembly, "that my son Aster has always been a paragon of sound, exemplary behavior. Even if he submitted to an uncontrollable genetic inclination to mentally unwrap an individual in a sexual manner, it would in no way jeopardize his ability to participate in completely normal social exchanges."

The room applauded in approval.

"Undoubtedly, yes!" the Superintendent proclaimed. "That's a truth!"

Mr. Tacca Bluebell waited for the applause to subside before standing. "Mrs. Bottlebrush, your characterization of Aster's participation in social exchanges as 'normal' implies that his resistance to the therapy may potentially be at odds with our established norms of social exchange, and thus potentially abnormal."

Opinions were averse to awkward public silences. A few seconds later, somebody's phone chirped.

"Fool Fact," the lady announced. "In 1994, eight hundred thousand Tutsi and Hutu people were murdered in the Rwandan genocide because a presidential directive had stated a peacekeeping operation had to be in the national interest."

Several in the room guffawed.

"Mr. Bluebell," Thymus Corkwood resumed between chuckles, "I just have to qualify your point with a friendly reminder that neither Aster's resistance to the therapy, nor the therapy itself, should justifiably, or truthfully, be considered 'abnormal.' Just as a natural genetic mutation is an adjustment to nature, so too is the Self Suppressor a scientific adjustment to nature, and so too is Aster's resistance to it, a kind of mutation, a natural adjustment to a scientific adjustment to nature."

"Oh, yes, I see your point," Mr. Bluebell grinned uneasily.

"Yes, well-said truths, everybody, well said!" Superintendent Spekboom nodded some more, his head happily remaining attached. "I believe we have arrived at an agreement, a truthful resolution to this agenda item. Don't you, Mr. Shadbush?"

"Yes. Yes, of course. We always do! And the Board concurs?"

The Board members all nodded.

"Any... objections?" Mr. Shadbush eyed the forum.

Nobody objected. The Opinions had collectively arrived at a Truth. Why object?

Nineteen

We have already seen several social, political, and cultural examples illustrating how the Opinions differ markedly from their Ancient ancestors. Perhaps one of the most dramatic differences is their lack of religious observance, notwithstanding the aforementioned practice of paying tribute to religious holidays celebrated throughout the Ancient world, whittled down to festive affairs completely devoid of their religious foundations. Various Opinion sociologists, including Mr. Figgle, had written plenty of articles raising the question as to whether a civilization lacking a tradition of spirituality, or a formalized religious establishment, could nevertheless support a sustainable social framework of healthy values and moral codes. It is not a given that a culture lacking reverence for a higher plane of existence can rely on secular institutions to guide their values.

The Opinions first examined why religious systems formed such an integral component of Ancient cultural life, right up to the demise of Homo Sapiens 1.0. Several popular currents claimed repeated attention. One was that belief in a higher spiritual power gave meaning to life. The modern Opinions discarded this notion, as it implied that life would lack meaning in the absence of a higher spiritual power. Whether or not there is in fact a higher spiritual power, this reasoning begs the question of whether any particular meaning prescribed to life affects the quality of life being itself. In the words of Bob Geldof, "The meaning of life is life itself." For the Opinions, asking whether life has a "purpose" or a "point" is exactly equal to asking whether the wind blowing this way instead of that way has a purpose—a nonsensical question from both our perspective and the wind's perspective. If we instead ask *why* the wind blows this way instead of that way, we can arrive at a reasonable scientific explanation, but we will never be able to answer the *meaning* of why it blows a certain way. Therefore, the existence or non-existence of a higher spiritual power is immaterial when considering life's meaning because life is a meaning unto itself—that is, life's purpose is to live, just as a wind's purpose is to blow. If life's purpose was not to live, then the Opinions deduced either there wouldn't be any life in the first place, or else everything alive would be endeavoring to end their lives as quickly as possible to resolve their paradoxical, contradictory existences, a tragic circumstance peculiar to select members of Homo Sapiens 1.0 who decide life has ceased to serve its purpose of being itself and is therefore voluntarily discarded.

What the Opinions found much more interesting and instructive was to examine why religious devotion throughout the cultural history of Homo Sapiens 1.0 always provided not only a model for behavior to codify their cultural norms, but also a sense of community, comfort, and consolation. Why was it that people always felt compelled to look to an elusive, supernatural, supreme being for reassurance they weren't alone in the ongoing struggle to maintain order out of a universe tending towards disorder, that there was always a watchful eye, or an admonishing finger, or a soothing hand? The answer, the Opinions concluded, is precisely because religious devotion enables humans to reconcile, and cope with, living in a universe tending towards disorder. Humans need to feel some degree of rationality, some degree of order in the way their fates unfold. That soothing hand or admonishing finger lends a measure of order over the unpredictable, cold abyss. A supreme being, no matter how remote or elusive, reassures that chaos does not in fact reign, that there is a cushion of community and security we can weave with the embrace of that guiding hand, a hand that reveals the benevolence of our inherent commonalities.

For the natural world, disorder has a name: entropy. For human civilization, disorder has an additional name: evil. Humans, genetically programmed with the capacity to commit evil acts, are the only species facing a two-front war with Disorder, those fronts being entropy and evil. Religion, spirituality, and belief in God are ways of dealing with these omnipresent, formidable adversaries. The Opinions, in examining the cultural and emotional benefits of faith-based constructs, were very interested in finding a way to contend with the roots of these constructs. The law of entropy was irreversible; the universe will always tend towards disorder. But the practice of evil is not a law of nature like entropy. It is peculiar to human behavior. It is peculiar to creatures with the intellectual capacity to commit such evil acts. What is the root cause of all evil acts? It didn't take long for the Opinions to arrive at the answer. It was selfishness.

Following the lead of notable moral and political philosophers like Rousseau, who famously asserted that *amour-propre*—vanity, or selfish pride—was what moved an individual to value himself above all others, the Opinions would formally pronounce the universal elimination of this selfish pride, and legislate it.

Over a century and a half ago, when the authorization requiring mandatory administration of the Self Suppressor therapy to the population was formally appended to the Opinion Constitution, the written justification stated a set of dictums outlining why the trait of selfishness needed to be expunged from the human genome. These dictums are quoted as follows:

When a person kills another out of malice, his motives disregard the value of that human life in comparison to his own. This is selfishness.

When a person steals from another, his motives devalue the human rights of those he steals from in comparison to his own. This is selfishness.

When a person exploits his position of power to graft or extort from innocent others, his motives demean the human value of those he exploits. This is selfishness.

When an employer exploits his employees through oppressive working conditions or unfair wages, his motives demean the human value of those he exploits. This is selfishness.

When a leader oppresses his own people to satisfy political ideologies or personal gain, his motives hold in contempt a people's confidence in the universally implicit social contract predicated on a leader acting in good faith for the welfare of those he leads. This is selfishness.

When a person judges another racially, he degrades the value of one human life in comparison to his own. This is selfishness.

When a person judges another ethnically, he degrades the value of one culture or nationality in comparison to his own. This is selfishness.

When a person judges another's gender, he degrades the value of one gender or sexual orientation in comparison to his own. This is selfishness.

When a person judges another's religion, he degrades the value of one set of spiritual beliefs in comparison to his own. This is selfishness.

When a person uses physical force or violence to subjugate or harm others, be they individuals or an entire people, his motives ignore the value of equitable respect and decency between human beings. This is selfishness.

When a person uses lies, manipulation, and deceit to empower himself at the expense of a community's welfare, his motives ignore the values of trust and goodwill binding that community together. This is selfishness.

When a person knowingly produces and/or distributes a product that is psychologically or physically harmful to others, his motives degrade the value of community welfare in comparison to his own personal welfare. This is selfishness.

When a person enters into an agreement or contract with another, be it a personal or business transaction, formal or informal, and knowingly dishonors the terms of the agreement through fraud or trickery in the interest of personal gain, his motives ignore the values of mutual trust and good faith between human beings. This is selfishness.

When a person possesses a disproportionately large magnitude of money or power that enables him to assist others in need, but chooses not to, his motives degrade the value of community welfare in comparison to his own personal welfare. This is selfishness.

When a person occupying a position of leadership promotes a policy benefiting one group of people, for purposes of personal advancement, such that another group suffers, his motives ignore the commonality and equality of human worth. This is selfishness.

This is why the development of the Self Suppressor therapy was of paramount importance to the Opinions. In the absence of any real evidence that a supreme being interferes with the course of human affairs, the consolation of a faith-based construct was simply not enough. The Opinions needed to know they had at least a fighting chance against one of the fronts in a two-front war. They needed to know that regardless of whether a higher spiritual realm existed, they could fight the capacity of human beings to commit evil acts. They could fight selfishness.

Thymus Corkwood, like all genetic scientists working to engineer and distribute the Self Suppressor, believed the Opinions had won the battle against selfishness. Together with a rigorous state-sponsored educational system instilling citizens with healthy values from early childhood on, the therapy had been proven to infuse its subjects with a newly invigorated genetic predisposition to care equally for the well-being of all sectors of society. This ideology meant that no single individual, no business, no local community, no income bracket, no intellectual level, and no occupation was deemed more or less valuable than any other. As long as a person was not incurring deliberate harm onto any other, that person's place within the network of social contentment was honored. Any disruption to that network needed to be corrected immediately, lest a tiny crack becomes a fissure, becomes a fracture, becomes a collapse.

Thymus was concerned whether Aster Bottlebrush's genetic peculiarity could potentially represent a tiny crack in the network. People might feel threatened about the prospect of a behavior associated with the primitive, pre-therapy human genome spreading throughout the gene pool. His recent analysis of Aster's antibodies indicated that the development of a therapy to express the estrogen receptor ESR1 gene, thereby turning on the libidinal instinct, was very possible indeed. If his preliminary studies were correct, then Aster's genetic peculiarity would not represent a threat to the gene pool. It could simply represent a new modification to the original Self Suppressor—and a most welcome modification at that.

But Thymus concluded this particular venture was way too sensitive to seek public funding. The public did not need to know about his theory just yet, as any suggestion of modifying a universally approved and widely acclaimed genetic therapy was bound to garner shouts of protests and calls for investigation. A much safer course of action for the present was to seek private funding. For now, it would remain a classified preliminary trial.

The first person who came to mind was his friend and colleague, Lupin Hollyhock, in direct line from distinguished Hollyhocks like his father Mistol and Mistol's great-grandfather Nalca. Thymus's company, Geranium Genome Gentrification, had generously helped to fund many of Lupin's projects at Thunbergia Therapy Thresholds, such as their ongoing development of Chimeric Antigen Receptor T-cells. Thymus was sure Lupin would be intrigued with the proposal.

Lupin was indeed intrigued, though with some reservations. Without access to more concrete data, he wasn't entirely convinced the modification would leave unaffected the primary altruistic component of the original therapy. Thymus assured Lupin that his analysis and preliminary testing suggested Aster's resistant proteins could be engineered specifically to modulate gene regulation controlling the expression of libido. Thymus also promised Lupin he would keep Lupin well informed during the entire clinical trial process. Should any adverse reactions to the new therapy arise, the project would be promptly abandoned. With Lupin's generous financial backing, Thymus could have a preliminary therapy in pill form within seven or eight months. If it passed all the phases of the clinical trials, every genetic lab in Opine could contribute to the most groundbreaking achievement in the genetic sciences since the inception of the Self Suppressor.

Lupin Hollyhock found Thymus Corkwood's enthusiasm infectious. Of course he would help to fund the new therapy. The very thought of Thunbergia Therapy Thresholds providing the resources that would ultimately create a trailblazing new therapy like Self Suppressor 2.0 was irresistibly intoxicating. They would be the toast of munificence in all of Opine!

Twenty

YEAR ONE FOR THE CHRISTIAN CALENDAR was marked by the birth of Jesus of Nazareth.

Year One for the Muslim calendar was 622 CE, marking the date of the Hijri, Muhammad's migration from Mecca to Medina.

Year One for the Hebrew calendar was 3760 BCE, marking the creation of the world.

Year One for the Hindu, or Vikram Samvat calendar, was 57 BCE, marking the date when King Vikramaditya of Ujjain defeated the nomadic Iranian people known as the Saka.

Year One for the new Opinion calendar marked the date when a nineteen-year-old Dr. Nalca Hollyhock discovered the adenovirus vector that would deliver the Self Suppressor therapy (the name "Opine" had been adopted long before this date). This occurred on November 9, one hundred fifty-eight years before the present narrative, the event now celebrated as Opinion Day. Citizens celebrated that day with variously colored bright T-shirts reading: "I am an Opīnion." The long vowel symbol was always a different color than the letters.

Thus, the current Opinion date was November 9, 158, a little over three months after Thymus Corkwood began working on the Self Suppressor update.

Opinion Day at the Catchfly County Culture Coalition Center followed the Opinewide celebratory tradition of philanthropic activities, keeping with the general profile of most Opinion holidays. The "season of giving" for the Opinions applied to all seasons, including tax season, a formalized version of a typical Opinion holiday. Opinion Day was simply another opportunity to spread the joy by spreading the wealth. The center's Large Conference Room was decked with harlequin confetti, streamers, party horns, noisemakers—and balloons, some of which were filled simply with helium for decoration, while special gold and silver balloons were reserved for the evening's customary philanthropic entertainment: The Balloon Endowment Fund.

The Balloon Endowment Fund was a kind of trivia game played by many businesses on Opinion Day, where each balloon was stuffed with money in the form of bills collected previously by every employee, and a single trivia question printed on a folded piece of paper. The trivia categories were history, arts and entertainment, and science, history being the favorite. The balloons are filled with helium, released into the air, and the first person to pop a balloon, using nothing but their hands, reads aloud the question within. Any player answering the first question correctly keeps the money in the balloon—temporarily. If a question is answered incorrectly, the money goes to the Balloon Pot. The game resumes, and when a player answers a question correctly, the player collects all the money in the Balloon Pot. The game ends when all the balloons have been popped. Each winner then has the option to either keep twenty percent of the winnings, or distribute some, or all of it, among fellow employees. The natural genetic tendency, of course, was to keep little, if any, of the winnings, since every employee winds up taking home money. The remaining eighty percent of the winnings is donated to various non-profit charitable foundations, who in turn provide funding for various businesses and organizations throughout Opine—everything from welfare aid, to scientific research and development, to humane societies, to grants for education, clean energy, the environment, and medicine. Opinion Day in Opine was a way to celebrate the anniversary of the end of selfishness by openly displaying the fruits of that anniversary.

Bubbling conversations about family, culture, and good news reigned as the employees feasted on vegan cuisine, pot luck Ancient dishes like South Indian crepes, ndambe (black-eyed pea, sweet potato, and okra stew), mapo tofu, vegan bánh mì, braised collards, soba, and efo riro (a western Nigerian vegetable soup). After dessert, the highlight of the evening. "Release the balloons!" it was announced, to whoops and wahoos. The first balloon was popped by Literary Consultant Sugi Blackthorn. A dozen bills flipped and fluttered along with a folded question.

"What is the name of the series of 1921 racial attacks in Oklahoma," Sugi read, "involving a white mob, with the help of city officials, against African Americans, resulting in the destruction of thirty-five blocks of African American homes and businesses and hundreds of deaths and injuries?"

Senior Data Administrator Mallow Garva began the timer. She only had one minute to respond.

"I can't remember," she finally said. "I know it begins with a 'T,' right?"

"The Tulsa Race Massacre," Mallow revealed.

"Oh, we can't have that!" Crocus Sophora snickered. "Naughty critical race theory, teaching about naughty past events! History should always be pleasant. Do you remember any patriotic, happy stories, Dr. Garva?"

"Of course," Mallow Garva smirked, "as according to race theory detractors, only happy stories are permitted to have happened!"

They all cackled and applauded.

"Money goes into the Balloon Pot!" Mallow directed, as the bills were scooped up and dumped in a large floral brocade porcelain bowl, and a few minutes later the next batch were launched. Rimu Titoki, a Music Consultant like Daphne Sweetspire, promptly sat on a balloon. Pop, and the bills flew out on either side. Rimu rifled through the bills until he found the question.

"What was the common name for Mao Zedong's br...br... *BRUHHHH!...*" Luckily, a quick-thinking co-worker handed him a canister. Rimu wiped his lips with a napkin before continuing. "...for Mao Zedong's brutal collectivization of agriculture between 1958 and 1962 in which the forced famine killed tens of millions of peasants and farmers?"

Rimu hesitated before admitting, "Nope. Used to know that."

"It was known as The Great Leap Forward," Mallow said. "Add to the Pot!"

"What a *great* name for a mass killing!" shot a man, followed by volleys:

"Workers of the world, starve!"

"Stalin's a tough act to follow!"

"Hey Joseph, if you had called your own five-year plans 'great,' maybe you could have killed more people!"

This repartee drew appreciative applause.

The next employee, Heather Smilax, bit her balloon, delighting her colleagues. The explosion sent her pecan bangs fluttering and her party hat flying. It took her a while to find the folded question, hidden in a balloon fragment.

"What labor leader was sentenced to ten years in prison for speaking out against struggling American workers being forced to fight in World War I? Oh, I know this. Eugene! Eugene . . ." Heather faltered. "Um . . . Eugene McCarthy?"

"Oh, not quite!" Dr. Garva grinned. "Eugene Debs!"

"The Sedition Act!" somebody offered. "A new, progressive take on the definition of free speech!"

"Ha ha, that's right," Mallow laughed along as the bills were collected. "Pot's getting fat! Next batch!"

Kaffir Bottlebrush caught a gold balloon in a vice grip until it exploded, eliciting a cheep from Daphne Sweetspire. Kaffir read the question to himself before reciting it aloud.

"Ah. I think I know this one. What is the general historical term for the German atrocities against the Herero and Nama in South West Africa, the British against the Aboriginal Tasmanians in Australian, and the Americans against the Yuki in California? Frontier genocide."

Mallow Garva's confirmation of his correct answer burgeoned a spate of cheers. Daphne trotted over to Kaffir, offering congratulations with a peck on the lips. Heather Smilax, Sugi Blackthorn, and a Music Consultant named Kauri Rangiora followed suit. Others hugged, patted his shoulder.

"All right, that's enough love, enough love," Mallow chuckled. "Bag up the bills for Mr. Bottlebrush! And Kaffir, tell everybody your preferred charitable foundation."

Kaffir proudly faced his colleagues. "I chose the Foundation for Capital Funding and Marketing Initiatives for Struggling Small Businesses."

Everybody clapped, and the next round of balloons were set afloat. It turned out to be a joyfully beneficent occasion, as one would imagine, given the fulfillment of the evening's main event, the obligatory dispersal of the balloon funds to a diversified buffet of foundations, including The Foundation for the Beautification of Corporate Facilities, The Foundation for Wildflower and Vegetation Filtration of Waterways, and the Foundation for Disabled, Senior, and Incarceration Housing Developments. After the foundation allotment was completed, Kaffir was able to gift a hundred crassulas to every employee and keep fifty for himself. Dr. Garva decided to give Kaffir the honors of carting the foundation bags to his office.

"Feel free to take some biscotti while you're there," Mallow said, handing Kaffir his key card.

Kaffir felt a bit uncomfortable walking into Dr. Mallow Garva's office alone. This would be the first time Mallow ever gave Kaffir his key card. When he walked in, the platter of biscotti on Dr. Garva's desk caught his eye, an inviting consortium of vegan varieties: almond ginger, almond raisin, lemon pecan, hazelnut cinnamon, cashew orange, spiced cornmeal, walnut pepper, and who knows what was buried underneath. He rolled the cart into a free corner. Then, a few feet away, he noticed the shamrock screen of Mallow's computer.

But it wasn't just a desktop of blue folders. A window was opened, displaying a list of hyperlinked names. Knowing full well it was not his place to look, Kaffir stepped forward and looked anyway:

CE CENTURY 20–21
POLITICAL SOCIOLOGY – BANK 47G

Jeffrey C. Alexander
Robert Bernasconi
Luc Boltanski
Judith Butler
Noam Chomsky
Simon Critchley
Robert Alan Dahl
George William Domhoff
Warren Figgle
Sally Haslanger
Bob Jessop
Brian Leiter
Seymour Martin Lipset
Thomas Humphrey Marshall
Robert Michels
Charles Wright Mills
Ralph Miliband
Gaetano Mosca
Thomas Nagel
Martha Nussbaum
Vilfredo Pareto
Nicos Poulantzas
Joseph Raz
Ian Shapiro
Gu Su
Charles Taylor
Max Weber
Cornel West
Slavoj Žižek

Feeling a jolt of guilt, Kaffir scooped up three cookies, began to walk out . . . then stopped. He turned around, scanned the left column of names, stopping at the ninth.

Warren Figgle.

He blinked, unsure if he misread a vowel.

Well, a coincidence, obviously. Mr. Figgle's first name was Jonquil.

Kaffir turned again, then turned back. More spasms of guilt couldn't stay his finger from clicking on the name's hyperlink. A new page appeared listing at least thirty scholarly articles. The first one read "Balancing Popular Interests With Public Policy: A New Analytical Approach—2032/1/19." He clicked on it.

Balancing Popular Interests With Public Policy:
A New Analytical Approach
January 19, 2032
Warren Figgle

ABSTRACT:

Throughout the first half of the twenty-first century, liberal democracies have increasingly alienated themselves from popular interests due to a weakening of vital social and political institutions. This is due to a variety of developments over the last two decades, such as the gradual disintegration of party systems, the increasingly dominant role of money in politics, the disconnect between education and popular culture, and the incursion of autocratic political ideologies into basic democratic principles, including access to healthcare, and civil rights. Furthermore, the consistently low turnout in political primaries has enabled dangerous fringe radical groups to promote candidates holding

> extremist positions, damaging the capacity of free elections to represent the will of the electorate...

There was a chime from the elevator down the hall. Kaffir hurriedly clicked the window close and rushed out of the office. When the door shut behind him, he saw Mallow Garva emerging from the elevator.

"Oh, Kaffir, did you get in okay? I forgot to tell you, my key card has been a bit uncooperative."

"Yes! Yes, fine. I... I took some biscotti."

Kaffir displayed the cookies. He could not be sure if Mallow noticed his hand quivering.

"Wonderful. You only took three!"

"Oh, it's enough. I'm pretty full."

Mallow motioned to move, then peered at Kaffir.

"Are you content?" he asked.

"Yes, yes I am. And you?"

"Yes, thank you. I'm just getting the bonus checks. Can't forget those."

"Right, right. Thank you."

"Of course. I'll see you downstairs."

"Yes. See you there."

Kaffir walked on. Before reaching the elevator, he looked over his shoulder to see Mallow doing exactly the same thing—looking.

Twenty-One

Thymus Corkwood sat at his kitchen table with his wife Nolana holding two cerulean pills, each exactly three-quarters of an inch in length. Finally, it was the prototype of the very first modification of the Self Suppressor. With the generous funding provided by Thunbergia Therapy Thresholds, under the auspices of Dr. Lupin Hollyhock—a transaction performed in the strictest of confidence for the time being—Thymus was able to engineer a trial therapy a month sooner than he had anticipated. What he was holding in his hand right now may very well be the first step in abolishing the decidedly unappealing side effects of the original therapy, regardless of the degree to which these side effects had sublimated into unspoken acceptance within mainstream Opinion society. As with previous trials, Thymus was continuing the practice of validating his personal and professional confidence in the safety of a new therapy by voluntarily administering the first dose to himself, and, in this special case, to his wife as well. He was very confident it would work, though what remained in question was exactly to what extent.

"A pill?" Nolana said, her gaze fixed on the little capsules.

"Yes," Thymus smiled. "Swallow it like a vitamin."

"I wasn't aware a therapy like this could be in pill form."

"It's a prototype. The final therapy will most likely be an injected viral vector, like the original."

He placed one in Nolana's palm, aware she was not entirely convinced.

"What about the side effects?" she asked.

"This is supposed to cure the side effects," Thymus grinned.

"I know, but... will it make us behave... unnaturally?"

"Nolana, like I explained, the prime functionality of the Self Suppressor should remain intact. It won't make us behave unnaturally. In fact, I believe it will make us behave more *naturally.*"

"Yes?"

"Yes, it will enable us to strengthen an already strong emotional bond through the expression of our natural, biological reproductive instinct. An instinct imbedded in the genome since... well, since biology itself was originally conceived."

"What if... what if something goes wrong?"

"No, nothing will. The idea of a pill is to use chemistry like a viral vector. Essentially a lipid is engineered to get a DNA strand out of the cell endosome into the nucleus. Cells in the gastrointestinal tract turn over quickly so the effect will diminish over time. It's not a permanent fix, just a test."

Nolana smiled warmly. "I trust you, Thymus," she said, and swallowed the pill with a sip of water. Thymus did the same.

"You won't feel anything for a couple of hours," he said.

For a couple of minutes, they sat staring at each other, each seeing in the other the uneasiness they tried to hide.

The next day, Dianella called Aster asking if she could stop over.

She sounded perturbed. Ever since the breast incident, Dianella had avoided contact with Aster, greatly saddening him, as they had been close friends for almost nine years. Although at the time Aster had impulsively interpreted touching Dianella's breast as another stage in the natural progression of their relationship, upon reflection he judged the overture impetuous and decidedly regrettable. How the community reacted to his newfound biological aberration, or deviation, or whatever they wanted to call it, mattered less to him than losing the regard and admiration of his favorite person in all of Opine. Aster knew he was a good person, a smart person, a *selfless* person, an upstanding citizen. He didn't feel at all compelled to prove his worth to the community. But he did feel compelled to prove his worth to Dianella. He never imagined he would lose her good graces. Dianella had even intimated on more than one occasion that she shared his sense they would make a good match. Why on Opine he had to go and ruin their prospects for a lifelong, loving partnership by asking to touch her breast, he still had no idea, even as the psychological underpinnings driving that behavior remained intact. While he regretted the action itself, he only regretted its consequences, not the innocent motives impelling the action. If only Dianella could know what it was like to be him. If only Dianella could crawl into his mind and understand that he in no way shape or form ever considered for an infinitesimal instant that touching her in that way would *harm* her. If only she could understand that he wanted to touch her because he loved her.

But apparently, the Self Suppressor was incompatible with that type of mentality. It was the Self Suppressor's job to suppress that mentality, at least indirectly through its side effects. Dianella saw

Aster's action exactly the way some community members saw it. An aberration, a deviation, an oddity. There was some talk in op-eds that his very DNA could somehow pose a threat to the entire Opinion gene pool. As if his genome was a danger to the State of Contentment! How absurd. Aster had done nothing but support and adhere to the cultural norms and values maintaining that cherished social balance. And in any case he had certainly not *selected* himself to resist the therapy. How could he be held responsible for his own biochemistry? Nobody chooses his or her own biochemical nature. One may just as soon hold a person responsible for his shade of skin, or the texture of his hair, or his cognitive abilities, or his natural talents, or lack thereof. Nobody in their right mind could ever condemn Aster for the nature of his genetic makeup. One would expect such an unjust sentiment to emerge from the Fools, not the Opinions.

Every since the Board of Education meeting addressing Aster's "issue," he had been feeling increasingly exasperated. He was tired of his classmates treating him like a natural wonder, asking the same question, over and over again: "What does it feel like? What is it like having the libido?" After a while it was a lot easier for him to dismiss it as "no big deal," or to downplay the effect as "hardly noticing it." He hated feeling ashamed about speaking out freely about a part of who he was as a person, as a human being. He hated that he had to apologize to himself for a natural quality beyond his power to control. He hated that he couldn't feel comfortable telling people the truth of how he felt, and they would just accept it, and move on.

Maybe there was some better way he could articulate to Dianella exactly how he felt. It would not be easy. The libidinal instinct was foreign to Dianella. He would somehow have to convince her that his craving to touch her breast, from his perspective, was both natural and good, that the physical gesture was in no way intended to besmirch the trust, loyalty and respect on which their relationship was based, but on the contrary, was motivated by a sincere conviction it would actually enhance the validation of those values. In essence, Aster would be saying, "I touched your breast because I love and respect you." Stating it in those stark terms, though, would be as impulsive and ill-conceived as the original action, he quickly concluded.

"Dianella," he began, "I'm glad you're here, I need to tell you … why are you crying?"

"Aster," she sniffled, "I saw something *horrible,* and I think it has to do with you."

"Me?"

Dianella began to relate how the night before she had heard strange sounds coming from her parents' bedroom. Sounds she could only characterize as animalistic, though not normal vocalizations one might expect from a dog or a baboon or a cheetah, but rather grunts and screeches and inflections of tone one might associate with a creature in distress. She went on to describe how she slowly crept down the hallway, the bizarre atavistic sounds increasing in intensity as she approached the door. How she carefully pressed her ear to the door, listening more to the grunting and growling and thumping and creaking. How she silently turned the knob and pushed the door open an inch and peeked in. How she saw her naked stepfather on top of her naked mother, his hips bucking like an enraged bull, her raised legs shuddering and shaking like they had been stun-gunned, her talons clawing at his back and neck. How the mattress too gasped and quivered. How his violent pummeling resembled an assault. How Dianella quietly closed the door, rushed to her room and sobbed in her bed for hours. How the next morning her parents were oddly anxious, their sentences splintered, their tones withered, Thymus's neck marred with scratches, her mother's with peculiar blemishes and contusions. How their explanations for the injuries were thoroughly unconvincing, vague stories about Thymus gardening in thorn bushes and Nolana falling in the basement. How the mere thought of confronting her parents about what she had seen was as repellent as witnessing the episode itself. How painful it was to admit to herself the reality of what she had seen, the reality of her parents engaged in the *act,* the act that should have expired, should have been obsolete from the world, and here it was, right in front of her, barefaced and sniggering and leering in all its unashamed barbaric nakedness.

Aster was at a loss of how to process Dianella's account, caught off guard by her distressed state snuffing out his plans for reconciliation. Though grasping the general idea, more precise terminology would clear his fog.

"They were . . . they were doing the . . ."

"Having *sex*, Aster!" Dianella nearly hissed the word. "They were having sex! And I know it has to do with you!"

"Why me? Why would I have anything to do with it?"

"Because you have the libido! What did my stepfather do, Aster? I know he was talking to you about it."

"What? I . . . Dr. Buckthorn was asking questions about my resistance to the therapy, and he was there."

"And what did my stepfather say, Aster? You have to tell me everything." She grasped his hands in supplication, her touch sending a rush. He felt ashamed she was so upset, and yet he felt a rush.

"He didn't say anything, really. He took a blood sample."

"What?"

"From my finger."

"Why?"

"Because he wanted to study my DNA, understand why my system was rejecting the therapy. He just wanted to help, Dianella."

She stared, unblinking.

"I have no control over it," Aster said. "I can't control who I am. I wish I wasn't like this, but I am."

He waited for a word, a blink.

"It doesn't make me a horrible person, Dianella. I'm the same person you always knew. Just because I have this . . . this genetic *glitch,* or whatever you call it, doesn't make me any less of a person than I was before it was discovered."

No reaction.

"It's not right for people to judge me over something I can't control!"

His sudden elevated tone smoothed the tightness in her face.

"I'm not judging you, Aster," she said.

"I think maybe you are."

"No, I'm not. I just want to know the truth."

"I told you the truth. And it's also true that I was never trying to hurt you."

She lowered her eyes, released his hands. "I know, Aster."

"Do you? You haven't been talking to me at all. It's like I committed some kind of crime."

"I . . . I'm not used to . . ." she looked up at him. "I'm not used to that kind of behavior."

"Well, neither am I. Maybe I shouldn't have asked you to let me . . . but I . . . it's hard to explain, Dianella. I like you a lot, and I wanted to be . . . closer."

"But I don't have what you have, Aster. It's different. I didn't understand it. You made it seem like you were doing it for the truth in art."

"It *was* for truth. That's what I saw in you. Is that wrong?"

"But what *kind* of truth, Aster? Erotic truth."

"Okay. Is that wrong?"

"It's foreign to us."

"Us?"

"People."

"Do you think I was trying to hurt you?"

"No, but Aster . . . we abandoned that Ancient instinct for the benefit of society. We collectively made that sacrifice long ago."

"I know, but again, I have no control over how I turned out. Maybe your stepfather can fix it."

"Aster, it would have been fixed by now. Didn't he give you the booster therapy?"

"Yes. It didn't work."

"Exactly. He's not trying to fix it, Aster. There's a reason why I saw what I saw last night."

"Wha-what do you mean?"

She drifted for a few moments.

"I have to go."

"Wait, Dianella! Do you hate me?"

The gasp and tenderness in her eyes entranced him. "*Hate* you? Aster, don't say that. Who hates anymore? I'm just confused. This is very confusing to me."

"So will you talk to me from now on?"

A light smile softened her response. "We'll talk."

Then she left.

Twenty-Two

KAFFIR BOTTLEBRUSH WAS FAIRLY CONFIDENT that Thymus Corkwood had Mr. Figgle's contact information. But Thymus was strangely not answering his phone or texts. An impromptu visit was the only option left.

Normally Kaffir would not knock on somebody's door unannounced. Ever since the Self Suppressor had spread throughout the gene pool, Opinions often carelessly left their front doors unlocked, always thriving on social interaction, always happy to receive visitors. But they also respected each other's privacy. It appalled them how the right to privacy was so often violated, and disrespected, by the Ancients. In particular, the Ancient indiscretions of public display, and their oftentimes flagrant disregard of human dignity throughout the mass media, were testaments to how the rightful tenets of individualism and personal integrity within a culture could be abused to the point of losing their sanctity.

It took two rounds of knocks before Thymus opened the door. He was wearing a butterscotch turtleneck sweater, gazing at Kaffir with intense wonder, as if this had been the first time a human being had appeared on his doorstep. His eyeballs seemed to protrude unnaturally. There was a two-inch scratch on the left side of his face.

"Hi, Thymus! I'm very, very sorry to bother you. I tried calling and texting."

"Oh? You did? Oh. D-did you? I must have, m-m-m-must have missed it."

Kaffir looked at him. His speech, his blinking, and his flicking facial features had the jittery aspect of a spooked squirrel.

"That's... that's okay. I didn't mean to intrude. I—"

"N-n-no intrusion!" Thymus's voice squeaked.

"Okay. I was wondering if you have Mr. Figgle's contact information."

"Fuh... Fig... gle?"

"Yes. I just had a question. Would you be able to—"

"Oh I don't nuh-nuh-know if I can do that. He's a private man."

"I would never give his number out. It's kind of important."

"Oh, right. How-wah... important?"

"Um... it's nothing terrible. Just a quick question. Are you... are you content, Thymus?"

"Content? Yes, ha ha ha ha ha ha ha, yes, of course I am!" Thymus's laugh was delivered with the measured report of a semi-automatic military style weapon (which did not exist in Opine). "And you?"

"Yes, Thymus. Very content."

"Well, that's excellent, we're both content. You're content, and, and I'm content."

"Yes. Is there anything... um... I can..."

"I can *give it* to you!" Thymus declared, jutting an index finger.

"What?"

"Figgle's number! Wait, I'll—"

Thymus spun around and trotted away. Thirty seconds later he was holding half a piece of notepad paper, hastily ripped, bearing a scribbled phone number. Handing it to Kaffir, he stood there, eyelids quivering.

"Thank you, Thymus. I promise I won't give this out."

Thymus didn't respond, but stood there with a suspended, pained grin.

"Thank you," Kaffir repeated. "Thymus, did something happen to you?"

"Happen? No, no, I just didn't get much, uh, *sleep.* Ha! Well… I should get more sleep tonight."

"Yes. Yes, I hope you do."

"Thank you. Goodnight, Kaffir."

"Goodnight."

Kaffir walked to his car reflecting on how sleepless nights had affected him in the past. He certainly could not think straight on very little sleep. But Thymus appeared wired, like he had guzzled a pot of coffee. That must be it! Thymus was overtired from too much caffeine! That must be it.

A few minutes later, both Thymus and Kaffir made phone calls.

Thymus's call was to his friend and colleague, Lupin Hollyhock. Thymus needed to meet with Lupin, first thing in the morning.

Kaffir's call was to Mr. Figgle.

To Kaffir's relief, Mr. Figgle was cordial and receptive to his call after an introduction and greetings were dispensed. Kaffir reminded Mr. Figgle they had recently spoken in the Aviary Lounge of the Catchfly County Culture Coalition Center. Mr. Figgle remembered

Kaffir, and even if he hadn't, any acquaintance to a distinguished genetic engineer like Thymus Corkwood need not fear imposition. Softening the tone with a repeated underscoring of how awkward he felt blindly contacting a preeminent professor of sociology, Kaffir assured Mr. Figgle he would be very brief, that he simply had a question prompted by pure curiosity, that the circumstances inducing his inquiry were almost too embarrassing to recount, that while he was sure his question would be instantly resolved with the most trivial of explanations, he didn't feel it could be ignored, perhaps for no other valid reason except that the issue could not be properly laid to rest without Mr. Figgle's awareness of his connection to the matter, however coincidental the connection may be. Mr. Figgle was intrigued. What connection? Kaffir went on to describe how on Opinion Day, upon rolling in the cart of Balloon Endowment Fund bags to Dr. Mallow Garva's office, he noticed a window open on Dr. Garva's computer listing hyperlinks associated with Ancient political sociologists, one of the hyperlinks reading "Warren Figgle." Kaffir thought it quite interesting that this Ancient professor of sociology bore the same name as Mr. Figgle, who, by some strange stroke of providence, had recently retired from a very similar academic position, namely Professor Emeritus of Comparative Sapiens Social Anthropology. Mr. Figgle sounded even more intrigued, and even amused, immediately suggesting Kaffir and he meet in person, as the implications of this "presumed coincidence" could not be done proper justice over the phone. Kaffir, wondering over Mr. Figgle's use of the phrase "presumed coincidence," eagerly agreed, beaming with the prospect of a tête-à-tête with one of the most distinguished experts in the field of Comparative Sapiens Social Anthropology.

Mr. Figgle suggested they meet in ninety minutes at the Erigeron Eatery in Ox Eye County, a lush garden establishment noted for their exotic vegan cuisine, particularly Morrocan tagine, seitan negimaki, meatless suya, and their delicious carrot turmeric soup with roasted garbanzos. Kaffir was delighted Mr. Figgle was open to meeting him that very evening. He thought it prudent to withhold from his wife Gaura the real reason for their meeting, pending some unexpected development made it necessary. Mr. Figgle would be offering Kaffir some more consultative direction on the release of an Ancient literary work, Kaffir told her, silently mollifying his deception with the reasonable possibility that such a topic of conversation may in fact turn out to be the only substantive outcome.

Mr. Figgle greeted Kaffir with his signature broad, squinty-eyed, bright grin, complementing the lively palette of bougainvillea, willow, and wisteria vines bedecking the Eatery. After the waiter brought some baba ganoush roasted eggplant dip with flatbread, Kaffir began by thanking Mr. Figgle for offering his insightful views on Wagner's operas at their last meeting.

"And now," Mr. Figgle said, "you would like to hear my views on your discovery of a mysterious hyperlink on Dr. Mallow Garva's database bearing my name."

"Yes," Kaffir said, a bit uneasy with Mr. Figgle's continual grin, "yes, that's right. I... I didn't purposely go in there to look. I just happened to see it."

Mr. Figgle waited.

"I thought the best course of action would be to immediately contact you, as I'm sure you'd be interested to know an Ancient scholar's name matches your own."

"Interesting, indeed!" Mr. Figgle's lifted eyebrows bloomed a battalion of creases above.

"And I was also wondering if you thought there was any basis for speculating whether there might be some kind of . . . some kind of connection."

"Connection? When you say 'connection,' do you mean a biological connection?"

"Well, I mean, is it possible that . . ." Kaffir faltered.

"Are you asking if there can possibly be a biological connection between that Ancient Warren Figgle you saw on The Find's database and the living, breathing Opinion you see before you, Jonquil Figgle?"

"It's a wild idea, I know," Kaffir admitted. "You're obviously two different people. But 'Figgle' is not a very common name. I thought perhaps your ancestral relatives may have somehow known about this—"

He paused when the waiter arrived to take their orders.

"I was saying before," Kaffir continued, "I thought maybe your past relations may have known about Warren Figgle, and adopted the same surname."

Mr. Figgle nodded. "A plausible scenario, and you're not far off the mark. The question is, am I *the* Figgle or *a* Figgle? That's the question, isn't it? Ha ha ha!"

Kaffir stared, the belly laugh making him feel more uneasy.

"Uh . . . *the* Figgle? I'm not sure I . . ."

"I'm sorry, Kaffir. It's indecent of me to play mind games like that. You're a good man with a good, valid question. Permit me to clarify. What if I were to tell you that I am not *the* Warren Figgle, but *another* Warren Figgle?"

It still wasn't processing.

"Another . . . Warren Figgle? But you are Jonquil Figgle."

"Yes, that is my Opinion name, not my genealogy."

"Genealogy?"

Mr. Figgle leaned forward, and his grin receded.

"Kaffir, the grand Opinion experiment known as the Self Suppressor has other sides, other facets, the most profound of which are not known to the general public. You, my friend, were inadvertently exposed to one of those hidden faces."

"I was?"

"You were indeed."

"How . . . how exactly?"

"You saw evidence of the Ur-Figgle."

"The who?"

"The Ur-Figgle. The original Figgle. I am simply a copy of the original."

"A *copy?* I don't understand."

"Kaffir," Mr. Figgle chuckled, "I'm sure you're familiar with the technology of DNA data storage?"

"Yes. Yes, that's a form of computer storage developed in the Ancient twenty-first century. Strands of the four nucleobases that make up DNA are grown on microchips in the lab."

"Microwells, they're called," Mr. Figgle said.

"Yes, on microwells, and these are used to encode data, much like a conventional hard drive."

"Ah, yes, and imagine if a converse technology could be developed, where a person's DNA can be encoded onto, say, a quantum computer drive."

Kaffir was stupefied. "You . . . you mean . . ."

Mr. Figgle's squinty broad smile returned.

"I am a copy of the original Warren Figgle, Kaffir."

"A copy?"

"Yes. A clone. It turns out that my genetic parent, the original Warren Figgle, member of the original Homo Sapiens 1.0, encoded his own DNA onto The Find's quantum drive. Thus I am *another* Warren Figgle, an approximate replica of the original Ancient Warren Figgle, biochemically speaking. Amazing, isn't it?"

Kaffir, dumbfounded, watched him laugh again.

"You . . . you're a genetic clone?"

Mr. Figgle nodded. "Not a *perfect* copy, of course. Epigenetic factors always come into play. Environment, the mother's biochemistry, so forth."

"So your DNA . . . I, I mean the . . . the DNA of the original Figgle . . ."

"Somatic cell nuclear transfer," the professor nodded. "It has to be done with somatic cells, not reproductive cells, because somatic cells contain two full sets of chromosomes. So you take the DNA from the original Warren Figgle's somatic cell, upload a digital copy of it onto a quantum computer drive, then transfer the data into DNA grown in the lab, and then finally transfer that DNA into an egg cell that has had its original DNA and nucleus removed. A technological advance, I might add, perfected not too long ago—seventy-two years, to be exact."

"And . . . your mother . . ."

"Yes, my dearly departed mother, Leilani Soapberry, graciously volunteered to carry and bear the digitally fertilized denucleated egg. The first and *only* successful genetic clone of a human being from the Ancient Earth! Marvelous, isn't it? I sit here before you, Kaffir, the only surviving Ancient living relic of that forlorn, ill-begotten civilization, a civilization that for all its tragic turns and vicissitudes has allowed us to thrive on their greatest achievements, and lambast their greatest fooleries!"

"But . . . but do we know *who* uploaded Warren Figgle's DNA to The Find?"

"Yes, of course! It was Warren Figgle himself who uploaded his DNA to The Find!"

"He . . ." Kaffir's mouth hung open. "He did? But how? How did he get access?"

"Kaffir," Mr. Figgle leaned forward again, lowering his voice for the first time, "it was *Warren Figgle* who originally processed, and buried, The Find."

Kaffir felt himself turning white.

"Buried . . ."

Mr. Figgle closed his eyes briefly, as if in reverence. "Millions upon millions of petabytes of human civilization's greatest accomplishments, their histories, their triumphs, their pitfalls, their centuries of science and culture, chronicles of their most brilliant minds, their most deranged minds, miraculous deeds, horrendous deeds, all organized and compiled and digitally recorded by Professor Warren Figgle over the better part of three decades. When he saw the writing on the wall, and the threads of society began to unwind, he encased the computer in the strongest material known at that time, AM-III carbon glass, and had it buried deep in the earth, where it would remain for eons, billions upon billions of years, until..."

He raised his arms, palms up, to indicate the entire world, Opine.

Kaffir sat back, his heart racing from both Mr. Figgle's revelations and a brewing paranoia that police would come marching in and arrest him. It took him several moments to take it all in.

"I must say," the professor continued, "I felt honored that my unique standing in the gene pool granted me certain privileged access to The Find, access enjoyed only by a very select few. I was privy to many controversial Ancient works and documents never released to the general population."

"Like Hitler's paintings?"

Mr. Figgle chuckled. "Oooh, yes, but that just scratches the surface. I even got to see the proclamation issued by Warren Figgle alongside his own DNA."

"Proclamation?"

"Yes, I'll never forget it. He wrote:

'Herein lies the legacy of I, Dr. Warren Figgle, who, on this twenty-fifth day of February, 2046 CE, having expended inordinate amounts of time, labor and money recording centuries of human history onto digital quantum media, and having expended inordinate amounts of money recording my personal genome onto the same, hereby bestow upon Eternity these gifts, offered to whomever shall deign to receive them. If the first time was tragedy, may the second be farce.'"

Kaffir waited for an elucidation, then asked: "Tragedy and farce? Why would he say that?"

Mr. Figgle responded first with an odd, ironic smile. "A reference to a quote by Karl Marx," he said, "but the reasoning behind this allusion is admittedly subject to pure conjecture."

Kaffir was numb, lost in a fog of answers multiplying into more questions.

"Why was this . . . why does nobody know about this? I'm assuming this is not common knowledge."

"It is not common knowledge," Mr. Figgle confirmed. "I referred to the grand Opinion experiment before. The Self Suppressor is only one half of that experiment—a crucial half, the public half, but only half. The other half is . . . well, me! Hee hee! You see, the creators of the revolutionary therapy, like Nalca Hollyhock, were not just interested in manipulating what ethologists like Richard Dawkins would call the 'selfish gene.' They were also interested to know whether a refined, gentrified version of the human genome could live side by side with the primitive, ungentrified version; whether the pure and impure could coexist without disrupting the finely attuned State of Contentment; whether indeed anybody would even *notice* the presence of the impure breed!"

Mr. Figgle took a certain dramatic glee in expounding the story, like he was sitting around a campfire with children.

"Are you saying you are some kind of test subject? A test subject for society?"

"Yes, essentially, a select group of scientists have formed a hypothesis and are testing that hypothesis, that hypothesis being a Homo Sapiens 1.0 specimen can successfully be assimilated into mainstream Opinion society without any adverse effects to the status quo."

"And to what ends?" Kaffir asked. "Why is it important to test that hypothesis?"

"Well, in the same way that the Self Suppressor strives for a more refined version of the Homo Sapiens species, the hypothesis strives to attain a refined version of the truth on which the Self Suppressor is predicated. Namely, whether the Self Suppressor is a categorical imperative, or an obligatory deterrent."

"A categorical imperative?"

"You've read Kant, I assume? Whether the Self Suppressor is a moral obligation all must follow regardless of personal interest or desire, or whether it is simply a cautionary measure imposed by our society."

"But we know the Self Suppressor works! Why question its efficacy?"

"It's not a question of questioning its efficacy. It's a question of whether it can properly be phased out in the future."

"Phased out? Completely?"

Mr. Figgle shrugged. "Too early to tell. That's why I am the test subject. Maybe there can be a screening process, a selection process. For example, Kaffir, from what you know about me, do you think

I *need* the Self Suppressor to function in Opinion society? Would you say I have successfully blended in with Opinion moral codes and norms, or do you consider me a contaminant?"

"You're not a contaminant, Mr. Figgle. But there are many people who *do* need the Self Suppressor."

"And I agree with that assessment. But does absolutely everybody need it? That question approaches the issue from an entirely new perspective."

This was too much to consider at once. Kaffir's head was swimming. "Mr. Figgle," he nearly whispered, "am I . . . am I supposed to *know* this?"

"Ha, well, Kaffir, were you *supposed* to read a senior data administrator's computer screen?"

"I probably . . . no, I probably should not have looked at Dr. Garva's computer."

No reaction from Mr. Figgle, save the grin.

"But Mr. Figgle . . . still, I don't think I'm supposed to know about this. My knowledge about this . . . might somehow cause problems."

Mr. Figgle's eyes narrowed. "Why? Can it be a sin to know?"

"Well, in this case . . . maybe it could be."

"Upon what basis makes you suppose so? Upon a truth? Or is it your . . . o-*pin*-ion?"

Mr. Figgle's spacing of the syllables was strangely sardonic.

"I'm not sure how to answer that," Kaffir said.

"Kaffir, you're a smart man. Let me ask you something. If you had to choose one word that encapsulates what precipitated the demise of Homo Sapiens 1.0, what would you say?"

"I . . . would say 'selfishness' is the word."

"Okay, yes, that's true, but let's go a little deeper. What would you say is the main regulatory impetus behind the standard selfish act? What exactly is the primordial human spark of self-interest?"

Kaffir was unable to think creatively.

"Kaffir," Mr. Figgle pressed, "think of the ironic name of our people."

"The opinion?" Kaffir said.

"Yes, Kaffir, the all-knowing, all-encompassing, almighty opinion. Ha ha! I jest of course. Kaffir, have you ever read the works of T.H. White?"

"I have. *The Once and Future King*."

"That's right, and also one of my favorites, *The Book of Merlyn*. It contains some of the most perceptive views about human behavior in all Ancient twentieth-century literature. Kaffir, it is not personal preference that plagues the opinion. You like this ice cream flavor, I like this one, you like this book, I didn't care for it, et cetera. Personal preference is personal taste. It is *obfuscation of the truth* that plagues the opinion. It is when a person has every opportunity to know the truth, but resorts to convenient prejudice. That, Kaffir, is when self-interest gnaws away at collective benefit. I memorized one of my favorite passages by Mr. White:

> 'Neither force, nor argument, nor opinion are *thinking*. Argument is only a display of mental force, a sort of fencing with points in order to gain a victory, not for truth. Opinions are the blind alleys of lazy or stupid men, who are unable to think. Opinion can never

stand beside truth. At present, however, *Homo impoliticus* is content to either argue with opinions or fight with his fists, instead of waiting for the truth in his head. It will take a million years, before the mass of men can be called political animals.'"

"*Homo impoliticus?*" Kaffir asked.

"He is referring there to Aristotle, who wrote that man is by nature a political animal, meaning that humans naturally bond together, form associations. Which is true—the survival of human civilization has depended on cooperative social structures. But Mr. White has issue with Aristotle's thesis, calling the human species impolitic—unwise, lacking the wisdom to maintain these associations. It is the uninformed opinion, he maintains, that renders those associations dysfunctional. A prescient critique. Of course, other great Ancient authors have addressed the corrupting influences of the opinion, like Swift in *Gulliver's Travels.* For a philosopher like Hobbes, the opinion had to be regulated by the sovereign to govern a society. We, of course, have discarded the opinion, and thus the sovereign with it. And you know, Kaffir, what is most amazing, is that while these great thinkers may not have fully appreciated the implications of their own ideas at the time, their insights were telling no less than the story of the human condition. The story of how the truth breeds community and peace, and how the opinion breeds divisiveness and destruction."

"Mr. Figgle, you are definitely... among the wise. But in this case, my own wisdom is failing. I still don't see the truth of the matter."

Mr. Figgle smiled warmly at Kaffir's candor.

"The truth is, Kaffir, you chose to look at Dr. Garva's computer screen. The truth is, you chose to ask me about it. The truth is, I chose to tell you the truth. Did either of us do wrong? Did either of us break a law? A moral code? Can either of us form any reasonable basis to conclude, without question, that what we did was absolutely right, or absolutely wrong? No, we cannot, for making such judgment calls, in the face of the truth, amounts to little more than foundering in the amorphous morass of self-righteousness. And now, Kaffir, what do you we do with these truths? What do we do with *all* truths? We live with them."

Kaffir hadn't noticed, but thirty seconds before, the waiter had delivered their meals. He was no longer hungry.

Twenty-Three

Lupin Hollyhock stared at a jittery, distracted Thymus Corkwood sitting on the other side of his office desk and could not believe what he was hearing. Four million crasullas from Thunbergia Therapy Thresholds generously donated to fund a launch of Thymus's exciting new genetic therapy at Geranium Genome Gentrification. And Thymus simply wanted to terminate the entire venture? And destroy all traces of months and months of research and development? Even if he evaluated the preliminary results of the first trial dosage as "inconclusive?" Since when was an entire scientific breakthrough, especially one of this scope and importance, completely abandoned, with all records of the developmental phases unceremoniously obliterated, simply because the project manager felt a bit unsettled over "inconclusive" preliminary results? There must be something more to this. Thymus didn't look well. He looked as if he hadn't slept in days. And how did he get that scratch on his face? Working in a thornbush? No matter, Lupin suggested he take a couple of days to rest, clear his head, and reconsider his decision.

His hands shaking, Thymus insisted that destroying all evidence of the venture was not only the best course of action, it was the *only* course of action. The pill form of the therapy may have worked, but it may have worked way too well. It brought out latent emotions and passions that had lain dormant for generations through the therapeutic inhibitors of the Self Suppressor. Once these latent passions were suddenly released, the biochemical rebound was very much akin to a sleeping magma chamber awakened into a volcano. While the effects of the pill wore off after around ten hours, the aggressive, primal yearnings and unrestrained libidinal acts it instigated would only amplify, Thymus feared, in its more developed, viral vector incarnation. Enabling previously checked sexual passions to run freely could plausibly escalate into intemperate, or even potentially hostile behaviors. Although he and his wife Nolana had, Thymus finally admitted sheepishly, engaged in the sex act, and it was indeed pleasurable on a purely physical level, there was a disturbing compulsion through it all to *derive personal satisfaction without discretion.* In other words, there was an undeniably violent selfish component behind the biochemical trigger activated by the therapy. This was what worried Thymus the most. He could not be certain that the prime functionality of the Self Suppressor would remain intact, as he had previously assured his wife.

Lupin was trying very hard to be convinced. Alternate interpretations, however, were impossible to ignore. Thymus was drawing conclusions on intuition, not on empirical facts. There was no way to know for certain if the therapy would have any undesirable side effects without further testing. What kind of scientific method discards a hypothesis without refining it? Does a negative result or error preclude further trial? Thymus could very well be on his way to fine-tuning one of the greatest achievements in the history of Opinion science, and he was willing to throw it all away after one measly pre-clinical test, the results of which were inconclusive, at best. The therapy obviously succeeded in expressing the libido instinct. All that really needed to be done was to regulate its potency, perhaps. Lupin didn't see see why Thymus was reacting so dramatically, so emotionally. That was not like him, and quite frankly, contrary to standard scientific procedure. The experience was most likely so unique, so uncommonly astounding, so foreign to his natural temperament, that his mental faculties were swayed more towards the visceral than the intellectual. He took the pill completely unprepared for the effects, was caught off guard, and made a snap judgment. Understandable, but he should take some time to regroup and reconsider.

Thymus countered that he was relying on intuition rather than firsthand experience. The therapy was potentially dangerous, and a potential compromise to the invaluable efficacy of the Self Suppressor does not hold up against an argument for pursuing further clinical trials. A vigorous genetic expression of the libido could act as a counterbalance against the original therapy's prime functionality. It was not worth the risk.

Lupin acknowledged his colleague's concerns and risk assessment as valid, though reminded him of the generous financial donation provided by Thunbergia Therapy Thresholds. Perhaps Thymus could share his research notes with Lupin, so that Thunbergia could explore its own independent development of a safer, less volatile therapy.

Thymus assured Lupin that it would not be long before Geranium Genome Gentrification would compensate him for the squandered funds. He reminded Lupin that his data, regrettably, had already been permanently deleted from the lab's database. Thymus neglected to tell Lupin that he still had copies on his home computer, though in any case, these would also be deleted in short order.

What Thymus didn't know is that his stepdaughter, Dianella, would be secretly calling Lupin that evening from the downstairs bathroom:

"Dr. Hollyhock?"

"Yes? Hello?"

"I'm sorry, it's Dianella, Thymus Corkwood's stepdaughter. I'm sorry to call you like this."

"Dianella? Oh, yes, yes! I remember you! How is everything?"

"Not great. I'm sorry, I had to look up your number."

"Dianella, I can't hear you very well."

"I can't talk loud. I need to ask you something very important."

"All right."

"I found out my stepdad tested Aster Bottlebrush's blood for something, and I think... I think he's trying to develop something out of... whatever he analyzed."

"Oh? What makes you say that?"

"Dr. Hollyhock... I saw something the other night that gives me good reason to think so. I... I feel uncomfortable talking about it. I think it has to do with Aster's resistance to the Self Suppressor."

"Uh-huh."

"I think it has to do with Aster... resisting the side effects."

"Uh-huh."

"I think it has to do with the libido."

"The libido?"

"Aster's libido."

"You . . . think your stepfather is working on something . . . based on Aster's genetic resistance to the therapy."

"I think he *already* developed something."

"Oh?"

"But he won't tell me. He's hiding it."

"You asked him?"

"I . . . I asked him about what I saw the other night, without telling him what I saw, but he and my mother lied."

"Oh, did they?"

"Dr. Hollyhock, if my stepfather is using Aster's DNA to turn on something that shouldn't be turned on . . . if he's trying to reverse the Self Suppressor in some way . . . it's wrong. Scientists like you and he gave us all a genetic therapy that *saves* us, makes us all better people. He can't be doing anything to reverse that."

"Oh, Dianella, I don't think he's trying to reverse it."

"Do you know what he's been doing?"

"Well, now, Dianella, it wouldn't be right for me to speak about your stepfather's business—"

"Dr. Hollyhock, I need to know. What is he doing?"

"I . . . I can't really say."

"But I *know* he made something from Aster's genes. I *know* he did. I *know* it has to do with libido. The Self Suppressor is supposed to suppress the libido."

"Well, that's a side effect, you understand."

"Yes, but why wouldn't they tell me the truth? I *know* how he got those scratches on his neck and face."

"Scratches?"

Dianella said nothing.

"Hello? Dianella?"

"Dr. Hollyhock, what did my stepfather do?"

"Oh, now, Dianella, I'm in no position to speak about your stepfather's business."

"What if I sent you something?"

"Pardon?"

"If I sent you a copy of his work."

"A copy... of his work?"

"Listen... I know I shouldn't have done this, but I'm worried. I'm very worried. If you had seen what I had seen... what they were doing..."

"Okay, okay, Dianella, what do you mean, a copy?"

"I have software that creates a disk image of his home computer."

"Oh?"

"He keeps a copy of his work files in his home office. I... don't know how to read them. It's all science language."

"Uh-huh."

"If I sent you a copy of the disk image..."

"Well, Dianella, does your stepfather know that... um..."

"I don't see how he could have done anything to *spread* Aster's condition! He was supposed to cure his condition, not spread it!"

"I don't think Thymus would do anything that would be harmful to the general public, nor jeopardize the work that much of his livelihood is based upon."

"Then will you review his notes? Please? And then you can erase everything."

"Well . . . I can certainly take a look, but I don't think Thymus would be very appreciative if he—"

"I wouldn't want you to get into trouble for something *I* did, Dr. Hollyhock. You don't have to worry."

"I understand. Of course I can take a look. Can you compress the file and send it through Dropseed? Do you own that application?"

"Yes, I do."

"Okay. Give me your number and I'll text you the address."

"All right. Thank you so much, Dr. Hollyhock! I can't tell you how thankful I am!"

"Anything I can do to help, Dianella, you're most welcome. You're most welcome."

Twenty-Four

Nolana Corkwood stared at her jittery, distracted husband sitting up on the other side of their bed and could not believe what she was hearing. Four million crasullas from his good friend and colleague, Lupin Hollyhock, generously donated to fund a launch of Thymus's exciting new genetic therapy at Geranium Genome Gentrification. And Thymus simply wanted to terminate the entire venture? And destroy all traces of months and months of research and development? And was he *really* describing the preliminary results of the first trial dosage as "inconclusive?" Was he *really* characterizing the mind-bending, transfiguring, intellectually and emotionally and physically exhilarating experience of two nights ago "inconclusive?" Since when was an entire scientific breakthrough, especially one of this scope and importance . . . especially one of such incontrovertibly unmitigated spiritual and psychological import . . . especially one that could potentially elevate the current State of Contentment to a level of sublime perfection hitherto never conceived by any other Opinion scientist, including the father of the Self Suppressor himself, Nalca Hollyhock . . . since when should the embryonic sparks of so remarkable and transformative an achievement be completely snuffed out, with all records of the developmental phases unceremoniously obliterated, simply because Thymus felt a bit unsettled over "inconclusive" preliminary results? There must be something more to this. Thymus didn't look well. He looked as if he hadn't slept in days. Nolana suggested he take a couple of days to rest, clear his head, and reconsider his decision.

Thymus tried to explain to his wife, in more layman's terms, exactly what he told Lupin Hollyhock. Despite the allure of short-term gratification, and the appeal of releasing a suppressed natural instinct, the long-term repercussions across Opinion society could be disastrous. Nolana had spoken of potentially elevating the current State of Contentment. Preserving the integrity of the State of Contentment was, for Thymus, the first and foremost concern. Circulating an unstable therapy could jeopardize that crucially dependable stability.

"But it doesn't have to be unstable if you refine it," Nolana said. "Wasn't that Lupin's main point?"

"Yes, it was one of his points, but I sincerely don't believe it could be refined to any viable, practical standard, and I also don't believe it could be done without compromising the effectiveness of the primary therapy."

"But you don't know for sure, without more testing. Right?"

"Nolana, it's opening up a can of worms, believe me. I thought there was a possibility, but after... I just think the risks are too great. If this get's out—"

"Thymus, listen," Nolana supplicated her husband with a throbbing gaze, fingers clutching his forearm. "You can't tell me you didn't enjoy it. You *did* enjoy it. You *did*."

He recoiled a bit. She hadn't looked at him *that* way since . . . that night.

"Nolana . . . I'm not denying that it was pleasurable. Yes, it was. But you understand, it was a drug, Nolana. It was a drug."

"It was a therapy *you* synthesized in your lab, just like you synthesize the Self Suppressor."

"I thought it could work. It's impossible to anticipate the results without testing."

"And what went wrong, Thymus? What went wrong?"

"It's . . . it's not an accurate biochemical representation of Aster's system. It was too powerful."

"It can be fixed! You can fix it!"

"It can't be done. Nolana, it's too dangerous!"

"You don't know that!"

"I *do* know that."

"No, you *think* you know that. You're just afraid of what you felt."

"I'm not afraid of *what* I felt. I'm afraid of how *much* I felt it!"

"Then fix it!"

"I can't."

"Why not?"

"I just know. If you were a genetic scientist, you would understand."

"I understand that I'm your wife!"

"Nolana . . . your hand . . ."

Her grip on his forearm had grown tighter and tighter with her rising vexation. When she let go, she rolled away from him, sobbing and shivering.

"Nolana? Nolana?" He placed a hand on her arm, noticing the blotchy red marks on his own. "Listen to me. It's for the best. I . . . I made a mistake even trying it."

"You're not even thinking about how *I* feel," she whimpered through hiccupping breaths. "You're not thinking about how it affects *me.*"

"I . . . I am thinking about you, Nolana. I'm thinking about everybody. Isn't that what we're supposed to do? Think about everybody?"

She kept sniffling and huffing.

"Nolana?"

"You said . . ." she began quietly. ". . . You said this will enable us to strengthen an already strong emotional bond . . . through the expression of our natural, biological reproductive instinct. That's what you said, Thymus."

Thymus reflected on this, sighing.

"That was my theory," he said faintly. "With human nature . . . it is practice that reigns."

Twenty-Five

A LITTLE OVER EIGHT MONTHS LATER, in mid-March, the Tecoma Tennis Tournament in Tecoma County was set to begin, prelude to the even more prestigious Whortleberry Open and host to one hundred twenty-eight of the finest players in Opine. Opinions loved attending spectator sports as the Ancients did, but truth be told, the ability of typical Opinion athletes was never quite up to par with their ancestral cousins. In particular, the frequency of blunders was dramatically higher compared to Ancient athletes. Baseball and football players dropped balls and missed catches. Hockey sticks missed pucks and sometimes whacked players (though the customary fist fights were nonexistent). Basketball shots were not as accurate and the players often fumbled passes and dribbling. Tennis players were more prone to faults and net balls. Somehow the expected professional prowess was just not there. Summer and winter Olympic games were held every four years, and these athletes, though relatively proficient in their craft, did not fare much better.

This phenomenon was not observed in the realm of intellectual and cognitive abilities. Scientists were unable to confirm whether the phenomenon was due to effects stemming from the Self Suppressor, though there did seem to be some coincidental correlation between diminished performance and the therapy's unveiling. Still, despite the diluted competitive edge, players and spectators alike enjoyed themselves, and Opine had their share of athletic celebrities.

The two participants for this particular afternoon's qualifying singles match in mid-March were the very popular Ms. Jade Oxalis and Ms. Narra Staghorn, as near to an equitable match as Opinion fans could expect. Ms. Oxalis was an all-court player, strong on both offense and defense, and quick on her feet. Ms. Staghorn was more of a "counter puncher," boasting vigorous endurance, especially at the baseline with high balls, and just as swift as her opponent. The outdoor bleachers were packed, spectators ready with some of their favorite snacks, including rice cakes, beetroot nori rolls, and almond and date balls.

It was an exciting match from the start, each player winning five games in the first set. Ms. Oxalis and Ms. Staghorn were performing nearly up to the Ancient standard, almost never missing the routine shots. Everything proceeded in typical fashion, until in the middle of the final game when an orange and green hummingbird with crimson throat swooped down over the court as if to declare its virile iridescence preeminent over the event at hand. This avian wonder, having inflicted no harm diverting the attention of the spectators, had also unwittingly succeeded in capturing the awe of not one but both players, Ms. Staghorn unfortunately being the one most directly affected, as her distracted focus resulted in the tennis ball lobbing off her racket, the wild trajectory sending it on a sailing arc completely out of play and well into the bleachers.

"The resplendence," several people marveled, their adulation escaping the auditory sensors of the hummingbird, who was already outside the perimeter of the tennis complex when the stray tennis ball found the termination of its capricious flight right smack on top of a preoccupied lady's cup of matcha and coconut shake, the impact sending the beverage's innards splashing all over the owner's periwinkle floral print bell-sleeved dress.

The lady at first gazed blankly at her decimated refreshment, and then screamed. She screamed once, twice, taking labored breaths between, and kept screaming. The volume and intensity of her anguish drew the eye of nearly everyone, including the two players, so distracted that the connection between the lady's outburst and the fate of the rogue tennis ball eluded their comprehension. Several neighbors rushed to her aid, offering their napkins and sympathies, some of them stuffing enough bills in her hand to finance the replacement of her bespattered dress on top of multitudinous matcha and coconut shakes. "It's okay, you're content," they said, a reassurance sure to successfully calm the rate of an Opinion's heightened respiration.

During this drama, nobody had noticed a young man and woman trotting down an aisle and disappearing under the bleachers, and nobody noticed a man wearing a light blue chambray button-down shirt and khaki pants using the diversion to solicit another spectator, one of several spectators he had approached during the course of the entire match as he unobtrusively slinked his way up and down aisles into various bleacher sections. This particular man was offering the newest pathway to attaining the cherished Opinion Contentment, a pathway in the shape of a little emerald pill, the generic form of a pill only recently in circulation, a pill that had adopted the designation "libill," a portmanteau of the truncated "lib pill," where "lib" could mean either "liberty," or "libido," or both. A lucrative enterprise this was, as the little pill had begun to arouse both keen curiosity and keen skepticism, the skepticism feeding the curiosity, while the declined offers in no way diminishing a most agreeable rate of return amounting to one hundred fifty crassulas for a single twenty-dose bottle. The man could easily have financed enough vegan snacks for half the crowd with the proceeds he had already gathered by the sixth game. There were those who immediately said, "No, thank you." Those who said "yes" were operating under the very reasonable presumption that a pill designed to foster more Contentment could not possibly pose any imminent threat to their physical or mental well-being.

Once the unfortunate lady's calamity had been sufficiently rectified, play resumed, nobody expecting an interruption of a similar profile, at least not until the ending of the first set. This expectation proved to be premature. Ms. Staghorn was leading the final game 40-30 when another woman's scream pierced the applause. It was coming from somewhere at the back. People craned their necks to see a young lady staggering out from behind the bleachers, hooked fingers yanking up a lilac ruffled wrap skirt caught just above her knees. Her hair was straggled and one end of her off-white off-the-shoulder blouse was pulled even more off the shoulder. An older woman emerged from under the bleachers pointing a black stun gun at her.

"He wasn't doing anything to me!" the disheveled young lady cried, still hiking up her skirt. "Why did you stun him?"

"He was attacking you," the woman said, then to the bystanders closing in: "He was attacking her!"

"No he wasn't!" came the retort. The young lady appeared very upset, her body language belligerent. "Stop pointing that at me!" She attempted a swipe at the stun gun, missed by several inches. The other woman backed away, stun gun still raised.

Several tournament officials approached, each holding a stun gun.

"Now, miss, hold on . . ."

"I saw that man on top of her," the older woman said to the security personnel. "He was attacking her."

"He was not! He was not! Leave me alone!"

"Miss, please, you need to calm down . . ."

"Stop pointing that thing at me! You stupid shit!"

Another swipe attempted, this one dangerously close. There was a crackling buzz from an official's stun gun. The young lady shrieked, juddered like a failing engine, and collapsed, her splayed limbs fluttering.

The older woman raised a sympathetic palm to her mouth, then knelt by the incapacitated victim. "Poor, compassionate girl," she muttered, "defending that deranged man. Officer, will you please give this to her later? For her therapy?"

She handed a few bills to one of the men.

"Of course, ma'am, thank you."

"Me too, sir, here," another spectator offered, and another, Opinion generosity again shining through, courtesy of the Self Suppressor.

And two spectators remained on the ground, immobile, as a result of a little indulgence, a little indulgence in the form of a little emerald pill.

Twenty-Six

Nolana Corkwood, formerly Nolana Whitebeam, working as a Screener for the Cockspur Coral County Congressional Committee, was tasked with interviewing a select group of county residents for service as a legislator in the Central Opinion Congress, the five hundred members of which rotated every month on paid leave, as previously described. The selection criteria were fairly straightforward. Any candidate must not have served in the Congress during the five years prior to the date set for the new monthly session. This was to ensure that every eligible citizen in a county was guaranteed an equal opportunity to serve on the Congress. In most cases, an eligible citizen will serve on some congressional committee at least once in his or her lifetime—if not the Central Congress itself, then a local congress. Although there was no law stating a citizen *must* serve, participation was always encouraged, and Opinion citizens were generally eager to contribute their time and energy fostering a healthy State of Contentment. As long as a citizen was in good standing, with no record of physical or mental infirmities to indicate a potential incapacitation, or dereliction of duty, he or she was automatically eligible. Once the candidate successfully completed a short interview by a Screener like Nolana Corkwood, the required fifty

Congress members from each county were selected, the preference given first to those who have never served, and then to those who have not served for at least five years.

In any given month, the congressional agenda items may change, necessitating an adjustment to the screening topics. One month the issue might be wildlife preservation; the next, occupational safety and health (the Opinions retained many Ancient health agencies, such as OSHA); the next, review of taxation and finance algorithms; the next, public infrastructure and aesthetics; and so on. On this particular afternoon in late March of the year 160, Nolana Corkwood had the pleasure of screening a very familiar friend and neighbor, none other than Mrs. Hebe Hornbeam, one of the main interlocutors helping to cement the bond between Nolana and Thymus following their most fortuitous, consequential car accident over a decade ago. One of the several currently pending congressional issues on the table was "Preservation and Relocation of Endangered Frog Habitats from Hydroelectric Power Facilities."

Nolana would also be raising quite another issue to her interviewees, an issue that was not, in fact, one of the most pressing, time-sensitive congressional issues on the table.

"Hebe, thank you for being so cooperative," a cheery Nolana was saying. "Just a couple more questions. I'm sure you've heard about that dam issue with respect to frog habitats."

"Nolana! I've never known you to use Ancient slang like that!"

"Oh . . . no, no, I mean 'dam' as in the barrier used for hydroelectric power."

"Ooooh, I'm sorry, Nolana, yes, yes. I'm such a wack-a-noodle.

Yes, some frog habitats have been suffering from the dams, yes. I do love frogs, you know. One of my favorites is the four-eyed one."

"Four eyes?"

"Well, the two fake ones on its rear end to scare off predators! Heh-heh!"

"Oh, the four-eyed one, yes, I see. So I imagine you are in support of facilitating the preservation or relocation of these endangered habitats?"

"Incontrovertibly, yes, of course I am in support!"

"And how do feel about such a campaign potentially affecting clean energy initiatives, like hydroelectric power?"

"Well, Nolana, there are alternate clean energy initiatives! We have solar power and wind. You know, I *have* been reading about the ongoing research exploring the therapeutic benefits of several frog species, like the Bufon . . . *Bufonidae.*"

"Toads," Nolana said.

"I'm sorry?"

"Technically, they are toads. 'True toads,' to be exact."

"Oh, yes, yes, true toads—that's the truth, heh-heh! Yes, there are many benefits from the skin secretions. Like the Ancient Chinese Chop Su, to treat heart conditions and even some forms of cancer."

"Chan Su," Nolana said.

"Excuse me?" Hebe blinked.

"Chan Su. I think you're getting it mixed up with chop suey, a Chinese dish."

"Oh, you mean china?"

"Yes, from China."

"No, you mean a plate? A china dish?"

"No, no. 'Dish' meaning food. A Chinese food."

"Oh, a Chinese *dish*. Heh-heh-heh! What a wack-a-noodle I am!"

Nolana chuckled along. "Hebe, I can see you definitely have an appreciation for the wealth of medicinal benefits offered by the skin secretions of various toad species!"

"Oh yes, I do, I do. A *deep* appreciation," Hebe nodded, solemnly pursing her lips.

"Then, let me ask you this, Hebe. Do you also have an appreciation for the therapeutic benefits of an experimental therapy that has been circulating lately? I'm referring to the 'lib pill,' which has been known to show promise counteracting some of the side effects of the Self Suppressor."

Hebe blinked, twitched her eyelashes, and stared a few seconds, a bit flummoxed.

"Do you mean . . ." she began tentatively, ". . . do you mean . . . the pill that's been going around . . . to bring back . . ."

"To counteract the side effects of the Self Suppressor," Nolana finished.

". . . to bring back . . . the libido instinct?"

"Yes, to bring back the natural human instinct of libido."

"Oh . . . well . . ." Hebe blinked some more, sitting back. Her eyeballs flitted in thought. "Well, Nolana, I'm not so sure something like that can safely assumed to be . . . safe. I don't believe it has gone through the proper channels."

"There's been some encouraging reports," Nolana said, "and I think the Administration of Palliatives and Therapeutics will approve it once Congress grants the clearance."

"But... I'm not sure... I'm not an expert, Nolana, but I'm not sure the Self Suppressor should be tampered with..." She took a few moments to ponder this. "Yes, yes, if you think about it, tampering with a monumental genetic therapy like the Self Suppressor might not be such a wise idea. I would be very cautious, Nolana, very cautious."

"But the drug was developed by Thunbergia Therapeutics, a very reputable biotech company, as you know."

"Yes, but without the required approval—"

"I've heard that it met the requirements of a Drug Efficacy Study Implementation."

"Yes, but if an unregulated drug is sold by scalpers—"

"But once it's been approved by Congress, we won't have to worry about scalpers."

Hebe appeared a bit rattled by the interruptions.

"Oh, I suppose..." she began, her bottom lip quivering. This was a very unusual, unfamiliar situation. Years and years of immersion in a firmly rooted moral code had upheld dictates of civic duty in Hebe's mindset. Nolana seemed to be casting doubt on the integrity of those dictates. Yet there couldn't be any doubt. We were talking about the Self Suppressor here. Any unregulated drug purporting to modify its corrective benefits in any way seemed to be an ominous portent.

"You suppose...?" Nolana waited.

"I... suppose it would be a mistake meddling with a therapy that has... only improved our way of life!"

"Would that be your position if you served on the Congress?"

"Yes. Yes, Nolana." Hebe leaned forward, resolute. "I have to be truthful. I believe it would be a mistake."

"I see."

"I hope that doesn't jeopardize my chances of serving! I would hope something like *that* wouldn't—"

"I wouldn't worry, Hebe," Nolana's smile returned. "Your candidacy will be considered by our panel, just like everyone else."

"Oh, I hope so, Nolana. I so very much would like to serve on the Congress. I've served locally but never once on the Central Congress!"

"Yes, I know, I have your file here."

"And . . . I'm always open to discussion, of course. The Congress always finds the truth in the end. And . . . the Self Suppressor *cannot* be compromised, Nolana. I'm sure you see that!"

Nolana retained her warm smile. "You're right."

"Am I?" Hebe brightened.

"Yes. Whatever the issue, whatever the problem, the Congress always finds a resolution."

Nolana closed Hebe's folder.

Cited for "questionable dedication displayed for upholding the State of Contentment," Hebe Hornbeam would not be recommended for serving on the Opinion Congress any time soon.

Twenty-Seven

BEING AN AMATEUR COLEOPTEROLOGIST, Thymus Corkwood was thinking about beetles.

The world of beetles was one of the most diverse and expansive in the entire animal kingdom, and most of them exhibited social behaviors typical of other insect families. There were always exceptions, however. One species, the clavigerite beetle, certainly employed some of the most duplicitous, malevolent survival tactics known in the entire anthropod phylum, at least in Thymus's estimation.

These sly beetles are capable of secreting chemical substances called pheromones that trick ants into accepting the beetles into their colonies. The social response triggered by the pheromones can even grant the beetles access to an ant nest. Once inside the nest, they literally steal the food out of worker ants' mouths through a process called stomodeal trophallaxis, a mouth-to-mouth transfer of nutritional fluids. These fluids are meant for other ants in the colony, not these diabolical infiltrators. Treated as nestmates, the beetles are then free to feed on ant eggs and ant babies. The clavigerite beetles were supremely adept at wielding this pheromonal disguise. Their success dated as far back as seventy million years before modern Ancient

Earth, all the way back to the late Cretaceous Period, contemporaneous with Triceratops and Tyrannosaurus.

Words like "duplicitous" and "diabolical" ring of anthropomorphism, and it is tempting to read premeditated criminal intent behind these behavioral methods. Thymus understood these creatures were not acting on intelligent, planned design in the way human intellect operates. They were acting on survival instinct. As insidious and treacherous these methods may strike us, they reflect the ongoing evolutionary reality, however unpleasant, of competition between species for natural resources.

Humans, of course, do possess the intellectual capacity to plan, to design, to premeditate. Words like "duplicitous" and "diabolical" can quite readily be applied to human behavior. In human terms, the insidious and treacherous behavior of the clavigerite beetles amounts to pretending that something *is* what it is *not*... and convincing others of the same. Deception, for personal gain.

Thymus refused to believe that his friend and colleague of almost twenty years, Lupin Hollyhock, had acted in the fashion of a human clavigerite beetle. He refused to believe Lupin had somehow infiltrated his "nest," stole his intellectual property, and passed it off as the intellectual property of Thunbergia Therapy Thresholds rather than Geranium Genome Gentrification. He refused to believe Lupin had developed that intellectual property, synthesized it, patented it, and pretended it was something that it was not—that is, pretended it was an improvement, an enhancement, a correction of the therapy Thymus had dedicated his career to developing, when in fact it was a corruption, a subversion, an impairment of that very therapy. He refused to believe Lupin had then taken the even more nefarious step of convincing others this stolen intellectual property was something that it was not. Thymus refused to believe it, but stubborn reality would broker no alternate.

He had put off the phone call long enough, and still dreaded it.

"Lupin, I need to know how you obtained the DNA sequence, and then I need to know *why* you did it."

"Thymus, hello! How have you been?"

"I'll feel better when you answer my question."

"Thymus, you sound a little perturbed. I assure you everything is—"

"Please tell me how you got the sequence."

"Okay, now listen, Thymus. Since you had abandoned the venture, we took it upon ourselves to—"

"How did you get the sequence?"

"Like I was saying, we developed our own model for the therapy, the vector, the route of administration, the biodistribution—"

"You're not answering my question."

Thymus heard an exasperated sigh.

"It doesn't matter how we obtained the sequence. All that matters is that we have developed the model independently, just as *you* had developed the model independently."

"Lupin, you *stole* the model."

"No, no. No, now, Thymus, that's, that's not what happened."

"How did you obtain the sequence? And what platform did you use? What vector?"

"Thymus, all of that is under patent. The serotype is under patent.

There's no legal issue, you understand. Now, we would be happy to license the platform to you, at a reduced cost. Once the patent expires—"

"I'm not interested in a license. It should never have been done in the first place. It's a *hazard,* Lupin, it's a hazard."

"Oh, well, now, I think you may change your mind once you see what we've done. We think, with a few tweaks, we can have a true game changer. We've had—"

"Lupin, the only miracle is that you somehow were able to access Aster Bottlebrush's sequence. How did you get it?"

"I . . . am not at liberty to say."

"What? Why not?"

"We've had good success with it, Thymus. Good results. Positive results."

"You don't understand what's at stake. You could damage the stability of the Suppressor."

"No, we don't believe that is the case."

"How much have you brought in already with the licensing? You must be bringing in a bundle."

"Thymus, you will be given your due credit, if that's what you're worried about. It was your original concept, I realize that. Why don't we work out an arrangement—"

"Do you realize there are generics floating around? Being sold in shopping mall parking lots, online, entertainment venues, even at *tennis* matches? Who knows how safe they are!"

"We can't control that. To keep prices down in the market—"

"You can't control that? These are not one-off treatments, Lupin.

You have to keep churning out the pills. It's a lucrative market for all involved."

"Once we have approval from the Congress and Administration of Palliatives and Therapeutics, everything can be regulated."

"That should have been the *first* step."

"Thymus, you know as well as I do how things slip through the cracks. When you want to get something going as important as this, you can always have drug efficacy studies. This is only a trial version, not a permanent one-off treatment, like you said. And remember, we follow the tax algorithms like any other—"

"It's out of control."

"You have my word that it is safe, and effective. Very positive results. I would like your firm to benefit from the proceeds—"

"Lupin, how did you obtain the sequence? Did you test Aster's blood?"

"No. Thymus, I can't... *fucking*... talk about this anymore..."

Thymus goggled his phone.

"Lupin... did you take a pill? Answer me that? Did you try it?"

"I'm... I'm sorry about my profanity, Thymus. It's been very stressful for me lately."

"Did you take a pill, Lupin?"

"Didn't you?"

"I did, and if you did, then you *know* it's unstable."

"It is *not* unstable. It is safe and effective."

"Lupin... it will destroy everything we've built as genetic scientists."

"Thymus, you will never convince me that a creature of *your* imagination will be the instrument of our profession's demise."

"It is not a creature. It is a monster. And I should have killed it."

"You don't need to kill it. You need to do what a scientist does. Nurture it, perfect it. Thymus, we're . . . you and I are attempting to perfect the greatest achievement in the history of genetic science! Doesn't that mean anything to you? It must have, if you yourself initiated the process."

"That's exactly what I'm trying to avoid: Perfecting my mistake."

"Okay, listen. I think we're both feeling overwhelmed from the novelty, the unprecedented nature of this enterprise. We should take some time to really ponder what we're trying to do. What we're trying to do not just for our livelihoods, not just for science, but for every Opinion out there. We really need to think very carefully about that."

"I have, Lupin. I have."

"Goodbye, Thymus. Please be content."

Thymus glared at his cell phone like it was Lupin himself. He tossed it on the bed, numb, insensate.

A few seconds later, his stepdaughter Dianella, who had been listening through the door, came into the room, sobbing almost to the point of choking. She collapsed into Thymus's arms and it took seven minutes before she could collect herself enough to sputter out what happened. She told him everything, that it was all her fault. She was ashamed of herself, and she should have known better. She should have communicated her distress to Thymus instead of scheming behind his back. It was all her fault. She was a horrible person.

Thymus held Dianella, and was not in the least bit angry with her.

He told her not to worry, that she shouldn't feel bad, that she wasn't a horrible person.

Because there was nothing that could be done at this point. He had deleted all his data. Now it was in Lupin's hands. It was too late.

And it was not Dianella's fault. It was his.

Twenty-Eight

For weeks, Kaffir Bottlebrush's head had been reeling, first from what Mr. Figgle had revealed to him, and now, more recently, the new Opinion social issue brought about by his own son's DNA. A new Opinion landscape was emerging, and Kaffir was privy to the two personalities who had lain the groundwork.

Kaffir had kept the broth of Mr. Figgle's words contained until it began to sizzle, and simmer, and seethe until the pressure burst through the lid. He told his wife Gaura less out of a sense of civic duty, and more because he just couldn't keep it to himself. Whether or not Opinion society should know a genetic clone of a very learned, respectable Ancient scholar was living amongst them was debatable, though Kaffir reasoned in either case Mr. Figgle himself would never be deemed a threat to the public peace. If he was indeed a test case for a select group of scientists, Kaffir guessed the man passed the test with flying colors. Nobody would have ever thought Mr. Figgle was anything other than a true Opinion citizen. A brilliant one, and an eccentric one, perhaps . . . and perhaps his skin tone was a bit light for a typical Opinion, but there was nothing in his behavior to indicate he was an outsider, an intruder, a being not of this world. Yes, Mr. Figgle was quite *normal!* Despite the fact that Homo Sapiens 1.0 and

Homo Sapiens 2.0 shared a common genetic heritage—indeed, their genome was one and the same—the Opinions had been conditioned to view the Ancients as an inferior, polluted variant to their own refined, immaculate biological and cognitive brand. Through the genius of scientists like Nalca Hollyhock, the Corrective Biological Sciences had forged the Self Suppressor, the ultimate sanitizer for the corrosive maladies sealing their ancestors' dismal fate. While it is true there were plenty of magnificent examples of human thought and monumental achievement preserved throughout The Find, and while the Opinions did not take for granted they owed the meteoric advancement of their own civilization to the remarkable wealth of knowledge therein, the idea that an actual specimen of Homo Sapiens 1.0 could live and *function* within their society was as unthinkable as an ape learning to build rockets. They may have been blessed with the wings of ingenuity but could never fly without peril. Even the most intelligent of them would be incapable of identifying with the Opinion State of Contentment.

Yet now it seemed one of the elements of that supposed inferior, polluted variant had made its way into Kaffir's own son, not because Aster was an Ancient clone like Mr. Figgle, but because Aster, as an Opinion native, had carried the pollutant naturally. But was it really a pollutant? Thunbergia Therapy Thresholds, the genetic lab responsible for developing the first trial version of a therapy derived from Aster's DNA, had been promoting it as an "enhancement." The new "lib pill," or "libill," had been sparking as much controversy as intrigue, the buzz charged with allurement grappling with skepticism. Online forums had described the effects of the pill as "exhilarating," "liberating," and even "cleansing," a term traditionally reserved for characterizing the elixir itself, the Self Suppressor. As of yet there had been no adverse effects reported, though all bets were off with an unregulated drug running rampant. Thunbergia was claiming that the therapy met the criteria for GRASE, or "Generally Recognized As Safe and Effective," in that it was essentially a grandfathered "tuning" of the Suppressor. In all probability the Opinion Congress would pull it off the market until approved by the Administration of Palliatives and Therapeutics. But that wouldn't stop generic companies from producing what was turning out to be a popular item. Dr. Lupin Hollyhock himself had sent a complimentary ten-dose original bottle to Kaffir and Gaura, with the following note of gratitude:

> Dear Mr. and Mrs. Bottlebrush:
>
> Please find enclosed a complimentary bottle of the trial version of our new Libido Reinstatement Therapy. This advancement in the genetic sciences would be impossible without your son's generous cooperation volunteering a sample of his DNA to the scientific community, a gesture allowing a fellow geneticist, Dr. Thymus Corkwood, to pave the way for our research and development of this most extraordinary minor modification to an already extraordinary corrective therapy. We are all indebted to your family, and will be forever committed to providing a safe, effective medical expression of the evolutionary benefits endowing your son's natural biochemistry.
>
> Fondly,
> Lupin Hollyhock

Kaffir had held the emerald pill, rolled it between two fingers, felt the gelatin protein coating, weighing the physicality as if doing so would reveal its underlying ambitions. The pill remained mute, and Kaffir was left to wonder whether he should endeavor to assess Dr. Hollyhock's expertise firsthand, whether it was a good idea to experience an artificially induced replication of the "minor modification" occurring naturally in his son's genome. Though it wouldn't make much sense to test it alone. He asked Gaura if she would be willing to try it with him. Lupin did assert it was safe and effective. She responded with an emphatic "no," without hesitation. She was not about to serve as one of Lupin Hollyhock's guinea pigs at the expense of her own son's genealogical reputation. If Aster was to be perceived by the public as some sort of evolutionary misfit, she was not going to be an accessory to promoting that view unless the therapy derived from his DNA was endorsed and approved by the Opinion Congress as a legitimate, beneficial, protective medical treatment. Experiencing the natural instinct of libido could wait. He understood her misgivings, and agreed. Though the smooth pill was still there, and its smooth silence could not be ignored.

He could not ignore it at home, and he could not ignore it a work, the smooth, emerald, gelatin protein surface of that little pill, inviting in its silence—not tempting or beguiling, but politely nudging: "Hello, would you like to try me? If you ever decide to, I will be here." That is what its silence said. What would it be like, to feel what Aster feels, to feel a burgeoning nascent energy welling up, like the first sight of the blue sun in the blue sky, or the first breath of dew-laden air? Would it feel profane? Scampish? Benignly playful? Lewd and indecent? Or, dare he speculate, perhaps it would feel natural? Perhaps it would feel just right? The pill remained neutral on such matters. "You can try me, if you'd like," it said in its silence, "but you don't have to."

Then, one day during his lunch break at the Catchfly County Culture Coalition Center, after spending two hours deliberating over the profitable merits of Flaubert's *Sentimental Education,* a work whose application for clearance had previously reached an impasse, the pill's neutral silence was articulated with new prejudice by a familiar voice and a familiar face, that of Kaffir's friend, neighbor, and colleague, Daphne Sweetspire.

With her tawny, wavy curtain of hair swaying and her scintillating eyes, Daphne cornered Kaffir before he was able to approach a lunch table in the Aviary Lounge. The usual animation in her features were pulsating with a singular, bristling vigor. Kaffir thought at first she had received some amazingly happy news.

"Kaffir . . . I tried it," she announced in a hushed tone. He lowered his eyes to see an emerald pill in her cupped hand.

"You did?"

She gave a quick nod, a singular effervescence beaming through a winking grin.

"When?"

"This morning."

"How does it feel?"

Daphne closed her eyes, took an inhalation of emotional fragrance, released it. "Resplendent," she said.

Kaffir thought about the bottle of emerald pills at home sitting on his nightstand. Daphne uncurled her fingers, and the one on her palm asked if he wanted to try it. Then she asked.

"I . . . I was actually thinking about it, but I don't know."

"You *must,*" Daphne stepped closer to him, still hushed. "You don't have to worry. It wears off. But it's enrapturing while it lasts."

"Yes? Well, if you think it's safe . . ."

"It is. Here."

She gripped the pill between thumb and two fingers, thrust it into his hand. He felt the warm, smooth, coated texture. He felt his fingers curl around it.

"I promise," Daphne said, "it's okay. It's *good.*"

Kaffir sat down with Daphne and two other colleagues to eat. He slipped the pill in his mouth with a bite of his tempeh sandwich and washed it down with a gulp of ginger beet juice.

Two hours later Kaffir went down two floors to the Music Consultant Wing and found Daphne sitting at her office desk. He asked if she could please follow him, that he had to show her an interesting literary passage pertaining to music, though was a bit unclear about the reference. Daphne looked in Kaffir's eyes and knew right away he did not really want to show her a literary passage. Without a word, she followed him down one floor to a gender-neutral restroom. Kaffir went in the restroom first, came out, took her hand.

When they entered a stall and latched the door behind them, neither said a word. Their sealed lips never parted and they never said a word as Kaffir tore off his pants, and Daphne wriggled out of her dress. They never said a word as Kaffir backed her against the stall partition and slinked into her as unmindfully as breathing. She entwined her arms around him and tried to whisper "resplendence" in his ear. But only a guttural *reh* came out.

And then, from the two of them, syllables of no organized language, simian in their unshackled primal roots.

Twenty-Nine

THE SHIMMERING CREAM MARBLE Opinion Central Congressional Building was essentially a Roman rotunda, with a main chamber combining the designs of the United States House of Representatives and the Knights of the Round Table. While the members of the Ancient House sat in armchairs at connected "segment form" desks arranged in semicircles on elevated platforms, the members of the Opinion Congress sat on pure marble benches with cushioned seats and backrests, arranged in five concentric circles, each progressively elevated, an aisle cut every ninety degrees, and the Facilitator's rostrum in the middle. The first circle seated fifty, the second seventy-five, the third one hundred, the fourth one hundred twenty-five, and the fifth one hundred fifty, for a total of five hundred, one of the members seated in the middle as Facilitator. Like the benches, segment form mahogany desks were fitted together and ran continuously around each circular row. Each desk was equipped with a pad, writing utensils, a canister for vomiting, and a microphone. In imitation of the United States Senate "Candy Desk," inside each desk drawer could be found multitudinous vegan snacks, from nuts to edamame to trail mix to roasted chickpeas. A list of agenda issues was always compiled before the completion of one session and placed on the desks for the next session. The more complex issues were saved for last.

Following the tennis court incident, the members wrapping up that month's session decided to place the issue of the "lib pill" as the very first agenda item for the incoming session. Something as unequivocally obvious as this should be resolved in no time at all. There could be no other alternative than banning the production of the "lib pill" immediately, under penalty of home imprisonment. The trial therapy, which had been released prematurely from Dr. Lupin Hollyhock's facility under the supervision of a Drug Efficacy Study Implementation program, had created too much of a stir in public Contentment and could thus not be endorsed as a trusted upgrade to the standard Suppressor therapy. The therapy had not been reviewed by the Congress, and until it was cleared for evaluation and approval by the Administration of Palliatives and Therapeutics (APT) it was not safe for public use. Legislation had to be passed immediately to abort further production of all varieties, generic or otherwise, pending final approval by APT, and a Congressional Directive had to be signed by the members ordering all existing pills in circulation to be immediately turned into the authorities, under penalty of fine. Any person found to be promoting or distributing the said therapy without authorization by the Opinion Congress would be incarcerated immediately under the provisions of home imprisonment. The Self Suppressor, and the maintenance of the State of Contentment, were too precious to be imperiled by what amounted to, at best, a dubious first draft of an alleged Suppressor "enhancement."

Mr. Lucerne Bindweed, the presiding Facilitator, was concluding the recitation of these recommendations from the preceding session when a member sitting in the second row, Mr. Burdock Foxglove, announced his name and asked for the floor.

"Yes, Mr. Foxglove, proceed."

"Thank you, Mr. Facilitator. I would like to respectfully ask the Facilitator if there is, in fact, undeniable evidence to support the charge that this 'enhancement' therapy, developed and engineered by one of the foremost genetic science labs in Opine, the same lab directed by one of the most distinguished genetic scientists in Opine, Dr. Lupin Hollyhock, poses a clear and present threat to the integrity of the current State of Contentment as it stands."

"Thank you for that question, Mr. Foxglove. Yes, as I understand it, there have been reliable reports of the therapy impelling citizens to commit indiscriminate sex acts, thereby imperiling the State of Contentment."

"Impelling citizens?" Mr. Foxglove inquired. "Do you mean the citizens were committing the acts independent of free will?"

"Well, as you know, Mr. Foxglove, the manifestations of human behavior are determined in no small part by the manifold interplay of genetic predispositions, so that any therapy designed to manipulate those predispositions necessarily plays a decisive role in impelling deviant behaviors."

Mr. Arum Fieldrush in the third row raised his hand, and was acknowledged.

"Do we know the behavior to be 'deviant'—in the pejorative sense?"

"I would say 'deviant' not so much in the pejorative sense," the Facilitator responded, "but 'deviant' in the unacceptable sense, as the therapy deviates away from the primary functionality of the Suppressor, causing adverse, unregulated effects."

"What do you mean by adverse effects?" Mr. Fieldrush asked.

"Adverse effects, in that these reports indicate the therapy is causing people to behave in manners unfavorable to the status quo—hello, yes?"

"Ms. Nepeta Goosefoot, please."

"Yes, Ms. Goosefoot, go ahead."

"How do we know it is unfavorable to the status quo? It was not my impression that the pill produced unfavorable results."

Many heads turned to look at Ms. Goosefoot.

"Ms. Goosefoot," Mr. Bindweed said, "when you say it was not your impression, are you saying that you yourself sampled Dr. Hollyhock's therapy?"

"Yes, I did, Mr. Facilitator, and I fail to understand, having personally experienced the effects of the therapy, how something so innocuous can be deemed unfavorable to the status quo."

"Innocuous?" somebody in the back row exclaimed.

"Um . . . I, um . . ." Mr. Bindweed dithered, for it was unseemly, and very uncommon, to interrupt a member without first requesting the floor. Mr. Bindweed reminded the individual of proper chamber etiquette.

"I apologize, Mr. Facilitator," the woman said, "but I would just like to say—"

"State your name, please. Into the microphone."

"Teasel Milfoil," she said, leaning into the mic. "I would just like to point out that a trial medication of this type cannot truthfully be described as 'innocuous.' Not when it causes people to lose control of their inhibitions, to the point their behavior exhibits an overt rejection of the mitigating properties built into the very therapy our society has relied upon for over a hundred years."

"Have you tried it?" Ms. Goosefoot blurted.

"No I have *not,*" Teasel retorted, "and I don't plan on trying it."

"Well, if you tried it, you may not think of it so much as a rejection as an improvement."

"I don't see people committing the sex act in public tennis courts as an improvement!"

"Now, ladies and gentleman," Mr. Bindweed interposed, "these interruptions are out of order. I would remind the... *BrrrrrUFFF-uf-uf!*" The Facilitator wiped his lips and carefully placed his canister of ejecta under the rostrum. "... I would remind the members to follow proper chamber etiquette when addressing the assembly."

Mr. Arum Fieldrush raised his hand again.

"Yes... uh, yes, Mr. F-Fieldrush," the Facilitator sputtered.

"Mr. Facilitator, I would like the members to know that I too tried Dr. Hollyhock's therapy, and I cannot say with certainty that it disrupts or weakens the State of Contentment in any way. In fact, I found the therapy to be... quite pleasurable, and nothing more."

"Mr. Facilitator?" somebody in the third row began.

"Yes, yes, one moment. Um, Mr. Fieldrush, the issue under consideration is not so much whether the therapy succeeds in producing agreeable, or gratifying physical effects, but whether those effects are in any way potentially detrimental to the . . . to the functional basis of normal social, uh, inter . . . intercourse. Yes, yes, I see you. Go ahead."

"I am Ivy Hogbean. I agree with Ms. Milfoil. A trial therapy of this type cannot be trusted. It needs to be reviewed by the Congress, like any other medical treatment, and then it needs to be approved by the Administration of Palliatives and Therapeutics. Only then could it be distributed safely to the public."

Many members nodded and muttered "truth, truth" in agreement. Ms. Nepeta Goosefoot raised her hand again.

"Yes, Ms. Goosefoot?"

"I would like to suggest that we recess, so that more members of the assembly have an opportunity to test a dosage of the therapy for themselves. By each member evaluating the effects subjectively, we can then make a fair determination, as a deliberative body, whether the therapy produces anything indicating an undesirable physical or psychological reaction, and weather it poses a potential threat to normal social intercourse."

Ms. Yareta Bugloss in the first row waved two arms.

"With all due respect to Ms. Goosefoot," she said, "I think the last thing we need is for the members of this deliberative body subjecting themselves to an irrepressible compulsion to perform acts of fornication right here on the chamber floor!"

This produced a round of guffaws, abruptly silenced by a plainly irritated Mr. Bindweed.

"Now please," he said, "good members of the Congress, I implore you to—"

"It's *not* fornication!" somebody in the back row yelled. "The sex act is natural! Natural!"

The outburst was answered with a sprinkling of snickers.

"Please," the Facilitator continued, "we *must* conduct this assembly in a dignified manner. Let's not lose sight of who we are. We are the people representing the people, the Opinion Congress! . . . Yes, yes!"

"Thank you, sir. Mangrove Solidago. I myself have never tried Dr. Hollyhock's therapy, but I have to agree with the gentleman in the back, despite the fact he spoke out of turn. The sex act is not fuh . . . *buh . . . BLARrrrrrrf . . .* excuse me . . ." Mr. Solidago took a moment to dispatch his canister. ". . . The sex act is not fornication. It is the natural, genetically programmed instinct to procreate."

Teasel Milfoil barked out a request.

"Yes, go ahead, Ms. Milfoil."

"The natural, genetically programmed instinct to procreate is different from the artificial, drug-induced programming to penetrate your next-door neighbor!"

"Oh come on, it doesn't do that!" somebody yelled amidst groans and snickers.

"Everybody, please, let's—"

"Excuse me, Mr. Facilitator?"

"Yes, yes, third row."

"I'm Mrs. Sesban Campanula. I have heard that the eminent scholar, Mr. Figgle, is actually a genetic *clone* of a Homo Sapiens 1.0 individual of the same name . . ." There was a collective gasp. ". . . and that he has been living among us as a normal, functioning, successful citizen of Opine all these years, with his libido firmly intact!"

Mr. Bindweed's index finger, which had been perpetually extended throughout the debate, was now wagging at Mrs. Campanula.

"Uh, that hasn't been confirmed, Mrs. Campanula!" he asserted. "Hasn't been confirmed!"

"I understand," the lady continued, "but if it is, then we should consider this very carefully. If a man who represents an *exact* copy of an Ancient human genome, with his natural libidinal instinct fully intact, a man whose genome was left unaltered by our editing technology—"

"Hasn't been confirmed!"

"I grant you that, Mr. Facilitator, but if such a man is able to conduct himself not only as a normal, law-abiding Opinion citizen, but as an *exemplary,* distinguished, admired and respected expert in the socioanthropological sciences, who are we to say that a mere *adjustment* of this editing technology, allowing the expression of what we all agree is a natural libidinal instinct, should be christened undesirable, or harmful, for the rest of the population?"

Cries of "Yes!" and "That's right!" punctuated the general murmuring.

"Now, wait a minute!" the Facilitator interjected, quickly yanking out his cell phone. "Now wait, let's all of us take a step back for a moment. Have we all heard today's Fool Fact? Listen to this: The Buddhist monk Thích Nhất Hạnh was exiled from his home country of Vietnam for thirty-nine years because he wrote peace poetry and spoke out against the Vietnam War, a conflict that lasted twenty years, killed millions of people, and accomplished nothing! What do you think of that? Ha ha ha!"

There were a few chuckles, but the assembly seemed unimpressed. Mr. Bindweed nervously pocketed his cell phone.

"Yes, all right, all right, we have a lady in the first row... yes, please."

The plump woman thanked Mr. Bindweed and announced her name. It was Nerine Bayberry, the same Nerine Bayberry who presided over the Revelation Ceremony at the beginning of our narrative.

"I would like everybody to know... I have heard those same reports about Mr. Figgle, and even if he is... even if..." She cupped a palm over her mouth, gave a slight heave. "*...klairf...*" Taking a few moments to breathe, she released her palm and gulped. False alarm. "... Even if it is true that Mr. Figgle is a genetic clone of the Ancients, he is certainly an atypical one. How many brilliant scholars of his caliber, and men of his impeccable character, do you think were walking around back then? And that's just as true today! So I think it's a gross misrepresentation to claim anybody of Mr. Figgle's genetic *type* is necessarily going to exhibit the same level of intellect and exemplary moral behavior we see from a unique citizen like Mr. Figgle."

"That's not the point!" Mrs. Campanula called out amidst a wave of murmuring. "He still carries the natural *libido* of any Ancient—"

"Wait, Mrs.—*please,* may I—" Mr. Bindweed tried, but Arum Fieldrush was shouting over the swell of grumbling:

"Mr. Facilitator! Mr. Facilitator!"

"Silence in the chamber, please! Silence in the chamber!" Mr. Bindweed tried again. "Mr. Fieldrush has shown the proper courtesy and will receive the proper courtesy!"

The Facilitator paused as the chatter continued.

"Yes, one moment, Mr. Fieldrush. I would like to remind the assembly, *again,* that there is absolutely *no* confirmation of the hearsay just referenced by Mrs. Campanula, and aside from that, we are not here to legislate Opinion policies based on the behavior of a supposed lone genetic outlier, be it Mr. Figgle or anybody else. Our policies are written *by* the Opinion people, and *for* the Opinion people, irrespective of any foreign . . . or, or composite . . . morphologies that may or may not have been . . . introduced into the gene pool. Yes, Mr. Fieldrush, you have the floor."

"Thank you, Mr. Facilitator, and you are right. I would like to respond to Ms. Goosefoot's prior suggestion of our members taking a test dosage of the therapy. While I believe this would place unwarranted pressure to experiment with a drug not yet formally accepted into the public sphere, I would like to respectfully submit to the assembly that nobody could deny the individual pursuit of happiness is harmless, as long as it can be demonstrated, beyond a reasonable doubt, that such a pursuit does not in any way detract from or interfere with the happiness of others, and as long as the pursuit is not demonstrated to be an ephemeral, self-destructive gratification, or an *addiction,* cloaked in the guise of true Contentment."

"Ah, ah, yes, a very good point, Mr. Fieldrush," the Facilitator waved an index finger like a baton. "This pill could very well encourage an addictive behavior! Yes, state you name, young man."

"Matico Reinrose. In response to Mr. Fieldrush, I don't believe therapeutically induced libido can necessarily motivate an addictive behavior. After all, the animal kingdom does not perpetuate the species through an addictive behavior."

"Ah, another good point," Facilitator Bindweed said, "it does not *necessarily* motivate an addictive behavior, but it could, it could."

Strangely, a silence fell over the room. People seemed to be taking a moment to absorb Mr. Reinrose's words.

"Would anybody like to . . . yes, hello, young lady. Go ahead."

"Vivendel Bugloss. I have taken the pill and I do not feel addicted."

The Facilitator waited, but that was apparently the extent of her remarks.

"Okay, we . . . appreciate your assessment," he said, "but I think we can all agree on the truth, which is that it is possible to become addicted to a drug, including one in its developmental stages. And especially one that instills a feeling of . . . euphoria. And we all know, from our Ancient Studies, how excessive euphoria can lead to self-destructive behaviors. Yes? The lady in the—yes, your name, please."

An older woman, her shoulder-length caramel pleated hair streaked with saffron, leaned into the microphone.

"Jasmine Starwort. A word, for the assembly, about who we are. We are Opinions, and we pronounce it that way because we do not pass laws based on opinions. Whether or not a pill makes a person feel good, whether or not it is addictive, whether or not it encourages or deters the pursuit of happiness, is inconsequential to the issue at hand. The issue at hand is not to poll the individual opinions of the Congress as to the subjective benefits or risks of Dr. Hollyhock's therapy. The issue at hand is to arrive at the truth of whether it is in the public's best interest to release a drug before it has gone through the proper screening process established by our predecessors, people like us, the citizens of Opine. We can not justify dishonoring the precedents instituted by, again, people like us, the citizens of Opine, without endangering the integrity of future precedents we intend to set ourselves. We do not deal with opinions in this chamber. We deal with truths. And the truth is, we have no way of knowing, in fact, if Dr. Hollyhock's new therapy is addictive, or harmless, or dangerous, or beneficial, until it passes the regulatory process our forbearers have designed to protect the rights and welfare of our citizens."

The Facilitator, along with the rest of the members, could not help but take a few moments to absorb Ms. Starwort's words.

"A truth, to be sure," Mr. Bindweed nodded. "May I make a motion, then, to draft and pass the prohibitive directives, as outlined in last month's session, with the express stipulation that such directives shall be repealed if, upon review by the Congress and duly appointed specialists at the Administration of Palliatives and Therapeutics, the therapy is accordingly evaluated and approved by the said authorities to be lawfully produced and distributed to the Opinion public?"

The entire chamber remained silent, save a shuffle of papers here and there.

"Do we have a consensus?" Mr. Bindweed raised his hand, kept it suspended. "Yes? No? Any dissenters?"

Silence prevailed. Some of the members looked uneasily around the chamber.

"All right, then, we shall put it to a vote. Are we in agreement?"

Still no response.

"Let's do that, then. All in favor of drafting the prohibitive directives with contingency stipulation, please raise your hand."

A majority of the members raised their hands. The Facilitator carefully counted three hundred and two, including his own vote.

"Oh, my... um... all against?"

One hundred and ninety-eight members raised their hands.

"Abstain?"

Nobody moved.

"The count is three hundred and two for, one hundred ninety-eight against. Thank you, the motion is passed. Well, now, let's hope the next discussion is a bit more conventional, yes? Heh heh heh."

The Facilitator chuckled, and nobody moved.

Thirty

UNLIKE THE INTERVIEW with Ms. Bellis Jewelwood of NPC News, Aster Bottlebrush was not nervous at all about his taped interview with progressive talk radio personality, Dropmore Copperpod, famous also for his news and entertainment media platform, The Copper-Podcast. In fact, Aster was quite comfortable sitting in the QCC (Queens Cup County) Studio Room, looking forward to speaking with Mr. Copperpod on live radio. And he didn't feel obligated to tell his parents about the interview. He would be eighteen in a week and was old enough to make his own decisions.

Why should he not speak out about what he now thought of as a natural endowment? There was no reason to feel ashamed. Feeling ashamed about his genetic resistance to the Self Suppressor would be like feeling ashamed about his hair color, or his eye color, or his height. When we are born, we are born not with what we ask for, but what we are given. Imagine an Ancient African American feeling ashamed that he was black! Or imagine Ancient people of Asian descent feeling ashamed about the epicanthic folds of their eyes! Or imagine somebody born with Down's syndrome or cystic fibrosis feeling ashamed because they were born with a genetic disorder, something they had absolutely no control over, like skin color or facial features or lineage! Will Opinions choose the path of prejudice, or stereotype, or bigotry, just because Aster's genes happened to decide, completely without his knowledge or consent, that they would not be suppressed by the Suppressor? How was he expected to respond to this biogenetic irregularity that was as much a part of him as every other atom in his entire body?

As for the recent Congress directive, he cared little for what they had to say. Were any of them like him? Did they know what it felt like to be an outcast, even though he was *not* an outcast? Or what it was like to feel guilty about something he had absolutely no control over? Or what it was like to be stigmatized as a threat to the gene pool, as if he had one iota of influence over the natural course of evolution? The more he thought about it, the more it seemed ludicrous. If anything, *he* was the normal one, the truly pure, unrevised, most faithful representative of the human genome. If he could be administered the Self Suppressor, and resist its therapeutic effects, while still conducting himself as an outstanding Opinion citizen—for all who knew him certainly regarded him as such—then why should he feel obligated, by some arbitrary, manufactured sense of civic duty, to discourage people from taking a therapy derived from *his* perfectly unrevised and authentic DNA, when this very therapy could afford people the chance to feel just as unrevised and authentic as he? Surely if a respected scientist like Thymus Corkwood had been concerned over the objectionable potentialities of exploring Aster's DNA, he would not have gone through the trouble of collecting a blood sample, and a similarly respected scientist like Lupin Hollyhock certainly would not have gone through the time and expense of developing a therapy derived from that sample!

Aster prepared assiduously for his interview with Mr. Copperpod, memorizing key points he wanted people to hear. And the people did hear. Dropmore Copperpod would later be very happy with the AQH (Average Quarter Hour) figures used to calculate ratings.

Once Aster settled himself in the studio's tangerine organic hemp armchair and the proper introductions were made, Mr. Copperpod got down to business.

"Aster, what does it feel like to be the young man behind this new supplement to the Suppressor, even if it's been temporarily suspended by the Congress?"

"It feels like an honor. If my DNA can help to eradicate some of the unnatural side effects of the Suppressor, then I am honored to serve as springboard for that effort. And it should not have been suspended."

"Oh, yeah? Why do you say that?"

"Because it obviously works, and there's no evidence at all that it's harmful. If libido is harmful, that's like saying nature is harmful. Why not give people the chance to try it out? Then we can decide for ourselves, as a society, if it's harmful."

"Well, Aster, I don't think anybody is claiming that libido is harmful. But don't you think we should wait until it gets formal approval before it gets released to the public?"

"No, because I don't think the Congress will ever approve it."

"Why not?"

"Because I don't think there are enough people out there willing to accept any modification to the Self Suppressor whatsoever, regardless of whether the modification, *could* be in the end, a correction. I think people are so conditioned into believing their precious State of Contentment is untenable without the support of a genetic restraint. But I don't think that's the case. I wonder if we even need a restraint. I wonder if the only support system we need is a common commitment to discipline and decency. Maybe Opinions don't need to be restrained."

"But Aster, it *is* the Self Suppressor that has enabled our society to maintain that precious State of Contentment you speak of."

"I'm not suggesting to get rid of the Self Suppressor entirely. I just mean eradicating the side effects. Reinstating the natural instinct of libido that we all, as humans, have a natural right to express."

"Well, of course it's too early to tell if that's possible."

"I'm living proof that it's possible. And people are finding out it's possible. I've even volunteered my DNA to other genetic companies to help develop the therapy."

"Oh, really? Well, in case anybody in our listening audience presumes a young man with a natural resistance to the Self Suppressor must be selfish, think again! I wonder how Hollyhock and Company feels about that?"

"They already have my DNA. And DNA can't be patented."

"Aster, are you at all worried about this new therapy possibly reversing the effects of the Suppressor?"

"No. There's no evidence to support that."

"But there's also no evidence either way."

"If there is evidence, then they can scrap the entire idea and maybe try something else. I just refuse to accept that a natural, genetic rejection of an artificial, man-made therapy is wrong. That's like saying being human is wrong."

"But everybody on Opine who've been administered the therapy is human, right? Are you saying any kind of genetic alteration achieved by scientific innovation is wrong?"

"No, I'm saying the *absence* of that alteration doesn't make it wrong. Look, I've done a lot of reading about this and human libido is... is important! I mean, why would nature encode every creature in the animal kingdom with the instinct to mate? It's pretty obvious, right? It's an integral part of what makes us all who we are, the propensity to reproduce, and that's a good thing. It's not just about sex drive. It's about passion. It's... it's not just about calm water and gentle breezes and blue skies, but also about... about *fire,* and longing, and striving, and even struggling! It's about expressing all the passions that make us human, not suppressing them! Why do we need a white-washed, antiseptic genetic version of ourselves if it's antithetical to nature's engineering? Nature's not stupid, you know!"

"Well, you're a bright young guy, and you've obviously thought a lot about this. I think the average Opinion, though, would call the Self Suppressor a godsend. A blessing."

"Okay. I'm not against the Self Suppressor. But if it's a blessing it doesn't make *me* a curse. And if I can offer something to make a god-send more of a godsend then I'm not going to be intimidated into hiding in a closet. I'm speaking out, for myself, and everybody."

Thirty-One

When two Boxwood Borough police officers showed up in their jade-green uniforms with gold embroidered double chevrons and "BB" insignias, Aster Bottlebrush was just finishing up a phone conversation with Dianella Corkwood, who had refused to see Aster in person.

Dianella explained in a very level but firm tone that she was disappointed with Aster's radio interview in which he touted the distribution of Dr. Hollyhock's therapy with not a shred of scruple. She thought him to be irresponsible and reckless offering his DNA to further promote the synthesis of a drug that not only had generated some very controversial, troubling reports, but even worse, had also been banned by congressional directive. She felt horribly rotten it was she who had volunteered her stepfather's research to Dr. Hollyhock under the mistaken conviction that Dr. Hollyhock would immediately denounce the project, when in fact it was her stepfather who had nixed his own plans after realizing the drug's dangerous impingement on the Self Suppressor, while Dr. Hollyhock, unbeknownst to Dianella, had schemed to exploit her erroneous judgment by undertaking himself the injudicious, unethical development and engineering of Thymus's ill-conceived work. She couldn't understand how

Aster failed to see the potential harm this drug could inflict on the populace without first being evaluated and cleared by the Administration of Palliatives and Therapeutics.

Aster was incensed but tried to control his tone. What she was calling a "drug" was really a replication of his natural body chemistry, and his natural body chemistry was an "unpolluted" expression of a natural bodily instinct. What both Dr. Hollyhock and her stepfather were attempting to do should be thought of not as a degradation but an advancement in genetic science. They were attempting to preserve the primary functionality of the Self Suppressor while eliminating its undesirable side effects. What could be dangerous or reckless about restoring a human instinct back to the state Nature herself had brewed out of the primordial soup? And who said the reports were troubling? Any new therapy is controversial. Nobody was reporting that the therapy made them feel bad, or sick, or mentally unbalanced! Aster suggested Dianella might think about trying the pill herself before jumping to unfounded conclusions! Maybe it would help her understand how he feels about her! But for the stifling, artificially induced constraints of the Self Suppressor, maybe the strong passions and emotions deep inside her would have surfaced long ago!

Dianella was in the midst of articulating how she didn't need a stupid, illegal pill to express her passions and emotions, and how she believed Aster to be *selfish,* that if he really had strong feelings for her then he would respect *her* feelings on the matter, when the Boxwood Borough police officers rang the doorbell.

The officers greeted with pleasant enough smiles to offset the stark blackness of the stun guns they gripped. Aster was informed that he had violated Congressional Directive 161-D by promoting the production and distribution of an illegal therapy through the voluntary tendering of his personal genome, and was thereby summoned to be held at the Incarceration Housing Development in Cockspur Coral County, until such time as his case could be tried in a court of law in front of a jury of twelve peers; that he would be given ample opportunity to secure an attorney before that time; and, finally, that if he could not secure an attorney, one would be appointed to him by the County.

Gaura and Kaffir Bottlebrush were stunned. Their son was fuming. They had no right to arrest him. A person's DNA was not bound by the law. The officer politely informed Aster that although his DNA was not bound by the law, the willful application of his DNA to promote an illegal substance was against the law. Aster retorted quite impolitely that there was no law prohibiting him from sharing his DNA with anybody he saw fit to receive it. The officer replied politely that sharing his DNA with the express intent of promoting the production of a therapy banned by Congressional Directive 161-D was against the law. Aster, with flaring indignation, replied there was no way to prove his express intent was to promote the production of the banned therapy. He in fact was donating his DNA in the interest of promoting current research and development aimed at enhancing new therapies in the Corrective Biological Sciences. The officer politely advised Aster to discuss that claim with his lawyer, but for now his safest course of action was to not resist and please calmly step into the officer's vehicle before they were forced to restrain him. To their credit, the officers kept smiling throughout the entire exchange.

In a huff, Aster complied, ignoring his mother's shaken voice assuring him everything would be fine.

"If I had known he was going to do that stupid radio interview," Gaura lamented, "I could have guided him. I could have given him some good advice. I could have at *least* told him what to say and what not to say. Maybe talk him out of it. I know he means well but he's still too young to understand how these kind of things affect people. You can't . . . go against the decisions of the Congress. The Congress *knows* what's right. A democracy always finds the truth, always finds what's best for Contentment. We have to . . . Kaffir? Kaffir?"

He was sitting slumped against the wall, shaking, one hand over his lowered head. It was only when Gaura kneeled down that she heard the sobs.

"Kaffir? What is it?"

The attempted speech was muffled by whimpers.

"Oh, Kaffir, it'll be okay. Don't worry so much. You know, juries are very lenient with boys his age. Young people can be impulsive. They know that. He just wasn't thinking. But he's such a bright, sensible boy. I'm surprised—and I've never seen him so *angry* before. He was just defending himself. I can understand that. A person can't be held responsible for resisting any kind of medical treatment or therapy. He just didn't think it was fair, and he reacted. The jury will understand that. We'll most likely have to sign something, and pay a fine. I just wish he had talked to us before—"

"I . . . did something . . ." Kaffir managed to sputter.

"What? You did what?"

"I . . . Gaura, I took wuh . . . one of the pills."

"What pill? *Oh.*"

Gaura recoiled a bit, then put a palm on his shoulder as the crying continued.

"Kaffir, maybe we should have discussed that before you did it. Are you okay? How do you feel?"

"I'm . . . I'm . . ."

"When did you take it? Kaffir?"

"It's . . . I'm okay . . ."

"Well, why didn't you say anything? I don't understand. I thought we agreed that we weren't going to be test subjects for our son's genes. I thought we talked about that."

He kept sniveling and shivering. Then, when he was finally able to control his breathing:

"I . . . I should have told you, Gaura."

"Yes. Yes, you should have, but it's okay. Please don't do it again. We'll throw the bottle out, okay?"

"It's . . . it's not just . . . taking the pill that I'm upset about."

She waited.

"Kaffir? What?"

"It's . . . what I did *after* . . . I took it . . ."

Thirty-Two

GAURA BOTTLEBRUSH stood next to her bed and watched her husband sleep.

She had taken the news of Kaffir's infidelity quite well. She didn't cry, or lash out in rage, or fling out a barrage of incriminations. She didn't feel hatred or contempt for either Kaffir or Daphne. It wasn't her husband who really committed adultery, and it wasn't even Daphne who incited the adultery. It was the pill. It had to be. Kaffir would never do such a thing under his own volition. And Gaura knew Daphne well enough to know she, too, was not the type to initiate a proposal disrespecting—*disregarding* the bond of marriage. The pill must have triggered a biochemical reaction causing them—no, *forcing* them to behave contrary to their natural psychological dispositions. There could be no other explanation. Kaffir loved her and . . . he had temporarily lost control.

Yet, could a pill be *so* powerful as to completely thwart resistance, with such absolute, unqualified potency? Is that the way her son always felt? Was Aster completely at the mercy of his innate libidinal instinct? Aster could have gone further with Dianella, but he didn't. He simply touched her, and she had let him.

But no, no, Dianella did not have the same condition as Aster.

Condition? And she hadn't taken a pill. What if she had? Would they have . . . ?

Oh, no, no, that was nonsense. Perhaps there were cases where natural libido could get out of hand, but it was unreasonable to assume the bulk of the Ancient population lacked the will power to temper their primal instincts. Aster could control himself, and Kaffir could have . . .

But Kaffir was not operating under the primal instinct. He had taken an artificially induced approximation of that instinct. The pill must be permanently taken off the market. It was a calamity. It was a dereliction of Opinion progress. It had to be wiped out for good.

Gaura grabbed the pills off Kaffir's nightstand, began to flounce out of the room, stopped, looked at the blue polypropylene bottle. Are the pills *that* effective? What would it feel like? What would it feel like to have that long dormant fervor bursting out of its confines, singeing every nerve ending into newly whetted appetites? Would she feel helpless, impotent against the throes of its sweeping dominion? Or would she welcome it, embrace it, enjoy it? Was the primal impulse to reproduce, central to the survival instinct of all living organisms, a thing to be repudiated, or a dictate of nature demanding submission, like breathing or feeling or striving?

Gaura took one cerulean pill out of the bottle, rolled it between thumb and index finger. She could show her husband that she was capable of untrammeled passion. A little pill did not have the power to wreck her family or control their lives. She would master the pill. If Daphne Sweetspire was not afraid to show it, then neither would she. Then she would be on equal terms with Daphne. And he would never even think about taking the pill again, unless Congress approved it, unless it was deemed safe and right and proper for the maintenance of Contentment.

Feeling her anxiety seeding doubt, she opened the bottle, popped a pill in her mouth and swallowed. Then she sat on her living room couch, clutching her own arms like a child wracked with guilt, and waited. While she waited, she thought about her family. She had a good husband. She had a good son. Neither of them did anything terrible. Neither of them acted out of malice, or out of cold, calculated deception. They were both, in different ways, victims of their own biological functions.

Nearly two hours later, Gaura was again standing next to her bed, again watching her husband sleep. She was a victim too, like Kaffir, like Aster. The world was against her son, simply because he was himself. They vilified him, imprisoned him, because he had the audacity to openly defend his natural right to *be* human. He was no less human than any other Opinion. He had no more control over his genetic makeup than any other Opinion. Her son was a good, decent, honorable person, a *remarkable* young man, an *exceptional* young man. They had no right to punish him, sully his reputation, portray him as a freak of nature, when he had done nothing less than serve as a pillar of his community. And Kaffir, Kaffir was no less innocent. A good, faithful husband; a good, caring father; a Literature Consultant for the Catchfly County Culture Coalition Center; and what was his reward? Being manipulated, wheedled into taking that pill by the wretched trollop, the wanton, slithering, scheming, lecherous, leering, wicked, foaming viper across the street. Kaffir got his just deserts, indeed! Falling prey to that vicious flytrap of a whore! Never would the torrid ogling of that temptress beguile him again!

She could show him right now that Daphne was nothing to him. She could wake him up and show him just how much more of a woman she was compared to that prurient, slimy miscreant. The frothing humors within her prodded on. But that churning concoction meant to foment surges of erotic energy was alchemized, repurposed, regressed into the primal embers igniting its ardor. She felt *rage.*

Gaura turned away from her husband, glancing at the digital clock on the nightstand. Salvia Hornbeam, Hebe's husband, would be attending his usual Ox Eye Symphony Orchestra rehearsal tonight. Only Hebe and Daphne would be home. Hmm. Yes, it would be better that way, wouldn't it?

When Daphne Sweetspire opened the front door, her features were bursting with ebullience. A new day smiling upon a spring blossom.

"Oh Gaura, how are you! Come in! Is everything okay? I saw a police car in front of your house before. Come in!"

Gaura stepped across the threshold and closed the door behind her. When she pulled the stun gun from her pants pocket, Daphne was still smiling.

After the crackling buzz, Daphne emitted a strangled yelp and fell backward. For a few moments, her body bucked like she was having sex. Her smile snapped into a quivering, rigid-lipped grimace.

Gaura stepped up to her, pointed the stun gun, and fired again. And again. And again and again. Daphne's body jerked, wriggled, and after a few more blasts it became more of a flitter of lingering muscle spasms.

When a shrieking Hebe Hornbeam bounded into the room, Gaura did not notice at first. The older lady clawed and grabbed at Gaura's raised arm. "What are you doing? What are you doing?" she kept wailing, until Gaura violently shoved the woman's midriff with her free hand.

Hebe lost her balance, tumbled backward, her skull cracking into the corner of her coffee table, the impact lurching the Tang Dynasty orange porcelain horse that Daphne had replaced. The piece skittered on its hooves a few inches, as if attempting to brace itself, before skidding off the edge, and shattered, once again, scattering shards across the floral ceramic tiles.

Gaura turned, and shot Daphne again, and again. And again. Daphne was no longer reacting to the volts of electricity coursing through her body. Her heart had stopped. She was dead. It was the first murder in Opine since the public release of the Self Suppressor.

Gaura looked at Daphne's body, her limbs rigidly angled, as if frozen in a dance move. She looked at Hebe, sprawled on the floor, out cold.

The sound of the gun clattering to the floor made Gaura flinch. She sank to the floor, unblinking, unmoved.

Then she began to cry. A gargled, coughing cry.

It took her fifteen minutes before she could call the police.

Thirty-Three

THE INCARCERATION HOUSING DEVELOPMENT in Cockspur Coral County was an area of ten residential blocks of detached small studio condominium homes, each consisting of a single combined bedroom/living area, galley kitchen with stove, and bathroom. Locks on doors and windows were controlled by the Home Security Administration computers housed in the county's main administrative facility. Refrigerators and cabinets were stocked with a week's worth of food, replenished in coordination with weekly waste disposal. Inmates could communicate with the incarceration officials through an intercom system. All the amenities one would expect from basic Opinion living conditions were provided, including heat, air-conditioning, supplies for personal hygiene, a vacuum cleaner, a television (not wired to the Internet), and even some magazines and books. No communication devices, other than the intercom system, were permitted. This was solitary confinement. Every inmate was alone.

Aster Bottlebrush, sitting on the drab pewter wool sofa in his prison quarters, was alone, in more ways than one. He was physically alone, taken from his home, taken from his family, locked up in a strange little house, and it seemed he was alone among the entire Opinion people. He was the only Opinion, to date, who possessed a natural resistance to the gene editing technology of the Self Suppressor therapy. He was the only Opinion, to date, who, as a consequence of this resistance, possessed a natural human libido. How utterly callous and deplorable of him, having the *temerity* to express a natural human libido! The impertinence, the audacity! Maybe he should be put to death! Maybe his very DNA was an abomination, a vile distortion of the Opinion natural order, a mortal threat to the integrity of the genome itself! Well, maybe that was their *opinion!* Aster knew the truth. And he also knew that regardless of whether the primary functionality of the Self Suppressor in his system had remained intact, he was not *selfish.* He was thinking of every Opinion citizen, thinking of their right to be *as human as nature intended them to be.* What could be more noble than that, to support the right to be as human as humanly possible? Let them continue to administer the Self Suppressor! Aster had nothing against the Corrective Biological Sciences. He had nothing against correcting genetic anomalies, or correcting genetic predispositions leading to destructive behavior. He was not out to threaten vital genetically motivated sociocultural values like community and philanthropy. But if this could be accomplished by correcting genetic side effects making us less fundamentally human, then it should be done! Scientists like Lupin Hollyhock and Thymus Corkwood had only just scratched the surface with Aster's DNA! This was the beginning of a new Opinion era, an era of new, uncompromising humanity! Aster was living proof that it could be done! Aster had a *moral obligation* to show people it could be done!

What would Ancients have done if they believed the State to have imposed unjust legal measures on its citizens? They would protest.

Aster needed to protest. He had to speak up, like he did on the radio. And he had to find some way to do it now. He couldn't wait, or the momentum he and his companion "lib pill" had generated would begin to dissipate. How could he protest if there was no one to hear him? Would he have to wait until his trial? The outcome of the trial was already decided. In their eyes, he had violated a congressional directive. Open and shut case. He needed to do something *now*. He needed to speak to those who could not only sympathize with him, but empathize with him, people who had already experimented with the pill and understood what it felt like to regain a sacred piece of their humanity...

Aster walked to the window, looked out to the adjacent unit. He could see somebody moving inside. Many of the units in this development, he was told, held people like him, people who had violated Congressional Directive 161-D. Aster didn't know it, but the man in the adjacent unit was a man who had attended the Tecoma Tennis Tournament last March, the man wearing a light blue chambray button-down shirt and khaki pants peddling generic "lib pills" to the tennis spectators.

Aster waited until the man walked to his window, looked out, and saw him. The two stared at each other for several seconds. Aster then raised an index finger, pointed to his right, then straight up, indicating he would return shortly.

The man stood there for three minutes.

Aster had turned on the gas stove and held a rolled-up magazine to the flame. He returned to the window, showed the man the burning magazine, a stolid look chiseled into his face.

The corners of the man's lips slinked up. Aster's lips echoed it.

Protest, Aster thought. Then he held the flame to the left curtain. When the fire began to creep up the length, he lit the other curtain.

The man stepped away from the window, grabbed a magazine, rolled it up, and showed it to Aster.

There had never been a single case of arson in Opine since the public release of the Self Suppressor.

A minute before, one of the congressional members who had approved the passage of Congressional Directive 161-D, Arum Fieldrush, happened to be driving down a road parallel to the northwest quadrant of the Incarceration Housing Development. Noticing smoke emanating from at least two units, he promptly altered his route to investigate. Security cameras recorded him emerging from his car, looking through two windows in Aster's unit, then running back to his car to get his cell phone. Mr. Fieldrush parked his car safely across the street and called the fire department.

What Aster had not anticipated was that the Home Security System was networked with online fire and smoke detectors. Once the detectors went off, computers in the county administrative facility alerted the staff, and protocol demanded the door and window locks be immediately disengaged. This was an Opinewide safety measure built into the network, though there had never been a prior case of home incarceration units catching fire. Aster's unit, and the unit next to him . . . and the unit next to that, the occupant of which had been prompted by his neighbor to start a fire . . . and the unit next to that, also on fire . . . all now had unlocked doors and windows.

When Aster heard the loud click and chime, he immediately rushed out of the unit, as did the others.

Arum Fieldrush saw them, but stayed in his car, hand on his stun gun.

Emerging from his incarceration unit, Aster was briefly astounded by how many other units were burning. It looked like at least six from where he was standing. The other prisoners, all men in their twenties and thirties, saw him standing there and jogged over.

The sight of these men voluntarily assembling emboldened Aster. He had never assumed a position of leadership, except on Student Council. Now, these men, their suppressive bonds burned away with Aster's direction, were looking to him.

"Listen, listen!" Aster said. "My name is Aster Bottlebrush. I'm the one—"

"We know who you are," one man said.

"Okay. Listen, we shouldn't run. We don't want to be viewed as criminals. They're going to lock us back up. But that doesn't mean we can't organize some time, and voice our rights. We should be able to decide for ourselves what we do with our own genomes, especially if it means having a say on what natural instinct to suppress and what not to suppress!"

They were all nodding. The air was redolent of the crackling, hot breath of the flames.

"We can even form some kind of a group, or coalition."

"A political party," one man suggested.

"Yes! A political party to voice our concerns to the Congress! We can canvass . . . and recruit members . . . and . . . and have meetings and consolidate our ideas, and come up with a publicity platform that makes people understand it is *not* wrong to adjust an unsatisfactory genetic therapy, and it doesn't make us *less* human but *more* human, and . . . and if nature has not forcibly denied *me* the libidinal instinct, then *no* Opinion should be forcibly denied the libidinal instinct . . . it should be an option, a personal decision . . . because our evolutionary instincts are what make us members of the animal kingdom, and makes us human, and makes us . . . *free!*"

They nodded more zealously, some muttering "yes" and "that's right."

"We can call it . . . the Lib Party! 'Lib' for liberty and libido!"

"Liberty and libido!" the tennis court gentleman echoed, and they all shook hands vigorously with Aster.

When the fire trucks and police pulled up, Arum Fieldrush got out of his car to report what he had seen. He began gesturing towards Aster and the other men, but they were already surrendering to another officer.

Thirty-Four

Nobody knew exactly how it started, but a rumor began to spread that one of the members of the Opinion Congress who had voted for the directive suspending all production and distribution of the "lib pill" had set fire to Aster's home incarceration unit. The individual, identified by security cameras as being in the vicinity of Aster's unit when the blaze occurred, was Arum Fieldrush.

Some people did not believe the report. Others believed it, and were appalled. They were appalled, and angry, that an Opinion would go through the lengths of attempting to burn alive the young man whose DNA provided the sublime adjustment to the Self Suppressor, simply because that Opinion vehemently condemned the very existence of the adjustment. And, according to the rumors, rumors gradually sweeping the land like a conflagration, Arum Fieldrush was not the only culprit. There were others, others who lit other fires. It was a conspiracy of dissenters. They had attempted to burn alive those lawfully awaiting trial, those accused of challenging the dictates of Congressional Directive 161-D.

The pro-lib people decided this was the truth. This was the new reality.

Those who supported Aster's "lib pill," all of whom had sampled the said therapy, and all of whom would go on to support Aster's new "Lib Party," felt an exhilarating, invigorated sense of release, which fed a sense of entitlement to their newfound freedom, which fed a sense of indignation over that entitlement under threat, which activated the primordial jaws of their humanity: rage.

They decided that if the anti-lib people were going to oppress and suppress and repress the pro-lib people, then they, the pro-lib people, would take it upon themselves to aggregate, to coordinate, to conglomerate, to gather their resources together and devise a suitable course of action communicating in decisive, unambiguous terms they would *not* be told do what to do with their genomes; they would *not* be bound by an unjust directive demanding they cease exercising their right to express a natural biological instinct; they would *not* be told to refrain from taking a genetic therapy that, in their firsthand estimation, enhances their State of Contentment; and they would *not* stand for those of opposing views perpetrating flagrant acts of political terrorism aimed at incinerating the living source behind their nascent crusade to attain genetic freedom.

They rationalized that reinstating their natural, biological instinct to reproduce was an inevitable consequence of their society's continuing objective of bettering themselves. Why should they not go back to the way things were, when human beings were their natural, pure selves? Why should they not be as human as they used to be? A revision to the Self Suppressor should not be viewed as a setback. It should be viewed as progress. Contentment in Opine would always be enhanced with scientific innovations of this sort. If Aster Bottlebrush hadn't spearheaded the advance, eventually somebody else would have. It was inevitable. If the revised therapy caused some problems... if the new treatment is found to have adversely affected the therapy's prime functionality... well, that was inevitable too, and they would deal with it, just as they had dealt with similar issues in the past. If they had to suffer a bit for getting what was owed to them, it would be worth it. Sometimes the status quo has to be upset in order to move forward. All in the name of progress, all in the interest of a bright future preserving what made them human. You couldn't stop it. One might even say that Aster Bottlebrush's natural resistance to an artificial genetic suppression would help institute Opine's new politics. The politics of inevitability.

These same individuals thus met, discussed potential plans for response, and ultimately judged it right and proper to literally fight fire with fire. As in Ancient democracies, the names of the members of any particular Opinion congressional assembly were posted for public record, as were the minutes of each assembly, and the results of roll call votes. Fired up with dosages of lib pills, the pro-lib people first marched to Arum Fieldrush's home, and set it ablaze. But the rest were just as guilty. They were part of the conspiracy. After all, how else would those incarceration units have caught fire? Who else would do that? The prisoners themselves? Aster Bottlebrush, burning down his own incarceration unit? What nonsense. The truth was clear. Anybody who had taken a lib pill would never doubt for a second what really happened. Social media blindly followed. It was inevitable it would come to this. When those in control are threatened, they lash out. The anti-lib people were lashing out. And the pro-lib people would answer.

So they identified the homes of those who had voted for Congressional Directive 161-D, and burned them. Not every single one. They wanted to make a statement, a strong statement. Several in each county would suffice. Their message would be heard, and seen.

And seen it was. O pale blue sun in thy blue sky, what doth *now* light upon thine eye?

Candles! Behold, ye free spirits, the lighting of the Flames of Liberty! Each burning home spewing forth majestic, bud-shaped, dancing, cheering flames, their hungry, writhing, wriggling tongues yearning, longing, craving, striving, reaching, up, up, *up!* Candles . . . for Opine's new birthday!

Welcome, all, to Opine! To a new birth, a new day, a new age!

Epilogue

As the flames hissed and lapped and licked, there was a young man and woman, not yet twenty, walking across a verdant field along the outskirts of Cockspur Coral County. They spotted a small park in the near distance, its perimeter of pink dwarf weigela shrubs enclosing a garden, trees, and sitting area with benches. The two headed towards it, giggling playfully.

"Oh, come on, let's just take everything off!" the young man gleefully suggested, and the young lady gleefully agreed. They began tugging and clawing at their clothes, hopping on one foot, kicking away shoes, whipping away garments. At one point the girl fell over, both cackling hysterically.

Behind them, in the distance, the flames and smoke of Opine's new birthday cascaded into the sky.

Holding hands, the two naked youths trotted across the lush warm grass, but stopped when they saw somebody standing on a hillock about a hundred yards away. It was Mr. Figgle! Forgoing his usual tweed blazer and chinos for a vibrant floral beach short-sleeve button-down aloha shirt, khaki shorts, and sandals, the professor tipped his lauhala hat and waved. The young lady recognized him first.

"Hi Mr. Figgle!" she called.

"Hello, children! Hello!" Mr. Figgle waved broadly, his smile also broad, and effulgent.

The youngsters waved back, and Mr. Figgle laughed heartily.

The young man then looked down, saw his own fully erect penis.

"Look," he said, pointing, and she goggled, her lips slightly parted. It resembled, to her, a curious turtle stretching out its neck.

"Oh, the resplendence," she said.

Their gazes bathed in it for several seconds.

"Come," the young lady said, clasping his hand, "we must look for a place that is shady."

They trotted along, then walked at a more leisurely pace upon reaching the garden. The late spring flowers were vivid, lambent, tumescent. There were pink hibiscuses and purple irises, red coneflowers and orange crown imperials, yellow sundews and lilac butterworts, azaleas and orchids and zinnias and nasturtiums. The two walked among the flowers, admiring the elongated, gleaming petals, a sea of gentle wings offering their torrid embrace.

Then they stopped in front of a tree boasting a full crown of glimmering lobed leaves. There was barely a breeze, though they noticed a rustling up above.

The young man took a few steps forward to get a better look, his companion following.

They peered up into the tree where something was moving among the leaves.

The two looked at each other, and smiled.

Author's Note

To CHRONICLE all the monumental, timeless works of literature that have inspired this novel would indeed be an endeavor at least as rigorous as the undertaking of the work itself. Three inspirational works are Howard Zinn's *People's History of the United States,* a mighty undertaking that left a profound, indelible impression on my perspective of this country's history; Timothy Snyder's *The Road To Unfreedom,* a perceptive and chilling historical account of how fragile democracies can be susceptible to the looming chicanery of tyranny; and Dr. Ian Shapiro's *The Moral Foundations of Politics,* part of the Open Yale Courses Series, offering an eloquent introduction to a subject as sweeping as it is vital. But it doesn't stop there. A free people can conquer tyranny and oppression only through heeding those great minds who, from the quill to the keystroke, have shown us the right way. Seek those good, learned souls, listen, and pass it on.

Dr. Matthew Marullo is the author of three prior novels: *The Octave Displacement* (2006), *Gludman's Proof* (2013), and *Till Times Are Done* (2019). Reviewers such as *Kirkus*, *Blueink*, and *Foreword* call Marullo's novels "unique," "clever," as well as "expertly" and "masterfully" written. Dr. Marullo lives with his family in Long Island, New York.

Made in United States
North Haven, CT
15 February 2025

65594380R00163